All Our Almosts

Allie Moffatt

To Erin, for your contagious compulsion
to fill the void at all times

1

I love Boston, but I don't know if Boston loves me back. Especially on nights like this, when my friends are late and I just watched a biker almost die making an illegal U-turn in front of a 66 bus and my nose has frozen into a solid block of ice. There's a group of kids—no older than 15, I swear—blowing vape smoke at me and God now it's starting to snow.

"Watch where ya goin', ya fuckin' lunatic!"

That was the bus driver to the biker, and you know what, he has a point.

You'd think I would be used to the cold. I grew up in Minnesota. Like deep north, rural Minnesota. But I always tell people: just because I've been cold before doesn't mean I like it.

And actually, despite the fact that I'm freezing my butt off outside of a Chinese restaurant on a grimy block of Allston, counting double parked cars and getting frostbite, I'm in the *best* mood. Because today was a good day. A great day, even. Well, maybe "great" is premature, I wouldn't want to jinx myself, but definitely a good day.

Because about an hour ago I got a call—and yes I answer the phone for unknown numbers, because what if it's something important and I miss it and then I never know what they were going to say?—offering me an interview with my dream grad school program.

I know! I'm so excited.

I went to Ashmore for undergrad, so I already know and love the campus. That's where I met my best friends, actually—the ones who should be here any minute. And the Ashmore Graduate School of Education is one of the best in the country for what I want to do. So the fact that I even got offered an interview is a good sign. It makes me think maybe I'm not crazy for considering going for a PhD in the first place. Even though it's a little crazy. But I definitely want to do it.

(I definitely want to do it, right?)

A low voice rumbles from my right, "There's the genius herself," and I spin around to see one of my favorite people in the world.

"Andy!" I squeal as he pulls me up into a full off-the-ground hug.

He mutters "I'm proud of you" into my hair, and that means a lot coming from him. I love the guy, but he's not exactly a words-of-affirmation kind of friend. He's more of a stoic-silences kind of friend.

Maybe that's not fair. He talks to *me* plenty, now that we've been friends for nine-plus years. And he talks to the rest of NASA too, just… no one else really.

Oh, I should explain. It's kind of stupid, but my best friends from college call ourselves NASA because it's an acronym for our names: Nolan, Andy, Sophie, and Amelia—even though Amelia only ever goes by Lia, but NASL is a bad acronym.

"Dr. Sophie Lindell," Andy says, setting me down and pulling back to look me in the eye with a little hint of a smile that means more from him than a full smile means from anyone else. "Sounds good."

"Well, I'm not in yet, so we're not counting our chickens." I lean over to the nearest tree and knock on the wood. "If Ashmore doesn't take me my next best option is in San Diego, so please let me be superstitious for another month at least."

"Did you tell your work you're leaving yet?"

I grimace and shake my head. "That falls under not jinxing it."

"Ah hah."

"Besides, I don't want to stress out the team until after the new exhibit launches. And I especially don't want to give them an extra reason to scrutinize me during my first project lead."

I love my job. I know people always say that and they're usually lying because they're usually a consultant for McKinsey or a mid-level grunt at Facebook or whatever, but I genuinely love mine. I've been working at the Boston Museum of Science since the week after college graduation, when they hired me to guide tours for school groups at a generous $13.25/hour ($1.25 above the state minimum wage!). And even with the horrible pay, I still really love it. I've been working my way up the ranks slowly over the last five years, and several months ago they finally promoted me to a Project Manager role on the exhibits team.

But exhibits take a long time to design and fundraise for and build, so the exhibit launch next month will be the first one under my supervision. I'm really nervous, but I'm really excited too. Sometimes. When it's not eclipsed by the nervousness.

Also, remember the grad school interview I mentioned before? Well, in my PhD I want to research the effects of extracurricular education—like museums—on student outcomes, so I *really* want to be able to cite this as a relevant experience. In other words: it has to go well.

"They all love you," Andy says in that deadpan way of his, referring to my work team even though he's never met them and has no way of knowing that. "Don't worry so much about their feelings and tell them when you want to."

"Yeah, okay," I reply, but it's muffled by the click-clack of my chattering teeth. Yes, they literally chatter like a cartoon character. I wasn't kidding before about not liking the cold.

"Should we go in?" Andy asks, eyeing me with an expression in his dark eyes that some would take as anger, but I know is just concern.

"Yes, please."

"Do we have a reservation?"

"Ooh…" I try to grit my chattering teeth. "I totally meant to do that."

"Don't tell me." Andy's looking at me like I'm Saran Wrap—totally transparent.

"Shut up! Shut your mouth right now, Andrew. It's a good system."

"Even using the word *system* is generous. I'd bet 80% of your to-do notes get lost before they happen. I still don't know how you got through college."

"Beep boop. I. Am. Robot. Andy. I keep information perfectly organized in my brain without writing it down. It is so cool to be me."

Andy rolls his eyes as he holds the door open, letting me walk in under his arm.

"Welcome," chimes the woman at the hostess stand. "How many in your party?"

"Four—" Andy starts but I jump in with "Five, please." Then, to Andy, "Elliot is coming too. Sorry, should have mentioned that."

He swallows down whatever comment was really on the tip of his tongue, then says, "Got it."

I'm not blind. I know Andy and Elliot have never particularly liked each other. But there's no open hostility there either, so it's workable. They're just very different people. Elliot—that's my boyfriend, by the way—is a perfectly good guy. He works hard, likes art and music, has a good relationship with his family… there's nothing not to like. I think it just takes a certain personality to crack the eggshell that is Andy Walsh's cold, hard exterior, and Elliot does not have that personality. At least, that's my working hypothesis.

There's no wait for a table, so the hostess walks us over to a circular booth with red pleather seats that some would call "well-loved" but I would call "disintegrating." The room is dramatically lit in reds and greens, and the pre-karaoke hype playlist is blaring.

Did I mention Fridays are karaoke nights here? We absolutely love this place. At least, Lia, Nolan, and I do—and Andy loves us.

"Should we get a pitcher of something?" I ask, opening my menu.

"I definitely need some kind of fried noodle situation for food, but… oh I forgot they have mai tai bowls for groups! We have to do it."

I look up at Andy in time to catch the tiniest twitch of his lips. So miniscule that only a trained eye would notice it. But I've been training for the Olympics of Decoding Andy's Microexpressions for nine years and I know that means he wants the mai tai bowl as bad as I do. In fact, I'm confident he's opening his mouth to say so when a shrill "Ahhhhh!" echoes across the dining room.

Lia rockets herself into the booth and pins me in a hug. "Sophie, you did so good! I'm so happy for you." Chaotic cheek kisses and laughter follow. I love her.

Lia is painfully gorgeous. Really. She has this long hair that curls just the right amount towards the ends, like little ringlets. And she has these big brown doe eyes—that totally belie her true evil nature, by the way—mile-long legs, and olive-tan skin. Her dad is Sicilian and her mom is French, but let me tell you: dad's genes were *strong*.

We met as randomly assigned freshman roommates, and it's a good thing we got along so well because otherwise I would've been extremely intimidated by her. She's a triple threat: smart, creative, and beautiful. She double majored in business and fiber arts—which is so cool in and of itself—and now she runs a (lucrative!) social media account that brings art school techniques to people without art school money. Power to the people et cetera et cetera. Her content is colorful and cheerful and unapologetically girly and I would genuinely be a huge fan even if I didn't know her. She was also an independent fiber artist in her spare time, because everything else wasn't enough.

"Hey, save some of that for me!" a voice bellows from the edge of the booth, and I know it belongs to Nolan—the N of NASA and our last missing piece. He practically drags his little sister off of me, then takes her place and squeezes me in a hug of his own. "Great job, Soph. We're rooting for you."

Nolan is big. I'm going to guess at least 6'3" and bulky (the boy loves the gym). He has a strong resemblance to Lia—same tan skin, medium-brown curls, light brown eyes—but completely different energy. He's like a great dane puppy: huge and innocent and lovable.

"Thanks," I laugh as Nolan lets go. "I admit I feel a little silly calling you guys out to celebrate an interview. I realize it's not that big of a deal."

"Stop," Andy says, blunt as ever. "It is a big deal."

The waiter arrives then to take our drink orders—one Signature Mai Tai Bucket™ plus waters for everyone—and by the time he's delivered the drink monstrosity with five colorful straws, the missing mouth for straw number five is here. I look up at him with a smile.

"Hi honey, thanks for coming all the way out here."

"Hey everybody," Elliot nods to the group. "How's it going?"

He's dressed for work—blue suit, dark blonde hair combed to the side, and bags under his eyes that say it's been a long week.

This is what other people didn't get about Elliot: he makes an effort, even when it's inconvenient. He came straight here from his office in Southie (the opposite end of Boston, if you didn't know) after a hard week of long hours, just to celebrate my interview—which isn't even conclusive good news yet, it's just a step in the process. He didn't have to come, but he did without complaint, and it means a lot.

Andy seems to realize that he's blocking Elliot's path to me, so he stands to make room.

"Thanks," Elliot says, sliding into the booth between me and Andy. "How's it going man?"

"Fine," Andy replies. And that's all.

(I could kill him sometimes. Just be pleasant to my boyfriend!)

Though to be *slightly* fair to Andy, he's not the only one of my friends with a weird vendetta against Elliot. Like Lia—I mentioned she's evil, right?—who leans towards him across the table and says, "Elliot, do you want to make a toast to your beautiful girlfriend's accomplishment today?"

Lia has never liked Elliot. Not since the very first day they met. She's always said he's wrong for me. In her words, he's "stuffy and cocky and dickish," but she just doesn't know him like I do.

Elliot doesn't know Lia well either, which is why he doesn't recognize the jab for what it is: her way of saying "why didn't you congratulate Sophie about the interview when you first walked in, you jerk?" (Her internal monologue, of course—not mine.)

So Elliot responds sincerely. "Oh, of course." He lifts his water glass, and I'm a little embarrassed that everyone else does too. This is really unnecessary.

"Sophie," he starts, tilting his glass towards me, "I think it's nice the way you chase your dreams, and this program sounds like it would be really nice for you. Cheers."

(Okay, he may not be the best at toasts.)

Glasses clink together and I give him a kiss on the cheek. "Thanks, honey. And here's a quick toast to us." I squeeze his arm then turn back to my friends to explain, "Yesterday was our third anniversary."

Only Nolan seems to brighten at the news—he's such a sweetie. "Wow, congrats you too! You have to tell me how you did it, because the dating apps are really not working out for me."

"They're not?" I ask just as Andy gripes, "I offered to help with your profile."

Lia barks out a laugh, then points a brightly colored nail across the table at Andy. "You are the last person who should help him. Your dating habits are insufferable."

"How are they insufferable?" he asks, feigning innocence even though he *knows* what he's like.

"You only ever date hot girls with huge boobs," Lia says, "and then get bored of them within like a month."

Andy rolls his eyes. "Nice to meet you, Pot. I'm Kettle."

"Get off his jock, Lia." Nolan elbows his sister before turning back to Andy. "And dude, it's not a problem with my profile. I swear it's a great profile." (God bless him and his confidence.) "I just feel like it's really hard to click with someone when you're talking online."

"When was the last time you asked out someone you met in person?" I ask, then nod towards Elliot. "You know, we met at a work thing."

"Ahh... I don't know." Nolan rubs the back of his neck in his boyish way. "When it's in person I chicken out."

I squeeze his arm in encouragement. "Just try it. As long as you're respectful and pay attention to her cues—"

"And remember I'll kill you in your sleep if I ever find out you harassed a woman," Lia adds without humor.

"Yes, that," I agree. "But with that in mind, I think practice makes perfect."

"So you really think I should like… go make small talk with one of the women at the bar? And then just ask if she'd want to go out sometime? Wasn't that move retired in the 90's?"

There are, in fact, two perfectly lovely blonde women seated at the side of the bar nearest to us. They look to be in their mid-20's, maybe sisters? Regardless, they're both dressed up with no dates in sight, and their body language says they're as open as anyone. But before I can tell Nolan I think it seems reasonable, Elliot starts chuckling to himself and mutters, "Don't do it, man."

"Dude, I thought you met your girlfriend in person. Why don't you think I should do it?"

Elliot shakes his head. "Just trust me, you don't want to date a girl like that. They're always more trouble than they're worth."

Unfortunately for him, those words are the exact summoning spell for the demon that lives inside Lia.

"Oh I'm going to love this," she says with a bite. "Say more, Elliot. What exactly is wrong with these women?"

"Lia…" I warn.

"It's not about these women in particular," he explains. "I just don't really believe in dating hot girls."

Now, look. I know what you're thinking. That sounds really dickish. But he's just not the best with words. He doesn't mean that *I'm* not hot—really, I know that! But I still feel all of the blood rush to my face and sweat break out along the back of my neck. I'm so caught up in trying to control my physiological response to that stupid (but ultimately harmless) comment that I don't even realize how many seconds of silence tick by before Andy spits out, "What did you just say?"

"Oh, come on guys," Elliot says. "You know what I mean. Hot girls are always the worst."

I want to stop time. Or better yet, rewind it two minutes. Maybe rewind it several hours and never have called NASA to go out tonight. It could've been just me and Elliot and this would be fine, because I get what he means. He's not insulting me, he's just… clumsy.

I don't want to, but I have to. I look up at my friends' faces. The men look incredulous, certainly not prepared to back Elliot up on this, and Lia looks like she'd gladly ruin her manicure for the pleasure of gauging his eyes out. Elliot doesn't take the hint.

"What? Don't look at me like that. I'm allowed to have a preference. I just don't like dating… conventionally attractive girls." He says it like someone begrudgingly using a politically correct term, and it's getting harder and harder to not take offense.

Look, I know I'm not a model, okay? And next to Lia I'm sure I look like a cave troll. But I try hard to keep a positive body image. And I think I'm… fine? Normal? To the extent normal is even a thing. I have straight brown hair (nothing to write home about), freckles (a controversially cute-or-ugly feature), hazel eyes (again, fine) behind glasses (okay, this one I acknowledge Elliot's point on—maybe I should wear contacts more), and I have a body that I try not to criticize because that road only leads to unhappiness. But even with my reasonably acceptable body image, I don't know what to say to that. I'm still coming up with a response by the time my mean friends take matters into their own hands.

"What the fuck are you saying, Elliot?" Andy snarls, and I don't think I've ever seen him angrier. Then Lia asks, "Are you high?" in a tone that's half explicit insult and half genuine question.

Color is rising on Elliot's cheeks, and I can already see how this is going to go. It's going to be ugly. They're going to fight and leave hating each other more than they already do, and it'll be impossible to hang out together after that. And God, I just wanted to have a nice night out! I can't deal with the conflict. I just can't.

"You know what," I say, clapping my hands together. There's a manic edge to my voice that I try to correct in my next sentence. "This actually reminds me of something I learned at work today. I have a friend who works in the museum's biology department, and she was telling me that there's an animal called a sea salp whose reproductive cycle alternates generations, so basically Generation A reproduces sexually, and then Generation B reproduces asexually, and then the cycle necessarily repeats forever. And the two generations have totally different anatomy and everything. So you know, it's totally normal for there to be weird mating rituals in the animal kingdom. Humans aren't the only ones. In fact, ours aren't even that interesting."

It's not my smoothest work, but give me a break, I'm under duress.

After an awkward beat, Nolan says, "I'm sorry, I'm lost. In this metaphor, is Elliot the asexual reproduction sea salp, or is that you?"

"It's not a metaphor! I'm just sharing something cool I learned today."

I turn to my left, intending to smile at Elliot to show there are no hard feelings about it at all, when my eyes catch on Andy's instead.

And in that one second of eye contact, I think Andy understands everything going through my head. It's always been like that. We don't need to spell things out with each other. Sometimes we just know.

"That's actually really cool," he says, holding my gaze as tightly as a physical touch. "Do the two generations look the same externally?"

Then Lia gets it—God bless her—and adds, "Yeah and what are sea salps anyway, are they like fish?"

I exhale for what feels like the first time in an hour, then tell them everything I know about sea salps.

And it's fun. It helps. Really. It's the perfect distraction from the flush I know is still riding high on my cheekbones. And Elliot, to his credit, lets me monologue for probably ten minutes straight before he says, "The alcohol bucket is empty so I'm going to get a beer from the bar. Anyone need anything?"

And you know what? I *do* need something. I deserve it, after that ordeal.

"Yes, a margarita please. Actually, do they have flavors? You know what, I'll just come with."

I don't look back at my friends as we head for the bar. I don't want to see them watching us.

We place our orders, and Elliot pulls out his phone to check work emails while we wait. I take the chance to fix myself up a bit, smooth my dress, make sure my makeup hasn't smudged under my eyes. And I know what you're thinking—it's not because of what Elliot said. I look how I look, and that's fine. I just don't want to seem messy.

I finish running my fingers through my hair and finally dare to look back at the table. Lia and Nolan are hunched towards each other in rapt discussion, but Andy's looking at me.

I give him a smile-and-nod. *I'm okay.*

But he doesn't smile-and-nod back, just keeps looking at me with that deep crease between his brows, the one that's always there when something troubles him and often there regardless.

"Hey, Soph." Elliot pulls my attention back and I look up at him. "I just got an email from Umair and he needs the slides tonight so I'm gonna have to bail. Sorry, honey."

"Oh," I say. "Okay, no worries."

And between you and me? I'm relieved.

Not because I don't want him here or because I'm still mad at him from before—which I'm not—but because the conflict will leave with him. Now everyone will just get along, and no one will expect me to do something I can't or say something I won't.

I carry my strawberry margarita back to the table and Elliot comes up behind me, explaining to the group, "I actually just got an email from work and have to bail."

"That's just fine," Lia says with a sardonic smile. "Have a good night!" Her dismissive wave paints an unambiguous picture of her feelings on the matter.

Elliot ignores her, turning back to me. "I might be home late, so don't wait up." Then he gives me a quick kiss and heads out.

Mercifully, my friends seem to realize I don't want to debrief what just happened. There's an immediate and unspoken agreement to switch gears.

Step one: Nolan heads to the bar for a round of shots. Step two: Lia sprints to the karaoke sign-up sheet as soon as it's out and signs us up for a slew of songs. But don't worry, we're polite about it. She always leaves a few lines of space between each song so other people can take turns too. Step three: somewhere between Nolan's excruciating rendition of "Fergalicious" and my duet of "Summer Lovin'" with Lia, the night takes a turn for the better. Even Andy—after two "please don't make me"s and three tequila shots—is successfully roped into a group performance of "Total Eclipse of the Heart," and my own heart feels full.

"——— •❦• ———"

With a hoarse voice and sore feet, I unlock the door to my apartment just before 2:00 AM. I moved in with Elliot about six months ago, and to be totally honest, it's been fantastic. There is simply no way I could afford a place this nice on my own. We have: climate control, a dishwasher, and *zero* mice inside our unit.

(I have seen a few in the laundry room, but you can't have everything.)

I take off my shoes and coat by the door and feel my phone vibrate with a text.

> Lia: you home yet? are you ok?
>
> Me: Yep got home safe and sound!
>
> Lia: i mean are you ok after the bullshit at the bar today
>
> Me: What? Are you mad at me?
>
> Lia: no i'm talking about elliot. PLEASE tell me you had a fight with him when you got home
>
> Me: He didn't mean anything by it. He's a goon.

I see an incoming call on my screen and seriously consider ignoring it, but let's be honest, I'm too afraid of her wrath. I hit accept.

"Lia—"

"Sophie, I know I have no right to interfere in your life, and I've dated my fair share of asshole men, but if my boyfriend said he didn't date hot girls to my face after three years together, he would not be my boyfriend anymore. Period."

"It's seriously fine," I say in my calmest tone as I head into the bedroom. "I knew what he meant."

"Please enlighten me then," she spits. And okay, drunk Lia is not gonna drop this.

"Look, it's not like he called me ugly," I say, more defensive than I mean to sound as I put her on speakerphone. "It's really not a big deal. We had such a great night and now I'm tired and just want to get out of this dress and go to bed. Can we talk in the morning?"

"Is he even back yet?"

I toss my dress into the hamper and grab an oversized sleeping shirt from a drawer. "He cares about his job, and he doesn't get to just turn it off. The schedule isn't his choice."

Lia exhales loudly into the phone. "No. No. I'm not coming off this Sophie, I'm not. I know you don't want to hear it but you deserve better than all of this. I swear he's getting worse."

There's a small—tiny—part of me that's thinking about hanging up on her. I never would, but I'm so on edge right now that the temptation niggles in my mind.

Here's the thing, Lia is an Aggressive Friend. Not just that she's an aggressive person and she's a friend—she's aggressive at being a friend. The kind of person who will yell "I LOVE YOU SO MUCH AND FUCK YOU FOR THINKING OTHERWISE!" The kind of person who showed up to freshman move-in day, saw me standing in our shared room, declared, "I'm so glad college comes with a live-in best friend," and hugged me tight before she even knew my name. The kind of person who will always answer the phone at 1:00 AM, 2:00 AM, or 3:00 AM, but will tell me hard truths when she does.

"I know you don't like him, Lia. You've told me. But I… we're just…" I exhale, scavenging for a string of non-pathetic words. "I love him. And we work. It works. Really. You don't know him like I do. We're stable, and we want similar things. It's good." It sounds more like I'm convincing myself than convincing her, so I switch tactics. "And look, I don't want to start over, especially not right now. I just want to focus on getting into grad school, and as soon as that happens you're welcome to annoy me with this conversation again."

A second of hesitation passes before Lia says, "Okay, Soph. I just want to say one more thing and then I won't bother you until you're officially a PhD candidate."

I snort. "I doubt that, but okay."

"I know you don't want to think about more changes right now, but now could be the perfect time. This could be your year of fresh starts. And I know it's scary to change everything at once, but you wouldn't really. You'll still be here. You'll still have NASA, always. And I can speak on behalf of myself and the boys when I assure you we'll gladly murder Elliot if that would help the situation."

"I'll think about it, okay?" I say, quieter than I mean too. "Good night, Lia. Love you."

"Okay," she says, resigned. "Love you. Sweet dreams."

I do not, in fact, have sweet dreams.

2

When showing up somewhere uninvited, it's common courtesy to plan your arrival for the least imposing moment possible.

I put a lot of thought into this—the time to arrive. And here's my thinking: Andy is a creature of immaculate habit. Every Saturday morning he goes for a long run, though the length does vary. He sets his alarm for 7:30, so it's fair to assume he eats some kind of breakfast then hits the pavement by 8:30, then factor in roughly two hours for a run. (Is that a reasonable time? I don't really know. But I did Google it, and Reddit at large seems to think it is.) Then after the run he usually makes lunch and does meal prep things before making his work schedule for the coming week, and often even does a few hours of work, too.

I'm always trying to get him *not* to work on weekends, but sometimes he wants to. He's a developmental editor with a little indie publishing house in Boston, and he really loves it. Honestly the only negative thing about his job—in his mind—is that it's *too flexible.* The man thrives on a rigid schedule, so he makes one for himself.

But anyway, I digress. The point is that I figure the ideal moment to arrive at Andy's place will be some time around lunch, after his run and before he starts any work. Of course he may feel obligated to feed me if I show up at lunch, but there's nothing to be done about that.

I walked here from my and Elliot's place. It took like an hour, which is normally more walking than I enjoy, but I had time to kill. It's now 11:00. That seems like as good a time as any, right?

I piggyback my way into the building thanks to one of Andy's neighbors and head up to his second floor unit. I contemplate just knocking, but that's weird right? So instead I send a text.

> Me: Heyyy... are you home rn?
> Andy: Yes. Why?

Good enough. I knock on the door three quick times before I can chicken out. It's only a few heartbeats before he opens it.

"Hi," I say with a small wave, very smooth.

"Hi?" he returns, surprised and confused in equal measure.

"Uh… What are you up to?" I'll note that my voice sounds just as surprised and confused as Andy's, even though I'm the one who made this choice.

"Nothing…"

"Can I come in?"

"Yes," he says, stepping aside to clear the doorway, "but if you want to hang out I have to shower first."

Only then do I realize he's still in his sweaty running clothes. Whoops. Slight miscalculation on my part. But what's done is done and we forge ahead.

"Yeah that's totally fine!" I'm going for breezy and I hope it comes across as I waltz in and set down my purse. "Wow, is this a new kitchen table?"

"Yeah... Sophie, I'm sorry but why are you here? I mean it's fine, but did we have plans today?"

"No, but I thought we could make some, if you're not busy. But if you are busy that's alright, I don't have to derail your day. Oh and sorry, I forgot to take off my shoes." I dart back to the shoe rack to remove my boots, but of course one of the zippers is stuck and I tug and tug on it and I just know Andy's watching me and figuring out more about my mental state than I want him to from my body language alone.

Out of my peripheral vision I see him walk over, then crouch down until he's eye level with me. I petulantly refuse to meet his gaze.

"You should stay," he says. "But I really do need to shower." He ducks a little further until I have no choice but to look at him. "And when I get out you're going to tell me why you're really here, right?"

I finally tug off my boot, and we both stand.

"Okay. Yeah. Definitely." I smile—at least I hope I do, though it might be more of a grimace. He gives me one more penetrating look before heading into the bathroom.

Andy's apartment is ridiculously nice by the standards of Boston, home of America's finest slumlords. The front door takes you into an open concept living space, with the kitchen on the right and the couch and TV on the left. On the opposite wall from the front door are the two bedrooms (that's right—TWO! in this economy!) separated by a bathroom in between. And of course he keeps everything spotless. No dishes unwashed, no sweaters discarded on the backs of chairs. The walls are off-white which is a little boring, but they have a decent amount of art on them (mostly thanks to Lia). It's honestly pretty perfect.

On the whole, NASA has moved around a lot since college ended, but Andy's lived here the whole time. In the intervening five years, I've spent many late nights on this familiar beige couch, drunk on gin and tonics or high on adrenaline. Mornings and afternoons too, heckling Andy while he cleaned or cooked, indulging Nolan's jigsaw puzzle addiction, or talking Lia out of getting bangs. I'm idly drifting through the memories when I hear the bathroom door click open.

Andy comes out wearing a white t-shirt and black sweatpants, his dark brown hair now black from the water. His face asks about ten silent questions as he approaches the couch where I'm camped out, and I decide to just rip the Band-Aid off.

I pivot to face him fully, my knees digging into the couch cushions as I blurt, "Elliot and I just broke up. But we're fine. I mean, I'm fine. But that's why I'm really here, I needed somewhere to go. Is that okay?"

Andy stops dead in his tracks, and I'm starting to realize this is a bigger imposition than I thought it would be.

"I know I should've called or texted before coming over. Sorry about that. I just had to get out, and Lia lives in a studio, and Nolan basically lives in a frat house, so I thought here was the best option, but—" Oh no. I can feel my throat getting tight. I really don't want to cry right now. I really, really, really don't. Andy hates when I cry. "Actually, could we maybe just not talk about it for a little while? Just a bit, and then I can go."

"Hey, Soph, it's okay." He comes up to the back of the couch where I'm leaning and oh God, I made him feel like he needs to comfort me. This is not how this was supposed to go! Because when he comforts me it makes me more emotional, and I'm really trying to hold it together here. But I can feel the tears pricking the backs of my eyes as he says, "You're always welcome here, and we don't have to talk about it. Do you, uh…" He looks around the room like he's trying to come up with a plan. "Do you want coffee? I was just going to make some."

I bite my tongue—not figuratively, I literally bite my tongue because I'm hoping it will help keep the tears back—and nod. He nods too, then turns to head into the kitchen.

Silence fills the room, interrupted only by the clicks of Andy taking the French press out of the cabinet and pouring in the boiling water.

"So are you here for the day or…?" He trails off, leaving me to fill in the rest.

"Actually," I say slowly, "I was wondering if I could stay here until I can find my own place. Which will be very hard since everything in Boston is on a September lease and it's February, but you never know, someone might die and create a vacancy. Not that I want someone to die," I shake my head quickly, "but I also don't want to bother you." Andy walks over but doesn't interrupt my runaway explanation. "I just don't know where else to go. I mean, I'm sure Lia would say yes if I asked to stay at her place, but she doesn't even have a couch I could stay on and I feel like sleeping in her bed with her indefinitely is a pretty big ask. I promise Andy, if you let me stay you'll barely notice I'm here."

Andy sits next to me and places both mugs on the coffee table (on coasters, of course). I watch his throat bob up and down with a swallow, and I think he must be running through worst case scenarios in his head: me leaving out dirty dishes, me playing music until 4:00 AM, me sitting on the couch crying over some elderly parrot I saw on the internet while he's trying to bring home a date. I'm so mortified over the idea of that last one that I almost tell him *nevermind, just forget it, I'll leave now!* but before I can open my mouth he's saying, "Okay. Yeah. Yeah, of course you can stay here."

"I can… You… You really don't mind?"

"Yeah. Yeah, no, yeah. Definitely."

He's nodding with increasing vigor, and bit like he's still talking himself into it.

"You really don't have to say yes. I get that it's a huge imposition. And I would never, ever ask for something like this if there was any way I could afford rent at my current place without Elliot's half, but I just can't. I don't make enough to cover it. And I can't keep living with him with the way we left things, so I'm just kind of… stuck."

"How did you leave things?" he asks. He's trying to hide how curious he is, but there's a little twitch in his brow that gives him away.

And I want to tell him about the break up—I do, he deserves an explanation—I just don't have it in me quite yet. So I simply say, "Badly." Then, after a pause, "But if I'm being honest, it was a long time coming."

He looks at me like he sees through my tissue and blood and bones straight to the core of all the things I'm not saying. Then he's saying "Come here" and pulling me across the couch. His long arms wrap around me, bringing the side of my face to rest against his chest as he holds me tight.

Sometimes I joke that his arms are my seatbelt. Because you know how the pressure of a seatbelt against your chest makes you feel safe? It started just for scary movies at first (which I don't like but Lia loves and makes us watch often). Whenever there would be a really tense or scary scene, I'd grab one of Andy's long arms and pull it across my body, the same way the strap of a seatbelt would cross over your chest, you know? But the seatbelt has evolved, and now sometimes I do it when I'm just cold or tired or stressed and he doesn't complain, just lets me grab his hand with a plaintive "Seatbelt, please?" and tuck myself into him.

This, right now, is a double seatbelt. Which is different from a hug, because a hug can be for anything, but a seatbelt is to keep me safe.

I told you Andy's not the best with words, right? I mean, he's actually great with words because he's an editor, but he needs to take his time with them. Needs to see them written down, then revise them and rework them until the point is conveyed perfectly. So I know he doesn't know what to say to me right now, and I don't blame him for it.

But the double seatbelt? Phenomenal substitute for words.

3

By mid-afternoon, everyone knows. And by everyone I just mean NASA because they are everyone to me.

Well, I mean, I do have parents. But they don't need to know yet. In fact, I'd much rather tell them in a week or two—or in the case of my dad, possibly never—once things are firmly squared away. If I called my mom now she would just worry, and there would be nothing she could do, and why make her miserable for no reason?

But the important thing is Nolan and Lia know, and they have never stayed out of anything ever, so of course they're here.

Not that I'm complaining. They went to my old place and literally packed boxes for me so I wouldn't have to see Elliot. Not everything, obviously. Not the furniture since I'll only be here temporarily, but enough to last me until I get my life in order. Clothes, shoes, coats, sticky notes, toothbrush, the book I'm in the middle of, my computer and charger—things like that.

The two of them huff into Andy's apartment noisily, each carrying a box and a bag with a few more waiting in Nolan's car. I point them to the spare bedroom off of the kitchen—formerly Andy's home office until he unflinchingly handed it over to me a few hours ago. (I still can't get over how quickly he agreed to that, by the way.)

"I love you guys. Thank you so much," I say as they set everything down. "Really, you didn't have to do that. I could've dealt with seeing him."

"Shush," is Lia's response, and she literally puts her index finger over my mouth. "Stop that. We wanted to."

"Yeah, it's nothing, Soph," Nolan insists. "Why don't you and Lia just hang out while Andy and I get the rest from the car, yeah?"

I think about arguing, but Nolan pulls me into a bear hug that physically silences me. He kisses me on the top of the head like the most softhearted big brother anyone could imagine (even though he's not really my brother) then pats Andy on the shoulder to cue their departure.

The moment Nolan's body breaks contact with mine, Lia's replaces it, arms wrapped tight around me. I bury my chin in her shoulder, praying she won't ask me about it but knowing she will.

"What happened, Soph?"

There it is.

I mean, she had to. She's being a good friend. I just hate that I'm bringing everyone down with this melodrama.

"I'm fine, really," I force out, but she doesn't loosen her grip. "It was just time to call it."

"Well he's a fucking loser who never deserved you, and you're going to be so much better off without him."

"Yeah, you're right," I agree, white-knuckle gripping my tears because I am not going to cry with everyone here. I'm not.

She doesn't let go of me until the boys come back in with the final boxes.

One thing I love about NASA? Most of our boundaries were completely torn to shreds by about year three of our friendship. Nolan doesn't even bother to ask if they can stay for dinner, he just opens one of Andy's cabinets and asks, "What kinds of pasta do you have? Should

I just make it from scratch?"

And boy, between the friend who's letting me live in his lovely spare bedroom, and the friends with generations-old Sicilian recipes in their back pockets, I've got it made.

What do I bring to this friend group? Not much—I'll tell you that for free.

With the boys getting to work in the kitchen, I pull Lia into my new bedroom to help me unpack. My room is right off of the kitchen, so normally the four of us would be able to chat at a normal volume through the open door, but Lia cannot exist with even a moment of silence so she's already playing music on her phone with the volume on max.

"Hey Andy," she calls, "can I have a cup?"

He brings her one, and she shoves the butt of her phone into it as a makeshift speaker. (Which works surprisingly well.) The sounds of rhythmic guitar float from the bedroom to the kitchen, mingling with the sounds of bags unzipping, packing tape tearing from cardboard, and frying pans clinking against each other. We fold shirts into drawers while the boys argue.

"Cayenne pepper and red pepper flakes are literally the same food, dude. They should be next to each other."

"Nolan, I don't know how to make this any clearer. It's in alphabetical order, and C and R are not next to each other." Andy sounds exhausted, like they've had this conversation before.

"Who alphabetizes their spice rack?" Nolan demands. "I would understand grouping them by like… flavor profile or country of origin, but alphabetical is insane."

"Who groups their spices by country of origin?" Andy asks, incredulous.

"Yeah, Nolan," Lia shouts over the music through the open bedroom door. "You're telling us you don't have time to wash your sheets but you have time to organize your spices by country of origin?"

"I wash my sheets!"

"Occasionally…"

I take it upon myself to pop into the kitchen and end the debate. "Andy, do you have a Sharpie?"

"Um yes…" He shuffles around in a drawer before turning to hand me one. I then pluck the red pepper flakes out of Nolan's hand and scrawl a big "C" on the front.

"Cred pepper flakes. Yup, that'll do it," Nolan nods, placing them back on the shelf next to the cayenne.

And I know I'm in trouble even before Andy's eyes lock with mine. I try to dart away around the kitchen table, but he lunges for me and he's too fast. He fakes left and I fall for it, then his freakishly long arms are wrapping around my middle and lifting me straight into the air. I can barely catch my breath from how hard I'm laughing as he carries me away, depositing me on the couch in my room and pointing a finger in my direction. "You stay here. You're banned from the kitchen."

"Just tonight or forever?" I wheeze. "Does that mean you'll cook all my meals while I'm here?"

He offers a wry look before heading back.

With dinner in the oven, the boys come into my room to help pull out the couch, and it doesn't take very long before we're all draped across it. It's like we have a mutual gravity—being near them just makes me want to get nearer.

(And anyway, I'm pretty sure anything with mass does have its own gravity, so there.)

Andy is the first to sit on the pull-out couch AKA my new bed, perching himself in the top corner with his arms crossed. Lia lies across the middle, perpendicular to Andy and taking up far more than her fair share of space. Andy rests his socked feet across her calves, which does make her yell "Ew! Man feet!" but doesn't make her move. Nolan sits on the floor, leaning against the dresser, and I arrange myself cross-legged in the space next to Andy and above Lia.

"I love those earrings, Soph," Lia says—*definitely not* throwing out any compliment she can think of to make me feel better about the breakup. "Are they rubies?"

"Um… I don't know." I say, touching one. And I really don't know what they are, but I do know I love them. Small, tear-shaped gems hanging from gold posts. I only realize I'm smiling after it's started.

"Yeah, they're rubies," Andy says confidently from my left, which prompts Lia to jab, "What, are you a jeweler now, Andrew? Oh my god, you know what they look like?" She flips onto her stomach to look squarely at her brother. "They look like that ring of Nonna's. The one you gave that girl on the second date and then she ghosted you."

"Nolan!" I laugh. I can't help it. It's so classically *him*.

"Dude." Andy shakes his head.

"Oh, that's what we're doing today, Lia? Okay, I'll remember this next time Nonna wants to see pictures of your art."

"You wouldn't," she hisses. "Nolan, the woman is 91, she doesn't need to see fiber art nipples. Let her live her final days in peace."

"Would you rather I tell her about the Ragu in your fridge?"

"Are you trying to kill the woman!?"

When the Mercado siblings start bickering, it's best to let it die a natural death. So I leave them to their devices and turn towards Andy, whispering, "When I'm 91, I'm confident I'll still want to see fiber art nipples."

"I'll inform your descendants," he replies seriously, and I feel a rush of gratitude for him that's completely disproportionate to the situation. I'm grateful for the room he's giving me in his apartment, of course. But somehow I'm even more grateful for his company on this couch during this unremarkable conversation.

I know that doesn't make sense. I've had a hard day—cut me some slack.

The night goes on much the same. Nolan serves a delicious homemade lasagna, which we eat while chattering about nothing across the kitchen table.

"I've never had lasagna with peas in it before," Andy says, "but it's really good."

"That's the Sicilian way," Lia explains.

Nolan doubles down, declaring, "It's the only real lasagna." But he's such a goon with his little posh act that when he takes a sip of his wine

I reach out and squeeze his cheeks. Red liquid spurts from his mouth all across the table, covering the lasagna we're still eating, and everyone groans and laughs and I think maybe this is why they keep me around—a spot of levity every now and then.

But I'm also not a total jerk, so I get up to grab paper towels for the mess I made. And people still serve themselves more lasagna, because we all have each other's germs already, so it's fine.

Once we've eaten our fill, Andy pours us each a second glass while I load the dishwasher. (I live here now, remember! I'm a hostess!)

"I've decided I'm definitely going to get tattoos," Lia is explaining as Andy fills her glass. "I just keep changing my mind about what and where. But I definitely want—"

"That makes no sense," Nolan cuts in. "How do you know you want them but don't know what you'd even want?"

"Did you guys know I have a tattoo?" Andy asks, and all three of our heads jerk up. I'm about to go into full-blown psychosis because I didn't know my best friend has a tattoo, when he shakes his head and says, "You all are too easy."

I slap his arm, but he's smiling with two dimples so how can I be mad?

Oh, I haven't told you about the smiles!

Here's the thing: Remember how I'm a professional Andy interpreter? A big part of that is in his smiles.

His default smile would not even be considered a smile for most people. It's a twitch of the lips. Nigh on imperceptible, unless you have my years of grueling fieldwork.

Then he has his polite smile. This is the only one I don't care for, because it's usually fake. I met his brother Owen last year, and the poor guy got only polite smiles from Andy all night (and it was Owen's birthday too—yikes).

Then there's the one-dimple and two-dimple smiles. Physically self-explanatory, those, but let me describe them to you anyway:

The one-dimple smile I gladly accept with open arms. It's a genuine show of Andy's happiness, and is worth its weight in gold. Likely to be seen when someone tells a joke that's actually funny, a person he likes walks in a room, he completes his 95th marathon with a personal best, etc. (I'm pretty sure he hasn't actually run 95 marathons, but basically.)

But the two-dimple smile… that's my kryptonite. The two-dimple smile shows up when Andy forgets himself and is just purely, unabashedly happy. It's hard to put into words unless you know him. Like… you know when dogs wag their tails with excitement and it just melts your heart because they have pure souls, and you want to do everything in your power to ensure nothing bad ever happens to them? It's like that. It's a glimpse into the pure part of his soul that's never been hurt or let down. And I love it so, so much.

Not like… *love* love. I'm not in love with him. But I definitely love him like a best friend, because that's what he is. My best friend in the world.

(Don't tell Lia I said that.)

4

"———— ·•· ————"

I'm not a morning person.

My alarm sounds at 7:30 on Monday morning, then 7:39, then 7:48. Eventually I force my eyes open with a groan, and that's when I remember I'm not in my apartment. I don't have an apartment anymore. Instead I'm in Andy's spare room, with its cream-colored walls and three sensible office plants. I don't know what kinds of plants they are, but they look fairly robust. I hope I don't kill them while I'm here.

Rubbing the sleep out of my eyes, I approach the mirror above the dresser—and can we talk about how Andy is so meticulously prepared for any scenario that he has a spare dresser with a spare mirror in his spare bedroom? Who does that? I mean I'm sure he got it all for free off the street on Allston Christmas, but still.

(We don't have time to get into Allston Christmas right now, but if you're not from Boston just picture a day where the entire city dumps their old furniture out on the sidewalk for grabs.)

The mirror is Dorian Gray's portrait. With the weekend's one-two punch of a dramatic breakup and consecutive late nights, I have certainly looked better. My hair is sleep-mussed, and yesterday's mascara is a filthy fog over the top inch of my cheeks

But it's not just that. It's a mental game, my self-image. Some days I can convince myself I look pretty, and some days I can't. Today is the latter, but it's not my first rodeo. I pull on an outfit that requires no ironing, accessories, or confidence: plain black pants and a gray turtleneck. I run a comb through my hair, grab a Q-Tip to turn yesterday's mascara into today's eyeliner, and we're ready to roll.

Yesterday passed in a daze. I kicked it off by sleeping until noon (who could blame me?) then proceeded to unpack the rest of the stuff Lia and Nolan brought over. When dinner rolled around, it felt like the least I could do to treat Andy to some takeout, especially because he *refuses to let me pay rent.* Yes, you heard that right. I am living rent-free right now. So yeah, I got us an absolute feast of takeout last night because he deserves it.

I told Andy it was because he's "my savior" and he seemed to hate that, so I will be referring to him as my savior as often as possible from now on.

Then the two of us proceeded to stay up way too late, despite having done the same thing the night before with Nolan and Lia, leaving me in my current sorry state of fatigue.

All that goes to say, I'm feeling somewhat low this morning, and planning to basically brush my teeth and head straight to the train. However, the moment I open my bedroom door I'm seduced by the smell of bacon. I have several kryptonites, and bacon is one. (Andy's two-dimple smile is another, as you know, but that one's a secret.)

I walk into the kitchen and find Andy riffling through the cabinets with his back to me. He must have his earbuds in, because he doesn't react to the creak of the bedroom door. And even though he works from home and almost never has phone calls let alone video calls, he's wearing a light blue collared shirt, black pants, and a black leather belt—the embodiment of elective professionalism.

Here's the other thing about Andy: he's made up of pieces that shouldn't fit together. He's pretty tall—maybe 6'1"—but kind of all limbs. He has a nose that's a little crooked and a little too big, dark hair that can't quite decide if it's straight or wavy, and eyes that are so dark brown they're almost black. But altogether, it kind of works. And let me tell you, his interesting looks paired with an elusive attitude? *Irresistible* to the ladies.

The man gets around, that's all I'm saying.

Only when Andy turns towards the fridge does he finally notice me. He takes out an earbud and runs his fingers through his hair—which he usually only does when he's nervous, but I guess is just sometimes a reflex?—and says, "Good morning."

"Good morning." I inch closer. "Whatchya got cooking there?"

"It's uh—" He takes out the other earbud and sets both on the counter. "It's nothing fancy, just bacon and eggs. Want some?"

I glance down at my phone, which says 8:04 AM, and decide I have time for the most important meal of the day. "Best friend, savior, and personal chef. You're a man of many talents, Andy Walsh."

"You have to stop," he says, shaking his head as he turns back to the stove. "I'm going to impose a tax every time I hear you say 'savior' in this house."

"What kind of tax?" I ask, taking a seat at the long wooden table.

"Well..." He takes out two plates and begins to serve us both at the stovetop. "When my brother and I got in trouble for fighting as kids, our mom used to make us chop firewood until we made up."

"You're joking!"

"I'm really not. She said the physical exertion would give us mental clarity or something. I think she just needed chopped firewood."

And I can't help it—I'm laughing out loud. "Oh my god, that explains so much about you."

"It does?"

"Yes! Like why you're always going on long runs because it 'helps you think' like a Grade A masochist."

"I thought I was your savior? Now I'm a masochist?" Andy puts a full plate, knife, and fork in front of each of us, then sits down opposite me. I immediately grab a piece of bacon with my fingers and take a bite.

"People can be two things, Andrew. Besides, I thought calling you my savior was a taxable offense."

"It is. I hope you're ready for manual labor." He gestures vaguely about the apartment with his fork.

"Don't worry, I'm very good with my hands." I give him an intentionally teasing wink as I lick bacon grease off my fingers. He flicks a piece of egg at me which makes me shriek. And by the time I leave for the train, I have a feeling today is going to be alright.

———— ••• ————

It's 8:58 AM when my butt makes contact with the office chair. I may not be Andy-level organized, but at least I'm punctual.

Have you ever been in the staff area for a museum? If not, let me describe it for you.

There's usually not a special staff entrance or anything, you just come in through the front door and make your way through the exhibits until you get to a staircase that's stanchioned off to the public. At the bottom of the stairs you scan your ID badge to enter a set of double doors, and then it's a pretty standard office setup: a bullpen of cubicles in the middle, with executive offices and meeting rooms around the sides.

I'm not nearly fancy enough to have my own office, but I like my cubicle. It has a corkboard in it with pictures of NASA and my childhood cats and a few sticky notes for ongoing projects, plus a calendar of "Badass Women in STEM" that Lia bought me as a gag gift but I actually secretly like. February is Mae Jemison.

I log into my email to ease myself into the workday, but the top message already has me leaning towards my computer screen with a furrowed brow.

My boss—who I generally like, by the way—wants me to make a presentation for our board of trustees *this week*. Surprise! She described it as "no big deal, just a few slides about what they can expect in the new exhibit and the run-of-show for the launch gala." And that's one of the scariest things I could imagine doing, but I'm completely spineless so I write back, "Of course, no problem! Will have that ready by Friday."

"Knock knock," a voice chimes, and I spin to see my work best friend, Mari. (That's an unofficial designation—I have no idea if she considers me *her* work best friend or not, but she's definitely mine.)

Mariane Gomes, Operations Manager, leans into my cubicle in a navy blue pencil skirt and collared white shirt, "no makeup" makeup on her light brown skin, and thick shoulder-length curls. Her cubicle is right next to mine, and beneath her nametag is a purple sticky note (provided by me) that says "Mariane rhymes with Johnny" with a little smiley face. (That's the Cape Verdean pronunciation, in case you didn't know.)

"I got you something," she says, smiling as she holds a cardboard coffee cup in my direction.

"Oh my god, really? Thank you." I take it from her hand with both of mine. "What do I owe you?"

"Nothing," she waves dismissively. "Dunkin was doing two-for-one for the Pats win."

"Oh right, weren't you and Paolo going to the game? Did you have fun?"

"It was freezing, but it was worth it to watch the Giants get their asses handed to them."

"I'm happy you're happy," I offer, having no idea what city the Giants are even from. (These teams play football, right?)

"Anyway, one month until launch day! How are you holding up?"

"I think good," I reply. "I mean, Shawna just asked me to give a presentation about the exhibit to the board on Friday, so that's horrifying, but I'm sure it'll be okay."

"Oof. Good luck. Our board is a mixed bag."

"You've met them?"

"Only a few. They're mostly nice, just…" She leans in theatrically to whisper, "don't be shocked if there are a few huge assholes in the room."

It's obviously a joke, so I force a chuckle along with a feeble, "Got it, thanks."

She straightens up and tilts her head. "Are you sure you're okay? You seem stressed."

"No, no, yeah, I'm fine. Really. I've got my to-do list sorted… mostly." I shuffle a few sticky notes around on my desk, then meet her eyes again. "It's all good."

"Really nothing's going on? Did you sleep okay this weekend?"

"Well, I mean… Elliot and I broke up on Saturday."

I realize immediately that I'm oversharing. This is work! I need to keep some things to myself! But there's no undoing it—Mari's eyes are already full-moon wide. I quickly add, "I'm totally fine though. Really. Just trying to shake off the brain fog still, I guess."

"Oh my god, I'm so sorry. Here—wait." She holds one finger up before darting out of my cubicle, then returns with her rolling chair dragging behind her. She places it directly next to me and sits down, taking both of my hands in hers as she asks, "What happened?"

And I know she's just being a nice person. But the force of her worried attention has my chest tightening, and suddenly I can barely control my expression. I just *hate* when people worry about me. I'm an adult—I should be able to handle my own stuff without making it into other people's problem.

So I pull my hands back (Sorry, Mariane! I know I'm a jerk!) and say, "Oh, nothing I didn't see coming. And it really doesn't matter. I'm doing fine."

"Okay well, I hope so, because I never liked that guy."

"Hah, tell me how you really feel."

"Sorry," she laughs. "Was that too soon? Do you think you'll get back together?"

"No, it's not that." I wave my hand dismissively. "Just a bit blunt. But we're not getting back together. I am moving on."

She quirks one perfectly shaped brow. "Moving on with someone in particular?"

"No, of course not." I roll my eyes, and I hope it comes off as playful. "It's been two days."

"I have ideas if you want to brainstorm." She scoots in closer and lowers her voice. "Do you know Mitchell in accounting? He's single and kind of cute—"

I cut her off. "I'm not going to start dating someone else right now. Even if I wanted to, I just moved into my friend's apartment. I don't want to be bringing dates around all the time when it's not even my place."

"You really think she would mind?"

"It's a he, and I don't know."

"Ohhhhh," she says, dragging out the syllable like she's realized something.

"Oh, what?"

She places an index finger over her mouth, then points it my way. "This friend. You're into him."

"I'm not!" I immediately yell, then remember where we are and bring my voice down a hundred notches. "I'm not."

"He's into you, then?"

"He's not."

"He could be," she insists. "A pretty girl just moved into his apartment. Maybe he's super into you and just waiting to make his move."

I shake my head, because it could not be more obvious that Mari doesn't know Andy at all. "It's definitely not that."

"How do you know it's 'definitely not that'?"

"Because we've talked about it!"

The moment it comes out of my mouth, I know I've said too much again—definitely too much for a work environment and definitely too much for my friendship with Mari.

"Wait, really?" she asks. "You asked him if he's into you?"

"I mean, well, it wasn't recent or anything. But yeah, in the past I've asked him if he wanted to… whatever… and he turned me down. But it was a long time ago and we're just friends now."

She gives me a scorching side-eye. "If he's not into you like that, then why would he be uncomfortable with you dating?"

At this point, my head falls into my hands and I let out an extremely unladylike, "Ughhhhhh, I don't know! I'm not awake enough yet for this conversation. Can we get back to actual work things please?"

Mari laughs it off—and that really is what I love about her. Then she stands and grabs her chair by the back as she says, "Actually yeah, I have to get ready for my 9:30. But you know you can come to me if you ever need anything, right?"

"Of course. Thanks." I force myself to smile—and again, I don't know why I'm so emotionally stunted that I can't accept friends' sympathy like a normal person. "Go to your meeting, I'll talk to you soon."

As soon as she's out of sight, I pull out my phone.

Me: Any chance you want to kill me before Friday?

Andy replies immediately.

Andy: Zero chance.

Me: Mmmm...I'm pretty sure you still owe me a favor for coming to Owen's bday thing with you

Andy: And here I thought letting you live in my apartment rent-free was a favor. Guess not.

Me: *pouty emoji*

Andy: Murder is not an eligible favor.

Me: *double crying emojis*

Andy: Alright, why do you want me to kill you?

Me: I just found out I have to do a presentation for the trustees on Friday and I'm stresseddd

Andy: Do you want to come work on it at the apartment? I can set a timer and remind you to stop worrying every five minutes.

Me: Yes I want that

Me: But no I have to stay here

Me: See you tonight <3

5

Andy

The night I first met Sophie, I was in a horrible mood.

It was the first week of my sophomore year of college and, unfortunately, my roommates were throwing a party.

I've never liked parties, or small talk, or people. But a merciless God left me living with three people who did. They were my friends—still are—but the point stands.

When the party started, I promised them I would stick around for an hour. The minutes ticked by slowly: 58, 59, then freedom. I ducked out at 10:00 exactly, grabbing a beer from a cooler and heading into my room, already dreaming of the feeling of a paperback in my hands.

I once read something about the different types of imagination: Some people read a sentence about a man tossing an apple in the air and can see it like a movie—the colors of the apple, its momentum as it's tossed, the man's hand as he catches it, the texture of his skin. Other people just see the words on the page. They understand an apple was tossed, but an image doesn't form in their minds. I've always been closer to the former, and grateful for it. So when I sat on my bed and cracked open a book and my beer, I was quickly lost to the world. So much so that I didn't fully process that the noise I heard—of a door opening and closing—wasn't just my imagination adding color to the story on the page. In fact, it wasn't until I heard a sharp female "Ah!" that I even looked up.

There was a girl standing in the doorway of my bedroom, looking as surprised as I felt.

"Oh my god, there's a person in here. Jesus, you scared me."

Gray shirt, jeans, freckles on her cheeks, big hazel eyes made bigger by her shock. I cleared my throat, buying time to think of what to say. I landed on "Uh…"

"Is this your room? I'm so sorry. Why did I think this room would be empty? Not that I make a habit of walking into people's rooms when I think they're empty. I swear I do understand boundaries. God, I'm never gonna get invited to a party again…"

I don't think I'd ever seen someone actually *blush* before, but her face was turning from cream to pink to red before my very eyes. She alternated between speaking to me and speaking to herself, like her thoughts and her words were in a race.

"It's… I… are you okay?" I asked, articulate as ever.

"Yeah," she laughed. "No, I'm fine. It's fine. I was just… I really didn't think there would be anyone in here. Sorry again. It was nice to meet you. Thanks for letting me come to a party at your place, and I promise not to barge in anywhere else."

She spun around to exit through the still open door, but was halted by something she saw to her left.

"There you are," said a voice. "I was looking for you. We're starting a new round, come on."

"Oh." She took a small step back. "I think I'm going to sit this one out, thanks."

"No come on, you have to join. I even made you a drink."

I was already crossing towards her by the time a man appeared in the doorway. Tall, backwards baseball cap, ripped jeans—obviously an asshole.

"No really, I'm okay," she tried to say, but he was already shoving a red cup into her hands.

"Here, take it, it's really good I promise."

"Oh, no thanks."

"Come on, you don't trust me? We've been talking all night."

He took hold of her elbow, and a more patient person might have had a more patient reaction, but I didn't. I inserted myself between them, because who gives a shit if this guy likes me or not, and said, "She said no."

The guy looked as offended as he was drunk. "Who are you, her boyfriend?"

"Yes, he is," the girl said without hesitation, grabbing my arm. Her eyes pleaded, *Go with it?*

So I turned back to him and didn't bother with pleasantries. "She's not interested."

The guy tried to counter with a pathetic "Whatever, she isn't even that hot," but the bedroom door was already slamming shut behind him.

Inside my room once again, the girl immediately dropped my arm and put space between us. She was pacing, shaking her head in disbelief.

"Are you... alright?" I asked feebly.

She scrubbed her hands over her face. "Yeah, I'm fine. Sorry. I know you don't want me in here, I just didn't want to talk to that guy anymore but I also didn't want to offend him and—"

"That's okay—"

"—I don't really know how this kind of thing is supposed to go. There were like 40 people in my high school class, so I haven't really been to parties like this before. Should I not tell people that? You know what, it's fine. I'm just going to go back out there. I bet with a few more drinks it'll be very easy to have fun. Thank you, again... for... this..." She gestured vaguely at the room, herself, and the doorway.

"And now I'm going to go."

"You can stay," I said without thinking. "If you want."

Her body stilled facing the door, and I was utterly confident that I'd just made an ass of myself. But then she looked back over her shoulder and asked, "Are you sure?"

"Yeah. I, uh… needed a break too." I reached towards my nightstand and lifted the book there in explanation.

The girl released the corners of her mouth into a smile—small but genuine—then flopped against the door in relief. "A man after my own heart. I swear I would give up my firstborn to be at home reading right now."

In the span of only a few moments, she seemed to completely relax. Her shoulders were looser, posture more casual. I wasn't really sure what to make of it. Did I do that? Did I make her feel more comfortable? There really was a first time for everything…

"Genre?" she asked, nodding to the book in my hand.

"Oh it's uh…" I turned the cover towards her. "Biography."

"Oof, tough. Will you still be my friend if I tell you I hate biographies?"

"I'm your friend now?"

"No, I guess not. You're more like my savior. Unless you think you can handle being both? That's a pretty big responsibility." Her teasing smirk reached its fingers into my chest and grabbed hold.

"Well, I've never had a friend whose name I didn't know."

"You didn't have any ghosts in your house growing up?"

"I actually did, but they were my enemies."

The girl laughed loudly at that, a resonant sound that crackled out of her. The fingers in my chest tightened.

Then the silence fell.

I became acutely aware of our relative positions: me all the way by the bed, her all the way by the door. Should I walk up to her? Should I say something? I shouldn't have asked her to stay. I shouldn't have stranded her in here with me, some miserable stranger who couldn't even remember how far apart people are supposed to stand, let alone remember enough words to form a sentence.

But when I actually looked at her face, she didn't seem miserable. In fact, she was still smiling as she glanced around my room, like she didn't mind the silence at all.

"The party isn't too loud and distracting when you're reading?" she eventually asked, and only then did I realize I was still staring at her. I snapped my gaze away—to the side, anywhere else.

"I—uh…" I cleared my throat. "I have a solution for that. Do you want to see?"

When she tilted her head in curiosity, I nodded towards the bedroom window. The glass pushed open to the warm night air and a fire escape just big enough for two. I climbed out first and offered a hand. She stepped onto the landing, then leaned forward against the metal railing, looking out over the dark street as the sounds of the party started to fade.

"Oh yeah, this is way better," she said. "Thank you."

I moved next to her, leaning against the railing and taking up all the remaining space. Our shoulders touched. She tilted her chin up to the night sky and squinted, trying to spot a few stars through the bright Boston lights. I had to consciously stop myself from watching her again.

"If you don't like parties," I asked, "why'd you come?"

"It's not that I don't like parties," she explained. "I just haven't been to many. I thought it would be more chatting and less… chugging? And anyway, my roommate brought me. Her brother lives here."

I mentally sorted through my roommates. Only one of them had a sister a year younger than us. "Your roommate is Nolan's sister?"

"Maybe? She didn't say his name. Hers is Amelia though, and she's having a great time."

"You could still leave."

"Hah, it's nice to meet you too!"

Fuck. Leave it to me to say something horrible the minute I stop thinking. "Sorry. I didn't… sorry."

She didn't seem to take offense though, just shrugged and said, "I feel like I should stick it out. It's actually my first college party."

"No…"

"Oh God, was it that obvious? What gave me away?"

"Besides what you told me earlier? Kind of everything," I admitted. "Didn't I see you ask if there was alcohol in the seltzers when you got here?"

Even in the low light, I could see the bright blush rising on her cheeks again. "So you've been watching me, huh?"

Fuck. Such a fucking idiot.

Before I could deny it, an uproar sounded from the living room, vibrating the fire escape beneath our feet. Both our heads snapped up to look inside, but we couldn't see past the empty bedroom and its shut door.

"I just don't get the appeal of that table game at all," she said, referencing the cause of the commotion. "I feel like I'm not even that drunk, but the sheer volume of Bud Light in my body is almost debilitating."

She took a seat on the metal landing, then leaned back against the window. Somehow it felt like an invitation, so I sat next to her. Our shoulders touched again.

"You were playing Wide River?" I asked.

"Unfortunately."

"Did you get to the no-hands level?"

"Horrible," she chucked. "I haven't had that much fun since my parents' divorce."

Something about that blunt statement from this summer morning of a person had me letting out a real, full-throated laugh. I realized we might have a few things in common.

Then she turned her face towards mine, leaning to rest her temple against the window. "I'm Sophie, by the way."

"Andy."

"Nice to meet you, Andy. And thanks again, for everything."

She turned back to look up at the sky, allowing herself a few moments of quiet before sighing. "I should probably go back in. My roommate will be looking for me." She stood and opened the window, turning back once to ask, "Maybe I'll see you around sometime?"

"Yeah," I replied. "Maybe."

And I wondered if I would. This girl who made me feel a bit more calm and useful and… normal.

I hoped I would.

6

February crawls through Boston with its claws out. Snow turns to slush. Salty footprints track through halls. Traffic cones and folding chairs stand guard on vacant parking spaces. The B line experiences 20-minute delays, with shuttles from Sutherland to Boston University East. Bar windows display painted shamrocks beside "Go Celtics!" scrawled in green.

Meanwhile, Andy and I find our roommate rhythm pretty quickly. Andy wakes up at 7:30 AM every day, Monday through Sunday, goes for a jog, then takes a shower before starting work. I am somewhat less regimented, waking up when God wills it and usually showering at night. Andy buys groceries on Thursdays and Sundays, and cooks for both of us every evening. I assign myself most of the remaining chores to balance things out—trash, bathroom, vacuuming, etc. (I don't want to be a crappy roommate *and* an imposition. It's like, pick a lane.) Oh, and we stop staying up until 3:00 AM every night, which was admittedly not sustainable.

So now it's day six of roommate-hood, and I'm very stressed, but not because of my living situation. It's because of this stupid presentation to the board tomorrow that I had to rush to get prepared on time, and am not confident it's any good at all. I can already see my night sprawling out before me: seated on the floor of my bedroom scrolling back and forth through my slides like the information in them is going to become more impressive upon the twelfth glance.

As a lifelong overthinker, I've developed some coping mechanisms for days like this. My favorite one is distraction. So as I disembark from the train and start walking home, I call my mom looking for Minneapolis's hottest gossip (among women of a certain age who happen to live in my mom's neighborhood). It's snowing pretty hard now, with a few inches on the ground already. The phone rings four times before she answers.

"Hi, sweetie!"

"Hi, mom. How are you?"

"I'm good, I'm good. I'm just whipping up some Snickers salad for book club, here let me put you on speaker." I hear the click of the phone as it's placed on the countertop, and her voice sounds a bit farther away when she asks, "Can you hear me still?"

"Yep, clear as a bell."

And then she's off.

My mom has the energy of a firework show. She's very entertaining and always has stories to share, and when she decides she wants to talk about something, there's almost no hope of wriggling your way out of the conversation. Today's topics include: the wonders of acupuncture, her boyfriend Billy and his new birding hobby, and a bit of drama she saw on Facebook.

"But anyway honey how are you? How's work?"

"Work's great," I report. "Same old, same old."

Between you and me, I haven't really kept her in the loop about the exhibit launch. It's not like a secret or something—I'll tell her about it afterwards. It's just that she's happy when I'm happy, so it's easier to report back once the stressful part is behind me.

"And what about Elliot?" she asks. "How's he?"

"Oh, um, we actually broke up over the weekend."

"You did? Oh my god honey, are you okay?"

"Yeah, it's all fine," I insist. "I feel really good about it. And I'm gonna be living with Andy until I can find a place on my own, and his place is really nice. He has a spare bedroom and everything."

"Andy? Really?"

I can see where this conversation is going from 1,400 miles away as I answer, "Yep."

"You didn't want to live with Lia?"

"Well, she's in a studio, so there isn't really space for me."

"Hmm."

"What's that 'hmm'?" I try to keep my tone light.

"I don't know," she says. "I just don't really see you living together. Andy's a nice enough boy, but he's sort of standoffish, don't you think?"

I shake my head but keep walking. "He only seems that way until you get to know him."

"Well you'll make your own choices, I'm sure. But I have to tell you, living with an emotionally repressed man isn't for the faint of heart. I would know, I lived with your father for almost 20 years." She laughs at herself, all Midwestern charm, but it doesn't land with me right now.

"He's not emotionally repressed, mom. Really, he's just shy. I promise."

I can feel her shrug through the phone. "It's up to you, Sophia." (She's the only one who ever uses my full name earnestly.) "But I'll be hoping you find a nice place of your own soon."

"Thanks."

After a beat, she asks, "You would tell me if you weren't happy, right?"

"Yeah, of course," I say immediately. "But I am happy. I'm doing great, really. The breakup was my choice and I'm honestly feeling good about it all."

She lets out a long sigh. "Good, I'm glad."

"Hey mom, I'm getting to the apartment now so I'll let you go, but have fun at book club. Tell Dianne and Margie I say hi."

"Okay, I will. Love you."

"Love you too."

"————— •❧• —————"

I feel a mess when I walk in through the apartment door. My cheeks are raw and my glasses are covered in melted snowflakes and the string of tension in my gut from work seems to have double knotted itself during the call with my mom.

Do you ever leave a conversation feeling bad and you're not even sure why? That's this. I'm replaying the call in my head as I unzip my boots and place them on the shoe rack, then hang my coat on the hook by the door. Did she sound upset with me? Or worried? I wish she wouldn't worry. Was I too snappy about the Andy thing? Maybe I should call her back and apologize. I'll do it as soon as I eat something.

Andy doesn't seem to be home yet, so I walk into the kitchen and grab a jar of peanut butter and a big spoon. And I'll tell you, peanut butter is a criminally underrated dinner. It's super fast and fills you up and tastes delicious. What more could a girl want?

No sooner do I place the first glob into my mouth than my best friend comes trudging through the front door, heavily laden with grocery bags like a lanky beast of burden. He sets the bags down and reaches up to take out his earbuds, the bottom four inches of his pants soaked from the snow.

"Hey."

"Hey, you," I mumble around the peanut butter.

He looks from the jar to me and back again. "You hungry? I stocked up."

Of course he did. Thursdays are grocery days after all—the regimented freak.

I swallow my unladylike mouthful, then cross over to him to grab some bags as he takes off his coat and shoes. "Honestly, I'm not that hungry, but do you want to do something tonight? I'm kind of fixating on work stuff and I think entertainment would help."

"Hmm," he muses, picking up the rest of the bags and placing them on the kitchen table. "Do you want to leave the apartment? I think it's Third Thursdays tonight at the Gardener."

"Andy! Yes! That's perfect. Let's do it."

Third Thursdays is this after-hours event at the Isabella Stewart Gardener Museum that happens on the third Thursday of every month, obviously. They set up bars all throughout the museum, and usually have live music and dancing, and you can still see all their normal exhibits too except with a way smaller crowd than usual. I haven't been in years but now that the idea is out there, I probably *have to* go for work… right? You know, doing recon about successful museum events, so I can make our exhibit launch better? Seems like the least I can do.

The momentum of this great idea has me up and heading towards the door when Andy steps into my path, catching my upper arms with both hands and halting my progress.

"Hang on." He physically rotates me back towards the kitchen. "Groceries. Refrigerator. And I want to change, then we can go."

"Right. Okay."

We quickly unload Andy's cloth grocery bags into the fridge and cabinets, then he folds them and places them into a drawer below the microwave. And if the fact that Andy *folds* his cloth grocery bags doesn't tell you the kind of person he is, I simply don't know how to make you understand.

He goes into his bedroom to change out of his snow-damp clothes and I sit back down at the table, reclaiming my peanut butter spoon and nibbling on another big scoop as I scroll through Instagram. Lia's account is at the top of my feed, right where it belongs, and I click through to her profile.

The top three posts are a pretty perfect encapsulation of her brand. The first is a ridiculously hot picture of her in a bright orange bikini outside in the snow. She's all long hair and longer legs, tan skin glowing against stark white as she lounges across her apartment building's front stoop. (Lucky neighbors!) The caption reads "All this snow makes me miss the beach. Thanks @stitchlady.official for helping me bring this suit to life and live my summer fantasy! Get your own sewing machine today with a 10% discount through the link in my bio" followed by a series of hearts and sun emojis. Of course she made the swimsuit herself. I mentioned she's my role model, right?

The second picture is of a handmade pink and red sweater. Lia's sweaters are art. And that's not me being hyperbolic about how good they are—her sweaters are literally art pieces that get shown in galleries around Boston. Don't ask me how she does it, but she crochets pictures and text *onto the sweaters*. And people pay big bucks for not only the original pieces but also printed photos as wall art. It's nuts. The one I'm looking at right now depicts the head and shoulders of a woman on the front of the sweater. Her eyes are closed, chin tilted up, and she's grabbing her own neck on the border between suggestive and violent. It's so… expressive. I can't imagine drawing something this beautiful on paper, let alone making it with yarn and a crochet needle. Insane.

The third post is a video that starts "Hello, ladies!" Lia's wearing a low-cut bodysuit and wide-legged jeans with her hair pulled into a perfectly messy bun. The white glitter around her eyes matches her bright white smile. "Welcome back to embroidery club. Today is lesson three, and we're learning a cute little stitch called the French knot…"

The video's about halfway through when I glance up towards Andy's bedroom door. To my surprise, I find him standing there, looking at me from the doorway.

He startles a little when our eyes meet—like one does when the person they're looking at looks back, and you have to avert your eyes and look around a bunch to make it clear you were just looking around and weren't specifically staring at that person… you know? It makes me smile and huff out a breath of a laugh.

"You ready?" I ask.

He clears his throat and looks back at me again, and his cheeks are actually a little pink as he says, "Ready."

He's the weirdest man alive.

I pocket my phone and head towards the door, but Andy doesn't follow. Instead, he walks over to the kitchen table where I left my peanut butter spoon (whoops). He takes the time to wash it and return it to the drawer before following me out.

"I love it," I say.

Andy doesn't reply, just tilts his head to the side a notch.

We're shoulder-to-shoulder in the Gardener Museum's famous Blue Room. It's famous because—get this—there was a literal *heist* here. It was back in the '80's or '90's I'm pretty sure, and real-life art thieves came in and cut the art out of its frames and just walked out the front door with, like, Rembrandts rolled up in their back pockets. But Isabella Stewart Gardener had put so much love and care into curating each room of this museum—which used to be her house, by the way—that she said in her will that nothing could ever be moved under any circumstances, so the museum just had to leave the empty frames hanging where they were.

It's a really good story, and honestly I'm sure the museum has made a mint off of it. Bummer about the Rembrandts, though.

"I just think it's amazing," I explain. My gaze doesn't leave the ornate gold frame, which now surrounds nothing but powder-blue brocade wallpaper. "They took a tragedy and turned it into its own kind of art."

"Still a tragedy," Andy returns flatly.

I turn towards him. "Would it kill you to look on the bright side?"

"Would it kill you to look on the main, obviously bad side?"

"Oh sure, I'm sorry. I forgot the first rule of a fun night out: focus on the bad side. Should we chat about our relationships with our dads next? Or maybe the untimely deaths of childhood pets?"

He fights a smile. "The empty frame looks ridiculous. Admit it."

"I will do no such thing."

The night goes on much like this. I point out my favorite pieces; Andy responds with shrugs and grunts. But by the time we've each had a few glasses of wine and listened to a strangely good bass/harp duo, his mask starts to slip.

"Not to be that guy," he says in a slightly tipsy whisper, "but I'm pretty sure I could've done that."

We're in the museum's New Wing now, having already wandered the entirety of the old mansion house. This area is basically one big room of white walls and sparse modern art, including the current object of Andy's ire: a large vertical piece covered in an abstract spray of blues and yellows.

"Ah, but you didn't," I whisper back. "That's the thing about art, you have to actually make it to get credit."

"Would we call this insipid Pollock imitation 'art'?"

"You are such a snob, Walsh."

I shove his shoulder sideways, but he catches my arm and pulls our bodies back together, clasping a hand over my mouth that makes me realize just how loud I'm being.

"I'm not a snob," he smirks, overcompensating for my volume with a whisper. "I just think my mom had something like this on her fridge when I was about six."

I drag his hand from my mouth and lean towards him. "Maybe this piece isn't the problem. Maybe you're a prodigy. You've set the bar too high."

"Maybe you're just too generous," he insists. "I want to know which piece in this room you hate the most."

I realize I'm still holding his hand with both of mine, and let it drop as casually as I can. "Okay, but in exchange you have to tell me which piece you feel an emotional connection to."

Andy rolls his eyes dramatically. "It couldn't just be which one I like best? It has to be an 'emotional connection'?"

"Yes. I want you raw and vulnerable, Andrew."

"You're the worst." He shakes his head, even as he starts to scan the gallery room. "Alright, divide and conquer. Let's give ourselves ten minutes to choose something, then we'll meet back here and show each other."

"Deal." I extend my hand. He shakes it once, firmly, before heading off.

When you think about it, Andy has a much easier prompt than I have. He just has to feel *any* emotion about a piece. My emotion has to specifically be hate. And as someone without an artistic bone in her body, I suspect the pieces I "hate" are actually ones I just don't understand. It's not the artist's fault I'm a plebian.

I glance over at Andy, who's scowling violently at a sculpture that—to be fair—does look like a pile of garbage on a table. But the overt disdain on his face is so funny to me that I have to bite my lips between my teeth to keep from giggling out loud.

People think Andy is hard to read because he's not very talkative, but he's really an open book if you bother to learn the language.

But back to the task at hand: a piece I hate.

On the wall to my right I notice a small white canvas with a vertical red line slightly off center. I lean in to read the artist statement, and it has lots to say about… the violence of menstruation? Jesus, deliver me. Okay this might be it. I take a few steps back to consider it from another angle, just in case there's something I missed, but nope. Still a wiggly red line that's supposed to be a statement about… "reproductive patriarchy" I guess?

I look around for Andy, trying to see if he finished early too, but when my eyes land on the back of his head I realize he's been joined by a woman.

She's tall and thin with a black french bob that looks incredibly chic on her but would make me look like I just got laid off from the Wonka factory. They're standing side by side in front of a painting, but the woman's face is turned entirely towards him. Unsurprisingly, Andy's posture looks much less invested.

As his girl best friend, it occurs to me that it might be my responsibility to educate him on female expectations for body language in polite conversation. This poor woman is giving flirting her all, and Andy looks like he's barely noticed.

Oh my god, now she's giving him her card! She's really going for it! You go girl. Andy takes the card from her and she walks away and wow, I couldn't even hear what she said but I could tell it was smooth.

I raise one hand in the air, frantically waving him over to me, and when he gets within earshot I whisper-yell, "Did you just get that woman's number?"

He shakes his head. "No, she gave me her business card."

"Andy." I take a breath, composing my patience. "Why do you think she gave you her business card?"

He shrugs. "I think she wanted to go to the contemporary art museum."

"As a date."

"She didn't say it was a date."

"Andy."

"What?"

"You cannot be that dense."

Andy cocks his head as if to say, *how can you be so sure?*

I raise my eyebrows to say, *because I have two eyes and a brain.*

Another fascinating layer to Andy's personhood: he's like catnip to women. Oblivious, elusive catnip. I have plenty of hypotheses about it, as someone who's spent the better part of a decade studying him in action. There's something about his stoicism and dry humor that makes people work even harder to win him over. And I kind of get it. Nothing makes your endorphins spike like getting a real two-dimple smile from him, knowing his smiles aren't freely given but *earned.* Also like… he does look good. I don't have to be into him to see he's objectively cute.

In all the time we've known each other, I've only seen him make the first move with someone once—yes, once, *ever*—and even then I had to practically script the texts for him behind the scenes. If there was a gold medal for romantic inaction, Andy would win it hands down, no contest, cue the American national anthem.

But—and this is the really perplexing part—out of everyone in NASA, he has had the most relationships over the years. He's always with someone, or seeing someone casually, or talking to someone, or getting asked out and not understanding that that's what happened. It's infuriating. Especially when I'm over here pulling out every tool in my arsenal just to get my boyfriend of three years to even notice me.

Ex-boyfriend, I mean. Elliot is my ex-boyfriend.

"Hey, where'd you go?" Andy's voice pulls me out of my head.

"Nowhere, nevermind." I grab his hand and pull him towards the wall. "Here, I'll go first."

When we stop in front of the depressingly wobbly red line painting, I start my explanation in the middle. "It's not even that I hate it per se. I'm sure there's something to be said for the artist's intent. I just…" I stick both hands out towards the painting, then look to Andy to see if he gets it.

"It's shit," he says.

"It's shit!" I yell. "Exactly!"

He lets out a single, surprised "Ha!" and it sets me off. In an instant I'm laughing too. Loudly. My hands come up to cover my face as if I could shove the laughter back in. Andy's fingers wrap around my elbow, keeping me upright.

"It's just—like—" I wheeze between giggles. "I could draw a red line on a canvas and call it menstruation and no one would hang it in a museum."

"Ah but you didn't," Andy retorts. "That's the thing about art, you have to actually make it to get credit."

"You are truly insufferable," I say in response to my echoed words from earlier, but I haven't stopped laughing and the words have no bite.

"Shhh!"

Both our heads snap up. To our right, there's an entire group of elderly women glaring. "This is a museum," one of them hisses, and I swear if I could melt my body into the floor by sheer will it would be happening.

"Oh my god," I whisper towards them, "I am so—" but I don't have time to finish before Andy grabs my hand and makes a run for it. He darts us through well-behaved museumgoers like we're in Mario Kart.

When we reach the far corner, he stops short and I barrel into him, laughing and breathless. His arms wrap around me—double seatbelt—and there's a warm rumble of laughter in his chest as he says, "I can't take you anywhere."

"Are they still looking at us?" I ask, face buried into his shirt.

"They're pretending not to."

"Goddddddddd," I whine.

"One of them was the artist."

"No! What? You can't know that—"

I twist away to look back at the group, but he catches my arm and pulls me back against him. There's a smile in his voice as he says, "I'm joking."

I'm more than willing to hide my embarrassment behind his tall frame again, with my arms trapped between our bodies so I can't get into any more trouble.

"Just a few more seconds, please," I mumble. "I can't show my face yet."

And he's the best, so he says, "Okay, Soph," and doesn't budge, just rubs a comforting line up and down my back with one of his big hands.

I hate that I'm like this. I'm such a panicker and I really do blush, which is humiliating. But Andy is calm and warm, and it's getting easier to focus on the rise and fall of his chest instead of the group of old biddies who just made me their nemesis.

One by one I pluck the thoughts out of my head until the only thing left is the feeling of Andy's palm as it moves along my spine. My pulse starts to slow, and his hand slows too, and suddenly I'm singularly focused on the exact place each of his fingers is touching me.

I'm tipsy. I know I am. And I know we've probably skipped right over the legal limit for how long friends are supposed to hug in public.

But I've had a rough week and the wine is making my skin buzz and it just feels good, being held by him.

Being held in general—I mean. Not specifically by him.

My arms move from where they've been trapped between our bodies, wrapping around his torso. He's solid and warm but also somehow all elbows and edges, and he adjusts us a bit until I'm tucked comfortably against him. One of his hands comes to rest at the base of my skull, fingertips just barely stretching up into my hair, and you know what? I would stay here all night if given the chance.

But I'm not given the chance. We're only there for a moment before Andy steps back, and every point of contact he breaks feels like a rush of cold water.

"Okay," he says, clearing his throat. "I still have to show you what I picked."

"Oh, right, yes." I clap once, shaken by the transition but hopefully acting normal. "Take me there. Confess your deep emotions, Walsh."

He nods his head sideways and I follow him. We end up at the piece he was standing in front of when Chic Bob Girl asked him out. It's an earth-toned canvas that from up close just looks like swaths of green and brown, but from a few steps back it suggests a patch of long, thin birch trees.

I look to Andy, waiting for his explanation, then look back to the painting because I know he doesn't like to feel put on the spot.

A few more seconds pass and still, nothing from my left. So I ask, "Does it remind you of somewhere specific?"

"Not exactly," is his only response, but I'm not letting him get off that easy. I start counting down from ten in my head, and by the time I get to two he continues, "I guess it reminds me of a specific feeling more than a specific place."

Now here's where the fine art of interacting with Andy Walsh comes into play. I can't act excited that he just showed emotion, because then he'll turtle right back into his shell. The key is to stay cool and collected, like you didn't even notice he shared a piece of himself. So I keep my eyes straight ahead on the canvas as I ask, "What feeling is that?"

And look, even experts make mistakes, okay? Because evidently that was too much too soon. He doesn't respond, just keeps looking straight ahead.

And can I just say that I am fascinated by his ability to straight up *not respond.* Can you imagine? Someone asks you a question or remarks something to you and you just *don't respond?* Meanwhile I'm the court jester over here, throwing pies in my own face at the slightest suggestion that it might please the gentry.

So as the court jester, I keep talking.

"I think for me… it makes me feel tense. Like I'm looking at the forest and I know I'm about to go in alone or something."

One more beat of silence passes before Andy says, "Not just alone. It's lonely." Then, quieter, "I hate feeling lonely."

"Yeah," I breathe. "Me too."

7

I get home after work the next day to find Andy seated in the corner armchair. He's been working out of that chair all week since I commandeered his home office, but he seems comfortable enough. There's a standing lamp next to him, casting warm golden light across the side of his face and onto the manuscript in his lap.

His brow is furrowed in concentration, and part of me wants to place my finger there and smooth out the deep crease.

But I don't, because that would be crazy.

In defense of my crazy thoughts, it's been a hard day. Not just because of my presentation to the board—which could have gone better—but because I kept catching myself thinking about last night at the Gardener. The feeling of my cheek against Andy's chest, the press of his fingertips on my back, then the abrupt way he pulled back, stopping tipsy-me before I could make things weird between us.

I *really* don't want to make things weird between us. Especially when I'm living here. Especially when, even after all these years, I still want to reach up and gauge my own eyes out every time I think about the night I made a move on him and was soundly rejected.

I was very drunk, in my defense! But the rejection was… *so* awkward. And we're much better as friends, anyway. Uncomplicated and easy.

Importantly—as I keep reminding myself—nothing actually happened last night. He saw that I was stressed and gave me a hug. That's the end of it. Especially now that Elliot's not in the picture, why should I feel guilty about a hug? Friends can hug. Friends can totally hug.

Andy glances up at me over the top of his glasses, and I realize I've been staring at him.

I snap my eyes away way too fast and say, "Hey, I'm home."

"Yeah, hey—Soph, shoes."

"Oh, right." I backtrack a few steps to take my boots off before I can traipse salt all over Andy's nice floor.

"You good?" he asks.

"Yeah, sorry, just a hard day and I'm feeling kind of out of it."

"What made your day hard?"

I didn't actually mean to bring that up. Rats.

"Just the board meeting was stressful, but it's fine. I'm gonna decompress in my room."

I start heading that way, but Andy interrupts my momentum when he says, "Decompress out here. I'm just gonna be reading. I have a little work to finish." He gestures to the manuscript on his lap.

I'm scanning my brain for a sentence that means *I think I should give us some space after last night's prolonged public snuggle* without using any of those words, but I'm not quite fast enough. Andy notices my hesitation and responds with a heartbreaking, "I mean—but—if you'd rather be alone that's fine."

And we can't have that.

Because here's the thing: You know how sometimes you meet a puppy and it's fresh-faced and new to the world, and it loves you instantly because it loves everything? And it comes up to you all wiggles and licks and sunshine, and you pet it and scratch it and coo and smile, and then it goes on to offer wiggles and licks to the next person too because it's only ever known good in the world?

Andy is not like that.

Andy is your friend's fifteen-year-old dog who hates toys and is blind and will probably bite if you move too fast. It has never liked a single house guest, and usually gets locked in the bedroom when people come over.

But when that elderly, satanic, gremlin of a dog comes up to you for a tentative sniff, you bet you're going to offer your hand out slowly, on its terms. And when—one day—it finally cuddles up next to you on the couch, placing its scratchy little dog butt against your thigh because it's decided you're safe—that's when you feel truly, irrefutably special.

And yes, Andy and I have been friends for almost a decade, so it's not like if I say "I'd rather read alone in my room tonight" he's going to think I hate him or something. But I just don't have it in my heart to turn down any offer of affection extended by him, even if that offer is simply reading in silence together.

So I say, "No, I don't want to be alone."

The better part of an hour goes by before Andy finally closes his work for the day. He excuses himself to change into pj's and comes back out in a black t-shirt and red flannel pants. I'm already in my very stylish gray cotton athletic shorts, wool socks, and a purple t-shirt with *Hudsonville Read-A-Thon* across the front.

Once he's sat back down on the far side of the couch, he taps my knee with his socked foot and asks, "How's your book?"

"It's good," I say, folding in the edge of the dust jacket to hold my place, "but it's the only one I brought so I'm trying to make it last."

"You could go to the library. Or I can lend you something when you're done. I have books, you know." He points towards his chest. "Editor."

A thought hits me like a minor epiphany. I look around the apartment again to make sure I'm not out of my mind before I say, "You know what? I'm just realizing that you don't have any bookshelves in here."

"They're all in my room." He nods his head towards the closed bedroom door. "Never know when I'll have a middle-of-the-night reading emergency."

"Ah, of course. Well in that case, yeah, thanks. I'll take you up on that."

I'm opening back to my place in the book when he asks, "Are you ready to tell me what's bothering you?"

"Nothing's bothering me," I reply, confused.

"You said the board meeting was stressful."

Right. I forgot I mentioned that. And I kind of assumed he would forget too.

(Elliot would have.)

"Oh, it was nothing, really. Some of the trustees are just annoying, but I don't need to whine about it all night."

"I bet Lia would have them killed for you," Andy suggests, in a small nod to our ongoing bit about Lia's relatives being in the Italian mob (they're not) and a large nod to her abrasive personality.

"No," I chuckle, "it's not all that serious. Honestly, most of it was my fault."

"I doubt that."

"No really." I put the book down on the coffee table then turn to face him, sitting cross-legged on the couch. He mirrors my position, leaning forward to rest his elbows on his knees. "First, they asked way more questions about the budget than I thought they would. Like I'm not the budget person, ask Raphael! That's literally not my job." I notice I'm yelling for no reason and ratchet down my volume. "Then one of them had a question about this video we're showing at the launch—and this is the part that's on me, because I'm pretty sure Shawna did tell me about that question. I almost definitely wrote it down, but I guess I lost that sticky note somewhere…"

Andy tucks his lips between his teeth, barely suppressing his smile—the smug jerk. I give him a glare that says I don't want a lecture on organization right now.

"*Anyway*, the worst part was actually after the presentation was over. There's this trustee named Jeff who's a biologist and really old—not to be ageist or anything but I feel like it's a salient part of the story. And he came up to me and was all like, *Good job today, honey. I bet your* parents *are really proud of you.*" I'm looking down at my hands as I continue. "Then he said it's a shame I didn't pursue a real science career because I might not be challenging myself enough here, or something like that."

When I glance up again, Andy is looking at me with focus. He doesn't respond—at least not yet—because he's not listening to respond; he's listening to understand.

"I think he meant it as a compliment," I explain, "but it hit a nerve. Like… this *is* a science career. I've always wanted to bring science to kids, and I'm doing it. It just really made me feel bad. And who talks to a professional colleague like that? *I bet your parents are proud of you.* Are you kidding me? There's no way he would've said that if I was a 26-year-old man instead of a 26-year-old woman. And the worst part is, I was so shocked that I just froze with this nervous smile on my face. I hate confrontation so much. I don't even know what I would do differently if I could go back. I guess I just have to let it go."

"If you want to let it go, then let it go," he says plainly. "But if you want to be mad, then be mad. You have every right."

"No, no." I wave a hand between us. "Being mad is just going to make my night worse and bring you down with me. Just… that guy sucks."

"That guy sucks," Andy affirms. "Fuck him. The museum is lucky to have you. And even the biggest asshole on the board realizes it, even if he says it in a condescending asshole way."

It's a sweet thing to say, but I'm feeling so deflated from the whole endeavor that I can't bring myself to offer more than a half-smile.

Something about the look on my face has Andy reaching over to take both of my hands in his. "Hey, don't be sad, okay? I'll make dinner. I have pizza dough—how about pizza and a movie?"

And I guess I'm more tired than I realized, because I feel tears starting to prick at the back of my eyes. But I am not going to cry over something as stupid as *this*. So I fight them back and say, "That would be great. Thanks."

Andy squeezes my hands once before letting go and heading into the kitchen.

It occurs to me then that maybe I'm not tired at all. Maybe I'm just not used to having someone take care of me every day, even in these small ways.

"What do you want to watch?" he asks as he turns the dial on the oven.

I clear my throat, then ask, "Is it masochistic that I'm in the mood for sci-fi after the day I had?"

"I thought I was supposed to be the masochist here."

"Well, you did just voluntarily subject yourself to that story about my day, so you're right, you're still number one."

"Sophie, it's fine." He opens the fridge and peers inside. "People like you have to get mad once in a while."

"What do you mean?"

"You know how you are," he replies. It's almost dismissive, as he starts to pile pizza ingredients onto the counter.

"No, I don't," I insist, and I don't know if I should be worried or offended about wherever this conversation is going. I turn my body towards him—chest pressing into the couch cushions—in time to see him shrug.

"The way your emotions are, you're barely human. You feel maybe half the normal range of human things." When I don't reply, he adds, "It's a compliment."

"A compliment," I repeat. "It's a compliment that I feel half the human range of emotions? Thanks. I'll keep that one in my heart right next to my other favorite compliment from today: I could've had a real science career if I wanted."

"No, I mean—" He turns and sees something on my face that changes his tone immediately. "No. Shit, I'm sorry, I said that wrong. I mean—fuck." He crosses the room, coming up to the couch until we're face to face. His hands hover near my shoulders for a moment but then pull back, never making contact. "I just meant that you're so understanding. You're *too* understanding. You almost never let things upset you and always find the best in people. For fuck's sake, you found the best in *Elliot* for three years. So if you get mad sometimes, it just means you're human like the rest of us. That's what I meant."

His pleading expression lets the air out of my anger.

"You never liked Elliot, did you?"

He shakes his head. "No. I didn't."

I'm tempted to ask him why, but have a suspicion the answer will only hurt my feelings more. Instead I just say, "Okay."

"You know," he probes tentatively, "I still don't know why you broke up."

But at this point I'm too exhausted to unpack it all. I haven't even unpacked it for myself yet, really. So I ask, "Another time?"

He nods.

"———— •••• ————"

Twenty minutes later, the pizza is hot and sliced and plated on the coffee table as the opening title for *Arrival* plays. Andy's on the far right side of the couch, and my place is on the far left, but about halfway through the movie I abandon sitting in favor of lying down, and Andy benevolently lets me rest my feet on his legs. I suspect he's still making amends for telling me I have 50% of the normal human capacity for emotion earlier, but I'll take it.

"If you were Amy Adams, would you do it?" I ask, pointing with my pizza slice towards the TV. "Would you go try to talk to the aliens?"

Andy half-shrugs. "I doubt I'd be anyone's first choice for it."

"Yeah okay, but if for some reason the FBI showed up at our door and said it has to be you. Would you do it?"

He thinks for a few seconds. "I don't know. I'm not a particularly brave person. And I can barely make conversation with humans, I doubt the aliens would like talking to me."

"I love talking to you," I say, because it's the truth. "Actually, sometimes you're too easy to talk to and I say things I mean to keep to myself. Like the Jeff story today. It's like I have no self-control around you."

"Well, if the FBI needs a Sophie interpreter I'll volunteer."

"You better," I say, smiling as I roll onto my side. "But I know what you mean. Connecting with people is hard."

"Are you kidding?"

"What?"

"It's not hard for you at all. You can start a conversation with anyone. I've seen you make a friend in ten seconds flat."

"That's not true."

He rolls his eyes. "You're so wrong that I'm not even having this discussion with you."

"Well okay, I guess making *conversation* can be easy if you're willing to just say whatever pops into your head. But making real friends is hard. I've always found it hard."

He doesn't argue.

The movie plays on for a few more seconds before my mind catches on something else he said.

"Wait—what do you mean you're not a brave person? You're much braver than I am. I bet you would've given Jeff a piece of your mind today."

"No way," he laughs. "Maybe we're both chickens."

An idea pops into my head. I look over at him, then pull my legs back and sit upright. "Okay, hear me out. Let's both do something brave tonight."

He looks down at the two of us in our pajamas, then at the time on his phone. "You mean like... leave the apartment?"

"Oh no," I laugh. "No way. We're way too far gone for that. But we can do something brave from here. We have the whole internet at our fingertips."

"You seem like you have an idea." He turns his body, resting one arm along the back of the couch and offering me his full attention.

"Well... if I tell you I need you to be unconditionally supportive, okay?"

"Okay." He picks up the remote and pauses the movie.

"I was thinking I could download a dating app," I say, then quickly add, "I know Elliot and I only broke up a week ago, but I'm not looking for *love* or something. I just think it would help me get him out of my system if I did a little rebound dating."

Andy tilts his head to the side, and it feels like he's x-raying straight through all the mush in my head. In those two seconds, his dark brown eyes ask me if I really want to go on rebound dates or if I just don't know how to be single anymore. They ask why I hate solitude so much, and when I became so dependent on external validation.

But his eyes aren't actually asking any of that, of course. It's ricocheting around my brain of its own volition. And in the absence of a response from him, the court jester in me is about 1.5 seconds away from saying, *Nevermind, that was a stupid idea—anyway want to hear a joke?*

But then he nods. "Dating app. Okay, that's doable."

"What about you?" I ask. "Anything you've been wanting to do, but haven't worked up the courage?"

His gaze dances across my face, and I'm not sure what he's trying to find there.

Eventually he clears his throat and says, "I guess it feels weird that my brother moved back to Boston but we never see each other."

"I liked Owen when we met. Why don't you invite him to Lia's thing tomorrow?"

"The art show?" Andy raises both eyebrows to the ceiling. "I don't know if that's his M.O."

"It's at a brewery. I think the main focus is going to be beer, then socializing, then art. Just invite him." I reach out and squeeze his thigh. "He can always say no."

His face twists for a moment before he says, "Fine, but let me do mine first before I back out."

"Yes!" I clap. "Be brave. You can do it."

I know what you're wondering, but it's not that Andy has a *bad* relationship with his brother. They just… don't have a relationship at all. Owen is two years older—30 to Andy's 28—and works for a big-shot law firm in the Seaport neighborhood of Boston.

I don't know much about what happened between them. (Andy's not a big talker—you got that, right?) But over the years I've pieced together a bit. They were definitely close as kids: they went to the same school, played soccer together, hung out with the neighborhood kids in their quiet northeastern Massachusetts town. Then their dad left, and they never quite recovered. Andy was 11 at the time and Owen was 13. Don't ask me any more about that, because I don't have answers. But that's when they started to drift apart—Andy choosing books, Owen staying out of the house as much as he could.

Owen moved to New York City for college, and a few years later Andy decided to stay in Boston and go to Ashmore. That kind of solidified the distance between them. They still both came home for Christmas and everything, but they didn't really know each other anymore, let alone have things in common. They would send each other a text on birthdays and stuff—it wasn't like there was active animosity, just no closeness either. Owen didn't even make it into town for Andy's college graduation, which I know hurt him much more than he'd ever admit.

Then, a little over a year ago, Owen's law firm transferred him to Boston out of the blue. He announced the news at Christmas dinner, and their mom was understandably over the Moon to finally have both boys back home, but from what I've inferred their relationship hasn't improved much since then. Like, for example, Owen had a birthday party a few months ago, and Andy brought me as his plus-one and *only* talked to me all night, despite my encouragement that he get to know his brother's friends. And… that's about it for Walsh brother bonding of late.

This is a really good idea. Andy will extend an olive branch, and maybe Owen won't take it, but at least he'll know he tried.

I unabashedly watch over Andy's shoulder as he types out a text.

Andy: Hey, Owen. I hope everything is good with you. Some

> friends and I are going to a happy hour/art show in
> Somerville tomorrow if you're interested in coming.
> We will be there around 4.

Then he pastes in a hyperlink to the event page. When it sends, the preview image pops up as a psychedelic medley of illustrated flowers, beer bottles, crying eyeballs, and middle fingers, with the boldly declarative title *Art Pop Your Pussy at Kalorama Brew.*

Andy's eyes go wide as he realizes what he just sent, and I can't stop the audible laugh that sparkles out of my chest. He flips the phone over on the coffee table so he doesn't have to look at it anymore, and that just makes me laugh harder.

"Done. Jesus," he groans, running his fingers through his hair and leaving behind a tousled mess. "Your turn. Do something."

I give his knee another squeeze, because I know that was hard for him and I'm proud of the effort he's making, then I pull out my phone. "Okay, I technically have the app downloaded already, but I haven't set up my profile yet."

Then poor Andy is then subjected to a full thirty minutes of profile set up minutiae with me. He helps trim down some of my long-winded prompt answers, and even—after *much* hesitation and arm twisting—weighs in on the pictures I use.

"What about these?" I ask, scooting next to him on the couch and flipping between two pictures of me walking down Beacon Street. In the first, I'm looking over my shoulder at the camera with a normal closed-mouth smile, bright green dress, neat line of rowhouses in the back. The second is the same, but Lia must have said something to make me laugh from behind the camera, because my mouth is cracked open and my eyes are squeezed shut.

His face is stone as he looks between the two, then says, "The second one."

"Are you sure? I feel like it shows more personality but I also look a little ugly."

He just snorts, then goes back to scrolling on his phone.

"What kind of response is that?" I shriek, shoving his shoulder. "You know I'm emotionally fragile right now, Andrew. You can't just laugh at me for feeling ugly."

I'm not actually offended, of course. And he can tell, because he shoves my shoulder right back, making me flop sideways onto the couch cushion.

"Yeah, right. Like you need me to tell you how you look."

"Well, under the circumstances," I muse, righting myself, "I am literally asking your opinion on how I look."

"Yeah, but you know you're beautiful."

He says it like a throwaway, staring down at his phone, as though he's told me I'm beautiful a million times before. And let me tell you— he has *not*. Not that he's said I'm unattractive or something. He just doesn't comment on my appearance. And why would he? He's a guy. But I admit I'm a little thrown right now.

"Are you still trying to make me feel better about the Elliot thing? Because I promise, I'm fine."

"Are you fishing for compliments? Because I promise I don't give a fuck about Elliot."

And I can't think of anything to say to that, so I just say, "Okay, fine," and add the picture to my profile. "I think I'm done. Want to help me swipe? It's actually pretty fun. I do it with Lia all the time."

"Yeah… I've actually used that app before."

"Oh, right. Weren't you helping Nolan with his profile too?"

"Trying to, but he's an obstinate motherfucker."

That makes me laugh out loud. "Okay then, you're a veteran who can help me in these trenches. Like what do you think about this guy?" I scoot over to show him my screen. Andy's arm is stretched across the back of the couch, and there's the perfect amount of space for me underneath it. Our sides are flush as he leans in to take a look.

"Thirty-four, consultant, likes travel and working out… eh." He gives a noncommittal shrug.

"Okay, you're right, that is painfully boring, but look at the picture with his cats! And it says their names are Rumpkin and Bumpkin. I'm sorry but I simply must match with him."

Andy pinches the bridge of his nose. "Jesus, Soph, you can be more discerning than that."

"Okay then, Mr. Know-It-All. What do you look for? Let me see yours." I stick my hand out, waiting.

"Well..." He reluctantly hands over his phone. "I try to glean if they seem smart. I know you can't tell much from a profile, but the wrong 'your' is a dealbreaker."

"Wow," I chuckle, "insufferable as always." I have his passcode memorized so I unlock it and scan until I see the app. "Don't you worry you swiped away on your soulmate because she made a typo?"

"Oh, 100%. And it would be a just punishment for my elitism."

"What about what they're looking for? Like if someone wants marriage and kids, is that a turn off for you?" I can't help but notice the list of unread messages in his inbox, several of which are... quite forward. I should've seen that coming. Catnip Andy.

"I mean, I do want those things eventually. But usually I'm just using the app for... something casual."

Realization dawns, and I feel my mouth fall open. "Oh my god! You just use it for sex!"

"Isn't that what you're doing?" A flush rises up his neck.

"Yes," I laugh, "but it's way crazier when you do it."

"Why?"

"You're so... you!"

"I have a feeling that's not a compliment." He runs his fingers through his hair again and looks away from me.

"No, no, Andy, please." I grab his hands and make him look at me, so he knows I'm serious when I say, "It's the biggest compliment. I just meant you don't love meeting new people, and you always need to plan everything out so completely. I'm surprised one night stands are your thing, is all."

The next second seems to swell into ten, as I realize I'm talking about sex with Andy while holding both of his hands. I'm acutely aware of the press of my fingers into his palms, the temperature of his warm skin against mine. I pull my hands back, then wish I hadn't because surely the abrupt movement made things weirder.

Andy shifts away slightly—okay yes, I definitely made that weird—and mumbles, "Well, we don't really talk about sex, so…"

"No." I swallow. "We don't." I spot the remote on the coffee table, and am about to reach for it to break the awkwardness when he speaks up again.

"Do—" He clears his throat. "I mean, are they your thing?"

"One night stands?"

"Yeah."

"I don't think so. I mean, I've had a couple, but that's part of why I thought the dating app thing would be good for me. I haven't had much experience being single in general. I usually…"

I trail off, stopping myself before I can say *I usually jump into a relationship with the first person who shows interest* so I don't sound pathetic.

But he doesn't make me finish the sentence. He meets my gaze and says, "Yeah. I know."

There's a subtle pressure change in the air between us—a warning pulse. His dark brown eyes flicker across my face, taking in every accidental tell in the twist of my lips and flush of my cheeks. He always seems to see too much of me. More than anyone else. More than I'm ready to show.

"So, um…" He hesitates, then asks, "How many dates?"

"Huh?"

"How many dates do you have to go on with someone before…"

I realize what he's asking, feeling my mouth fall open but hearing no sound come out.

"Sorry. That was weird. Pretend I didn't ask."

"No, it's okay. I'm just worried you'll judge me."

"When have I ever judged you?"

He asks it so sincerely, and the worried furrow of his brow reminds me that he never would.

"At least three," I admit. "Sometimes more. Does that make me a prude? I'll kiss on the first date, but doing much more than that right away has just always felt too vulnerable."

"That doesn't make you a prude."

I give him a sideways glance. "Are you just saying that because I'm the first person to use the word prude since the 1950's?"

He laughs, and it takes some air out of the ballooning tension. "No, though that's a bonus."

I open my mouth again, then stop myself.

"What?"

"What *what?*"

"Just say what you were going to say, Sophia."

I tuck my knees up in front of my chest. "Are you sure about that? Because I was going to ask you how many people you've had sex with, but then I realized I kind of don't want to know the answer."

"You don't?" he asks earnestly, and the question makes my temperature spike about a million degrees.

"Not… I mean… not because I'm like… jealous or something. Oh, Jesus." I drop my face into my palms, hiding from myself. "I totally made this weird. I swear I didn't mean it like *Tell me how many girls you've slept with because you're mine and they need to die*, I just meant—"

"I didn't think you did," Andy tries, but I can't stop talking.

"—like as a friend I was curious, because I've heard every single hookup story that Lia has ever had and I feel like that's a best friend thing, to talk about that stuff, but then I realized that it's not really our dynamic and I shouldn't be asking for that amount of detail."

"It's not our dynamic?"

"Clearly! Look at me!" I point to my face that's 700 degrees Fahrenheit and fluorescent pink.

"That seems like a *you* problem, not an *us* problem."

Andy leans forward, casually picking up another piece of pizza from the coffee table, and his nonchalance is making me insane. I need to steer this conversation back to safer waters or I will physically die. So I do the first thing I can think of: without warning, I lunge forward and take a huge, messy bite of the pizza in his hand.

"Hey!" He shoves me back onto my half of the couch, laughing as he attempts to protect his slice. "Get your own, weirdo."

I fall back against the couch cushion, giggling around the cold glob of cheese now hanging from my mouth.

Tension dissipated. Mission accomplished.

When we eventually press play on the movie again, I split my attention between the big screen on the wall and the small screen in my hand. Patrick (34, consultant, likes travel and working out) starts the conversation by commenting on a picture of me in a bookstore carrying a stack of three huge novels to the register.

> Patrick: i love this series
>
> Me: Oh awesome! I'm reading it now. I'm almost done with book two and am really mad at Merenia for the whole secret message thing. No spoilers please!
>
> Patrick: let me know when you get to the end, the cliffhanger is torture
>
> Me: Ahhhh ok will do!
>
> Me: Also I have to ask, do you actually call your cats Bumpkin and Rumpkin or do they go by nicknames?
>
> Patrick: usually they get called b and ru, unless my niece is over, she named them, i think it confuses them when their real names come out
>
> Me: They are so cute! I'd love to meet them someday
>
> Patrick: wanna come over now, i'll send my address

And look, I'd be the first to admit I'm mostly looking for a hook up right now, but even by those loose standards, it's an abrupt proposition.

> Me: Maybe we should meet for drinks to get to know each other first. Are you free next weekend?
>
> Patrick: how's next friday

8

I wake up the next morning feeling… good. Lighter than I have in recent memory. After all, I have two reasons to be excited now: a brewery trip with my best friends today, and a perfectly low-pressure rebound date next weekend.

I get out of bed mid-morning and check my phone for the weather. Shockingly, Boston in late February is still—as Nolan says—"colder than a yeti's ballsack," so I throw on jeans and a fitted maroon sweater. Standing before the mirror, I pull my hair into a high ponytail and pop in my contacts. And you know what? For the first time since the breakup, I actually feel pretty good about my reflection.

I pick up my favorite ruby earrings from the top of the dresser, rolling them over in my hands a few times. I don't even notice I'm smiling until I've secured the second one in my ear.

Spoiled as I've become with Andy's cooking, I'm a little disappointed when I don't find him in the kitchen this morning, so I decide to keep breakfast simple, grabbing a box of Chex from the cabinet and sitting down at the long wooden table to eat it dry. I've just shoveled the first handful into my face when I hear the bathroom doorknob turning.

The next moment is like a movie. Both because it happens in slow motion, and because it's hotter than anything else I've ever seen in real life.

The bathroom door swings inward. A plume of steam cascades out, and through it walks Andy, a white towel slung low over his hips, a second towel roughly tousling his hair.

And sweet baby Jesus.

I realize that, up until this moment, I'd still been thinking of Andy as the scrawny 19-year-old I met at a party the first week of my freshman year—all limbs and angles, too tall for his own skin. He's still lean, but he has definitely grown up in the intervening nine years.

My eyes catch first on his arms, raised to dry his hair with only an effortless, utilitarian flex of biceps that shouldn't be nearly as sexy as it is. Then my gaze drops to his chest, his stomach, the dark trail of hair leading down…

"Oh, you're up," Andy says as he lowers the towel from his face. "Sorry—I would've put clothes on if I realized…"

I avert my eyes as quickly as possible. "No, no, I'm sorry. You're good. Carry on."

I stare into my bowl of Chex like it contains the lost texts of Sophocles, waiting a full three seconds after his bedroom door snicks shut before daring to look up again. What is wrong with me???? A single week without sex and it's like my brain has already turned to horny mush.

(Well, that's not entirely true. My brain has a history of turning to horny mush for Andy.)

I know, I know. It's never going to happen. Nor do I even want it to, really! I wouldn't want to ruin our friendship with something as superficial as sex. Especially since he already turned me down once, you'll recall.

It's been long enough that I can laugh about it now. (Sort of. Maybe.) It actually almost seems surreal, that I straight up asked him if he wanted to hook up. I've never been that bold in my life! Needless to say, I never made the same mistake again. But every once in a while something like this happens, and it reminds me why I did it—while also burning a scorching hot hole of embarrassment straight through my chest. I pray to any and all Gods that he's completely forgotten about that night by now. And anyway, I eventually found a way to turn those feelings off.

Well… if not turn off, at least tamp way down into oblivion.

That is, until a few years ago.

It was an uneventful Saturday in an uneventful month, and Andy and I set out to watch all of the *Lord of the Rings* movies in a row to pass the time. It started as nothing. I was cold and asked for a blanket. Andy brought one. Then Andy was cold too and tucked himself under the other half. Our knees touched and neither of us moved away, but that was excusable, plausibly deniable, even *normal* for us to maintain that small point of contact.

We talked and watched and talked some more and eventually the first movie ended and the second began.

Halfway through, Andy made popcorn. We fought over the last handful until Andy scooped up the kernels and jokingly put them in my mouth. I clamped my lips over his fingers, sucking off the butter as he pulled them free. And it was fine—just a joke. (Kind of.) I laughed, and he laughed at my laughter, and then he was pulling me down across his chest. We fought and twisted and fell until our laughing died down and all that was left was the curl of our bodies into each other. Him flat on his back, my head resting on his shoulder.

And there we stayed.

I swear in that moment I could feel my pulse just under my skin. Could've counted my heartbeats from the pressure of it. The movie kept playing but I didn't take in a single second of it when my entire attention was focused on the press of Andy's warm body against mine.

The second movie ended. Andy sat up, reached for the remote, pressed play on movie three, then laid back down, exactly as he had been. Our silence was a shield and I followed suit, tucking myself into his side without ceremony.

When I stirred awake in the middle of the night, I was still on that couch, lying across Andy's sleeping chest. The TV cast a faint, cool light over the room, and I took in a deep breath. The body beneath me smelled like laundry detergent and… *Andy*—a faint muskiness that was familiar and comforting, like the soft embrace of bed after a long day.

And it just felt… right. It felt like I should've been there the whole time. It horrified me, actually, how good it felt to hear the rise and fall of his breath. To feel the warmth of his skin, the weight of his arm curving around me.

I repositioned myself by just an inch, my cheek moving against his shoulder.

"Soph?" Andy whispered, almost under his breath.

Shoot.

"Yeah?" I whispered back.

"You awake?"

I hesitated. "A little."

"Should…" he started but trailed off.

The radiator clanged. A siren passed outside.

"Should I get up?" he finally asked.

It was a yes or no question, so I simply said, "No."

He said nothing else, and eventually I drifted back into sleep.

By the time I awoke the next morning, Andy was already up and dressed and acting like nothing happened. But I couldn't stop it. That old longing had bubbled back to the surface.

I tried to remind myself that I'd already humiliated myself with him once and gotten an answer: we're just friends. Just. Friends. I refused to humiliate myself a second time.

It was moot anyway, because a few months later I met a guy named Elliot at a conference and we hit it off. He was handsome in that old-money, waspy kind of way. He took me out to nice restaurants and had season tickets to the symphony and made me feel special, for a while. And it was just so nice to have someone. Even if there was no magic. Even if—in between our "I love you"s—I was never sure if he actually *liked* me.

Maybe that was enough, I thought.

Maybe that's all I could ask for.

But even so—even after all that—didn't my heart still catch with every innocent touch that passed between me and Andy? A tap on the arm, a pull of the hand, a head on a shoulder.

And when I woke with my cheek pressed to Elliot's chest, didn't I sometimes keep my eyes closed for just a minute longer, imagining it was someone else?

Didn't I even—sometimes—think of him when Elliot was pushing inside me?

No. Definitely not.

"——— •❃• ———"

Andy and I don't interact again until it's time to head across the river to the brewery. It's pretty much right off of the 86 bus route, so we take the cheap transit option. When we plop down onto the hard blue plastic seats, Andy seems lost in thought.

"Hey, where are you right now?"

He shakes his head a little. "I'm here."

But he's not. And there's a (growing) part of me that worries it's because of the combined moments of weirdness between us recently, not the least of which was my fault earlier today.

"Sorry about earlier," I try. "I didn't mean to like… completely stare you down this morning."

"No, that's okay." He blushes the slightest bit as he says it, but otherwise seems unaffected. So alright, if that's not what's bothering him, time for guess number two.

"How are you feeling about the Owen thing?"

Andy shrugs, then turns to look out the bus window. "He wasn't sure if he could even come."

Bingo.

I tuck my arm into the crook of his. "If he shows up, do you want me to stay with you or do you want time alone with him?"

"I don't know."

"We can play it by ear." I know he's freaking out, but I also know he doesn't want me to make a big deal about it, so I just rest my head on his shoulder in solidarity. "Maybe we can stick together to start, but if you feel like you want to talk to him alone you can squeeze my hand and I'll take it as a cue to clear out."

"Okay." He tilts his head down at me, and a small smile tugs at his lips. "Nice earrings, by the way."

I smile back. "Thanks."

"———— •♦• ————"

We walk up to the large red brick building only a few minutes after the event is supposed to start. Gigantic, colorful banners reading *Art Pop Your Pussy* are hanging everywhere, depicting a mandala of repeating iconography with little to no apparent theme (horses, skull and crossbones, cacti, and flaming hearts among them). There's music playing from the crappy outdoor speakers, and a steady stream of hipsters flowing through the doors.

Inside the cavernous open-concept space, we're met with an assault on all senses: the smell of fried food, the glare of neon lights, the twangs of an obscure singer-songwriter over the sound system. The bar is in the very center of the room, with vibrant fiber artwork hanging from all the walls.

"Look who it is!" someone cries from our left, and Lia runs over to squeeze us each in a hug. She's wearing a tight black skirt, bright purple thigh-high boots, and a purple crop top turtleneck (a garment that begs the question: what weather is this designed for?). Her hair is up in a high ponytail, and she's wearing purple eye makeup with shining silver earrings. She looks gorgeous, so I tell her as much.

"Thanks for getting here on time so I can actually say hi to you," Lia says. "We're expecting it to get crazy soon."

"This isn't crazy yet?" Andy murmurs.

"Where is yours?" I ask, scanning the art on the surrounding walls.

"Oh, it's in the far corner." Lia points behind the bar. "I'm actually supposed to stay by my work, but when Nolan gets here come find me."

"Of course." I squeeze her arm before she dashes away through the crowd, then I take a second to survey the room. The overall vibe is Sexy Hippie Artist. To my left, a woman with long pink braids is talking to a tall man with a mustache and insect tattoos crawling up his arms. To my right, a woman with a shaved head and cat eye makeup is flirting with a veritable Clark Kent.

I lean sideways towards Andy and whisper, "Maybe this is Nolan's chance to finally meet someone in person. Everyone here is super hot."

"You think Nolan can pick up someone here but you and I can't?" he jokes.

"Oh, speaking of, did I tell you I made a date for next weekend with that app guy?"

"Already?" He pulls back in surprise. "You don't want to, I don't know, get to know him first?"

"I'll get to know him on the date. That's like, the whole point of a first date." I quirk an eyebrow, daring him to contradict me.

"Well then," he says, shifting his gaze out to the room, "with you off the market and Nolan being Nolan, it looks like I'll have my pick of the lot."

"Stop!" I laugh, swatting his arm. "Nolan is objectively a catch. He's just... really bad with women?"

We're both laughing at the truth of it when a beefy hand clasps over each of our shoulders.

"Hey friends!" Nolan exclaims, poking his head between ours. "Whatcha talking about?"

We exchange a guilty, wide-eyed look before I say "Nothing, nothing—hey you" and grab him around the middle in a hug. "Want to go over and see Lia's stuff? She's in the back corner. Andy's brother might stop by too but we're not sure if he'll have time."

"Oh," Nolan says, realizing that Owen's possible presence is a big deal. And of course he does—it's downright weird that he's never met his best friend's brother before. "Do you want to hang by the entrance for a bit in case he makes it?"

"Nah," Andy says. "I wouldn't wait around."

Andy's back is to the door, so I'm the first one to see Owen come in.

There's certainly a family resemblance between him and Andy, but no one would ever confuse the two. Andy's about an inch taller and noticeably leaner. They have the same shade of dark brown, wavy hair, but Andy wears his longer. Andy is also clean-shaven, where Owen has a neatly maintained beard. But ultimately, their eyes are the biggest difference: Andy's are a rich chocolate brown, while Owen's are an almost uncanny light blue.

I take and squeeze Andy's hand once to remind him of our plan before I stand on my tiptoes and wave. "Owen!"

He notices me and starts heading over. He's a little overdressed, in gray slacks and a white button down, but who cares. He came, and I couldn't be happier for Andy. Even having met him only once before, I can't resist pulling him into a hug the second he reaches our circle.

"Hey Owen, it's so good to see you."

"Great to see you too, Sophie." He releases me and extends a hand towards Nolan. "Hi, I'm Owen, Andy's brother."

Nolan takes Owen's hand in both of his, shaking enthusiastically. "It's great to finally meet you, man. I'm Nolan. I can't believe it's taken this long."

Owen and Andy look at each other then. I can almost hear them mentally weighing the pros and cons of a hug versus a handshake. Eventually they settle for the most awkward choice imaginable as Owen offers a small wave from across the circle.

"Hey, thanks for inviting me. I've heard of this place but never made it up here."

"Yeah," Andy says with a nod. "No problem."

"How are you?" Owen asks cautiously, like Andy's a scared kitten he just found on the side of the road. It's the wrong approach.

"I'm good. How are you?"

"Good. Good. How's work?"

"It's good."

"Yeah?"

"Yeah."

My heart sinks watching Andy retreat into himself. Sometimes I just want to shake him and tell him to *say more, say anything, try harder!* But I know that's not fair, because he's nothing if not trying. Still—it is literally, physically painful to watch.

I love the full version of Andy so much. The version that's silly and pedantic and set in his ways and comfortable with silence, the version that snarks and scolds and listens closely to every word you say. I hate seeing him protectively offer up only a tiny sliver of himself to the rest of the world, like it's the only part he thinks other people can't hurt. I wish I could tell him that the full him—the real him—is the most likable and lovable person I've ever met, and that anyone who thinks otherwise can roll over and die.

But at the same time, if I'm being honest, there is a tiny part of me that feels special, knowing not everyone has a chance to experience him the way I do.

I wonder about that sometimes—whether it might really be just me. He's had a lot of girlfriends over the years. Did they get to see every facet of him? Did Carly ever see him belly laugh over the misuse of the word "nonplussed"? Did Steph notice he always has to try out a recipe twice in private before he'll make it for anyone else? Did he dismiss Nour's insecurities with a look so earnest and piercing that it felt like the world had narrowed to just the two of them?

Maybe.

Or maybe they only saw glimpses of that Andy, my Andy.

In the most secret and unfair part of my heart, I hope they didn't. I hope his full self is only for me.

"Been working on any projects lately that I should check out?" Owen asks, trying to mask the discomfort written all over his face.

"The last couple books have been thrillers," Andy replies.

"Oh, yeah, cool. I could read a thriller."

"Okay."

"You should send me the title."

"Sure."

Then the silence starts to stretch.

And that's all folks. That's well above the quota of social discomfort I can handle here in the ninth circle of small talk hell. I place a hand on Andy's arm and say to his brother, "Thanks for making it all the way out here. I know it's a trek from the Seaport. Is your office there too or do you just live there?"

Owen looks relieved at the interjection, and I briefly hate him for it. He doesn't get Andy at all.

"Live and work," Owen replies. "It's pretty nice actually. Less than ten minutes walking door to door, and the building has a pool and a gym and everything. I'm pretty sure it even has something called a 'pet spa'. And lots of bars nearby. It's great."

"That sounds incredible. I don't know if you heard but Andy and I are actually living together now." I loop my arm through the elbow of the roommate in question.

"You are?" He sounds genuinely surprised, and looks to his brother for confirmation. Andy nods, then looks down like the eye contact was painful.

"You just moved recently?" Owen asks, looking back at me. "How's it going?"

"It's going great, his place is beautiful. Or… I guess it's *our* place now. Definitely better than anything I could afford on my own."

"So it was a financial decision?"

"Kind of." I shrug. "Honestly, I don't want to get into the whole sob story, but trust me, Andy really saved me." Then I wink at Andy, trying to pull him back into the conversation with a taunt about his savior complex.

Andy places his hand over mine and squeezes—our signal.

"You know," I say, turning back to the group. "I saw a sign that said they're giving out free samples of their IPA. I'd be happy to grab some for everyone. Nolan, will you come help me carry them?"

"Sure… Soph is there a reason you're being weird?"

"What? Shhh!" I pull him towards the bar. "We'll be back soon."

I wave quickly over my shoulder then cross the room with Nolan in tow.

"Ow, loosen the grip, Soph."

"Sorry." I drop Nolan's arm when we reach the bar and not a moment sooner. I wasn't risking his complete bumbling of social cues until we were out of earshot. "I just didn't want you to blow the plan. Andy and I made a signal for when he wanted to talk to Owen alone."

"Is that what the lovey-dovey hand holding was about?"

I shove him sideways. "It was not lovey-dovey hand holding."

"Sure looked like it to me."

"Can you read lips?" I ask, ignoring his idiocy.

"Um… maybe? You want me to read theirs?" Nolan spins around—extremely conspicuously—to face Andy and Owen across the room.

"No, shh, stop!" I grab his shoulders and spin him back towards me. "You have to be cool about it, but I can't see that far. My contacts prescription is old. Can you see what they're saying?"

Nolan leans forward against the bar, much more subtle this time, and glances over his shoulder at the brothers. He puts his 20/20 vision to use with a slight squint. "Well, their mouths are definitely moving."

"That's not nothing," I reply, then turn to the bartender and order four IPA samples.

"Andy looks pissed, though."

"Shoot. Can you tell what he's saying?"

He takes a moment to watch, then reports, "I think Andy just said 'It's not like that.'"

"That's vague."

"Oh my god." Nolan grabs my elbow, then spins to look away from the boys and face me completely. "I think they're talking about you."

"What! How can you tell?"

"It looked like Owen said 'She's hot' and then they both looked over here."

"They looked over here?" I shriek. "Why are you still looking at them then?"

"I'm not! I'm looking at you."

And sure, Nolan is facing me, but his posture is the exclamation point at the end of the sentence *I love spying on people!*

"God, can you act more natural? Here." I take two of the beers from the bar and shove them into his hands. "Hold these."

When I look up to his face, his eyes are full-moon wide. "Oh my god. You *want* them to be talking about you."

"Pfft." I wave my hand between us.

"You like Owen!"

"What? No I don't!" I'm definitely blushing now, but it's not even true. I mean, I like Owen fine as a person but I'm certainly not *into* him. I would never even consider it!

I grab the remaining two beers off the bartop just for something to do with my hands, but Nolan puts his beers back down and leans down to my eye level.

"You are being super weird right now. Look me in the eyes and tell me you don't like him."

I give him my best incredulous look. "I genuinely don't like Owen like that. I've only met him once."

"Then what's this?" Nolan flicks one of my cheeks, referencing the frustratingly obvious blush there.

"It's hot in here," I protest. "And it's completely normal to want to know if people are talking about you. It doesn't mean you have a crush on them. Just keep watching. Try to catch more."

"No. I'm not enabling you. We're going back over there."

Nolan grabs the beers again and starts marching back before I can stop him. I stagger behind, trying to look casual but also kind of freaking out. I mean, there's no way Owen actually likes me, right? But I don't know what else that conversation could have been. I guess Nolan's lip reading could have been wrong? Actually, that seems like the most plausible scenario.

The brothers don't notice us approaching right away, and we catch the very end of their hushed conversation.

"You don't know her," Andy is saying.

"I don't," Owen replies, "but I know you."

"Do you?"

A beat passes between them. Owen retracts the hand he had been resting on Andy's shoulder. Both men seem to realize we're there at the same time.

"Sorry," Andy says, and it's not clear if it's meant to Owen or us. But when his eyes catch mine there's a clear plea there, and I know I'll do anything to fix this for him.

"Hey guys," I smile big and hand over the full glasses like I didn't notice a thing wrong. "Beers for everyone. Should we head over to Lia's art? She said we should come over as soon as we're all here." I take the spare beer in Nolan's hands for myself, then nod my head towards the back.

"Yeah," Owen exhales, visibly weary. "Good idea."

When we find Lia, she's talking excitedly to a tall girl with dark brown skin, bright blue eye makeup, and long twists in her hair. Lia spots us and waves, then comes to grab me and Andy by the hand and pull us closer.

"Welcome to my lair," she says with a beaming grin, depositing us near a wall where two knit sweaters are hanging. "I'm going to make you stand here and guard my post for a second so I can get a drink."

"Wait, before you go." I grab her shoulder. "Let me introduce you. This is Andy's brother, Owen. Owen, this is our friend Amelia."

When Owen sees her, something about him visibly shifts into gear. His scowl from the Andy conversation is replaced by a warm, cocky smile. Then he leans in and takes her hand, saying in almost comically honeyed tones, "Amelia, so nice to meet you. I understand you're the woman of the hour."

And there goes Nolan's theory that he's interested in *me*.

Not that I'm disappointed or something. I really don't like Owen like that. It just, you know… it feels good to feel wanted sometimes.

Whatever.

"Well, I'm just one part of a pretty big show, but yes I'm excited to be here," Lia replies, and honestly I'm proud of her for staying civil in the face of such overt flirting. She does this weird thing where she always needs to have the upper hand in romantic situations, and tends to snap when other people make the first move.

Don't ask—I don't get it either.

Owen doesn't take the hint, shamelessly scanning her from head to toe and back again. "Gorgeous and talented, it must be my lucky day."

Lia's gaze mimics his, taking stock of Owen's dark hair, blue eyes, strong build, and slightly-too-formal clothes. When she meets his eyes again, she responds with a simple, "Ew."

Nolan nearly spits out his drink. Andy blushes crimson. Owen seems, at most, mildly discouraged, with a devilish grin still pulling at the corners of his lips.

And me? I have far, far exceeded the amount of awkwardness I can handle in a day. In sheer desperation, I pivot to face the woman next to Lia with a too-loud, "Hi! I don't think we've met before. I'm Sophie."

"Hey, I'm Rayna," she says with a wave and a shy smile.

"Oh, you're Rayna! Lia's Rayna! I thought you looked familiar. So nice to finally meet you. Are you a hugger? Can I hug you?" When she nods, I pull her in tight.

Lia and Rayna have been seeing each other casually for a few weeks. Nothing serious yet it sounds like, but enough that I've heard the name and know Lia's excited about how things are going.

"Lia told me you do makeup content and I admit I totally went and followed your account. I've watched kind of a lot of your videos, and I developed a secret dream that someday you'd help me figure out which eyeliner shape looks best on my face."

"Oh my god, you follow me?" Rayna replies, a new brightness blooming in her expression. "Don't worry, I got you. Everyone's so focused on contouring right now, but eyeliner makes just as much of a difference for how people see your face shape."

"Okay not to interrupt this love fest, because I'm so excited for you two to meet," Lia says, wrapping an arm around Rayna's waist, "but I really do want to grab a drink. Do you want to come with, babe?"

"Oh, sure. We'll talk more later."

I squeeze Rayna's arm in agreement, then let them go off to the bar.

In the wake of their departure, Andy immediately turns to his brother. "Great first impression."

Owen shrugs. "Didn't realize she's gay."

"She's bi," he replies curtly. "Try to keep it in your pants."

"Oh sorry," Owen returns with equal bite, "did you and Sophie want a monopoly on flirting at this event?"

"Owen."

"What?"

"That's not—"

"Oh, we weren't—"

"What's wrong with you?"

"It's not like that."

"Oh shit…" Nolan says from the sidelines.

"You know we're just friends," I insist, more flustered than I should be. "And we should focus on Lia's art anyway. She'll want our thoughts when she gets back."

Reluctantly—practically melting under the heat of the awkwardness—Andy, Nolan, Owen, and I turned to face the wall.

Before us are two sweaters, one mounted higher on the wall than the other. The top sweater is mostly light blue, except for the image of a woman's eyes and forehead peeking up above the bottom edge—crocheted in amazing realism with darker shades of yarn. (Lia really is good at her craft.) The woman has on heavy makeup and long lashes, with small, shining white beads sewn on around her eyes.

Below that, the lower sweater depicts the woman's shoulders and chest. The dark blue yarn shows her wearing a low-cut top, with the same shimmering white beads glittering across the top curves of her breasts. The negative space between the two sweaters stands in for her nose, lips, and neck. We stand in silent observation for a few minutes, until Lia and Rayna walk up holding bottles of beer and each other's hands.

"Okay, I'm ready," Lia says excitedly as she joins our line. "We're going left to right. Andy, what do you think?"

"They're great, Lia," he says. "I haven't seen you use beads before but it adds a lot."

That's about as verbose as Andy will ever be and Lia knows it. "I'll take it. Soph?"

"I am obsessed," I say, immediately pointing to specific areas of the work. "I don't know if this was your intention, but she looks really sad to me. Something about the blues, coupled with the beads around her eyes that shine like they're tears. It's like she wants so badly to look beautiful, and puts so much effort into her appearance, but feels like it's never enough. Maybe her self-image relies on external validation, but there's self-loathing underneath that she's not addressing. I even think you can see that in the shape of her brows. She looks determined, like she doesn't want to cry. I also think the two pieces separately would tell a completely different story than they do together. Like the bottom sweater alone would be more of a blanket commentary on female objectification, while the top alone would give me almost a pop art feel." I turn back to face Lia. "Am I anywhere close to right?"

"There's no right and wrong, but this effusiveness is exactly why you're my best friend." Lia blows a kiss, which I catch in my hand and plant on my cheek with a smile. Then she asks, "Nolan?"

"I mean…" he exhales, "Yeah, it's great, but you're not going to actually wear them, are you? I don't ever want to see the bottom one on my sister. That's just nasty." He's blocking out the view of the lower sweater with his hands, which Lia bats downwards with a level of violence only siblings can get away with.

"*Ma sei scemo?* It's art."

I'm never sure exactly what the Mercado siblings say to each other in Italian, but I assume that one basically means *you're an idiot.*

Finally, Lia pivots to face Owen. And honestly, it's a tremendous show of good will on her part that she even asks, "And you?"

Owen's hands are in his pockets. "It's good I guess."

I see Lia's mouth open, and I just *know* whatever comes out of it is really going to dampen the vibe, so I jump in as quickly as I can. "Do you think you'll do any more pieces in this style? With the vertical stacking? It's such an interesting effect."

Lia's mouth closes, then she looks to Andy out of the side of her eye. His clenched jaw and heated face broadcast his stress, and—miraculously—it's enough to make her drop the brewing fight. "I hope so," she says, looking back at me, "but probably not until I have another exhibit space lined up that's this big."

Without looking at him, I reach to the side and take Andy's hand in mine, squeezing once. Just to remind him I'm there.

9

Days pass in the comfort of our new routines. Andy—who I'll remind you has been cooking dinner for me every single night since I moved in—has started making breakfast for both of us too. And look, I do feel bad. But also he's just so good at it, and it's so delicious, and he really doesn't seem to mind cooking, and it's not like I asked him to do it! It just became a pattern. Every morning I come out of my bedroom and comment about how good something smells, and every morning he says he made extra just in case, and every morning he looks genuinely happy as I take a seat across from him at the table. He eats with perfect etiquette as we plan our days and joke about our friends and even just enjoy each other's quiet company.

This morning breaks from the routine, however, when I burst into the kitchen shouting, "SNOW DAY!"

"What?" Andy asks over his shoulder, filling a pot of water at the kitchen sink.

"HR just emailed. The museum is closed because of the storm!" I can't help myself. I run and jump onto his back. He catches me easily, hoisting me up with two big hands under my thighs. "We're going to have so much fun!"

Once I'm properly balanced on his back, he reaches to turn off the tap. "We still have to work."

"Yeah but who cares? We can work together. We can sit on the living room floor or something and make a day of it. I'm talking snacks, maybe a background movie... It'll be a great day!"

"We have a table." Andy carries the pot of water over to the stove with one hand, the other still holding my leg to keep me steady.

"That's so much less fun and special than the floor. Didn't you hear? It's a snow day!" I pat rhythmically on his chest, wiggling my shoulders and kicking my legs and making his task essentially impossible.

He sets me on the ground, then turns to face me. For a moment it looks like he's going to object. But in classic Andy fashion, it only takes about two seconds of expectant eye contact to fold him like origami paper. He sighs, "Okay. Go get your computer while I hard boil these eggs."

"———— ❀ ————"

I can admit, the floor set up is less than comfortable, but that's not the point. Andy's seated on the floor in front of the couch, computer on the coffee table. I'm lying on my stomach across the living room rug, computer and sticky notes sprawling in front of me.

We put a crappy movie on in the background. It's a Netflix Christmas special, which may be two months out of date but felt thematically appropriate for the snow day. And despite the floor-induced back pain and cloying dialogue, we both have productive mornings. I draft my remarks for the exhibit launch (Did I mention I have to give a speech? I'm nervous, but I'm sure it will be fine...) and Andy catches up on client emails. It's only when he lets out a dramatic groan that our concentration breaks.

"What?" I ask.

He shakes his head. "This guy is killing me."

"Why?" I shift positions until I'm sitting cross-legged.

"He never listens to my suggestions and his draft is full of plot holes."

"Is this the guy who wants to introduce a brand new character in the climax?"

"Mhm."

"He emailed you? Can I see?"

Andy shuffles out from behind the coffee table and places the computer in front of me on the rug. When I read the text on the screen, I can't help but roll my eyes.

Andy

I don't think you understand the intended tone of the work. Readers are supposed to think a happy ending is inevitable until Chapter 26. If they have all the information earlier on the story will lose all mystery and nuance. Please try rereading with this in mind. I look forward to seeing a new round of edits soon.

Hank W. Bristol

"Okay, first of all, Hank W. Bristol seems like a real jerk. But have you tried using a compliment sandwich?"

Andy gives me an incredulous look.

"I'm serious. Here, watch, I'll template it for you."

I take maybe 60 seconds to type out a response, starting with praise, then constructive criticism, then praise again, using what Andy's told me about this manuscript already but leaving blanks where he can fill in the details.

Dear Hank,

Thanks for this clarification. I see what you mean, and agree it is a great strategy to leave subtle breadcrumbs for the reader to pick up throughout the work without ever leading them directly to the answers. The manuscript does this very well in ______.

I think this structure would be even more effective if _______ is introduced or foreshadowed earlier. That way the reader won't have to suspend their disbelief about the coincidental timing of ______.

Let me know if you'd like help brainstorming ways to do this. I think with these few additions, the work has the potential to be a real page-turner.

All the best,
Andy

"I don't know," Andy says. "It doesn't really sound like me."

"Well edit it, Mr. Editor," I quip, pushing the laptop back towards him. "Make it sound like you. But leave in the compliments, butter him up a little. Once he likes you he'll be more receptive."

"Are you saying I'm unlikable the way I am?" His tone is joking, but also maybe a little not.

"I love you just the way you are," I insist, "but I also have the privilege of knowing the whole you and not just email you."

"So *email* me is unlikeable?"

"You said it, not me." I raise my hands in feigned surrender, keeping the mood light, and Andy's expression turns devilish. He sees an opening—lunging forward to grab the spot on my ribs where he *knows* I'm most ticklish. I shriek and topple backwards, batting his hands away, but it's hard when he's bigger than me with crazy long arms and

I'm already wheezing. He grabs my waist again, and I can't help my peals of laughter as I flail on the rug. He's absolutely ruthless, and it's only by luck that I catch hold of his arm and pull him down too, compromising his offensive. He falls gracelessly, landing across my chest, arms and legs tangled in mine.

"Not another move, Walsh!" I gasp, trying to hold his arms against his sides. "Hands where I can see them."

"Okay, okay," he smiles. "Truce."

He props himself up on his forearms, putting a bit of space between our chests. And only then do I process the position we're in.

I'm on my back, hair splayed out, chest rising with each panted breath. Andy's lying over me, and God he's so close. He smells like clean laundry and something muskier, heavier. He smells like *him* and it's comforting and masculine and as familiar as the look in his eyes. Only a few inches of air and a decade of boundaries separate our faces from each other; even less separates the rest of us. Our bodies line up in all the places that count, his gaze locked on mine, and my brain is short circuiting. Trapped under the weight of Andy's body, convincing myself that maybe—just maybe—that look in his eyes means he's started to feel some of the attraction I've always felt.

I'm frantically searching through reasons why it could be okay to stay like this. Explanations that sound like friendship. Excuses to press more of myself against more of him. But Andy beats me to it. His voice is a low scrape as he says, "You're so—"

My phone buzzes on the rug next to me. I want to know the end of his sentence more than I want my next breath but I *shouldn't*, so I reach for the phone. Mariane's name is on the screen.

"Oh, I have to take this." I still sound breathless, and that's as embarrassing as anything. Andy pushes up to his knees to free me, and I press accept. "Hi, Mari. What's up?"

I stand—too flustered to have this call with Andy watching me right now—and start walking towards my room. I mouth "sorry" back towards him, gesturing towards the phone, then close the bedroom door behind me.

"Darn it." I trudge back into the living room a few minutes later in the midst of a completely new thought spiral. "Apparently there's a typo on some of the signage we sent to the printers. I just had to call and ask them to halt the job, which they had already started, so we're going to have a penalty fee." I sit back down on the floor and immediately start angry-scrolling on my computer. "I knew we shouldn't have let that intern proofread the signs. But he was so excited and I felt bad saying no. See, this is why people shouldn't leave me to manage things. I'm too much of a pushover."

"You're a great manager," Andy says automatically, but he has no idea.

"Objectively, no I'm not. I have messed up a lot on this project. This is just Example A. And it's okay, right? Management is a growth area for me, and that's alright. I just hate feeling so incompetent."

"You are not incompetent. Look. I already got an email back from Hank." He turns his computer screen so I can see. "I couldn't have done that without you."

I take a few seconds to skim the response he got before looking back up at him. "Yes, you could have."

"No, I couldn't have."

And I love him for having faith in me, but clearly he doesn't get it. I'm shaking my head as I say, "This whole experience has made me wonder if I'm crazy applying for a PhD. I just don't know if I'm cut out for it. My professional strengths are things like that." I gesture vaguely towards the email on Andy's screen. "I'm good with vibes and vibes only. The second I have to do logistics I become a hot mess. And education research is like… *all* logistics. Maybe I'm not ready. Maybe I should just defer and try again next year. Then I can pick more schools in New England and I won't have to go so far anyway. I probably should have thought of this a long time ago—"

"Sophie." He cuts me off, taking hold of my upper arms. "You're catastrophizing. Stop. Come here." He stands and pulls me up with him, then leads me to the coat rack.

"Where are we going?"

"We're going to have a snowball fight."

I barked out a surprised laugh. "Why?"

"Because we need a break. Come on."

<hr>

"Rules?" I ask as we descend Andy's front steps into nearly a foot of fresh, unshoveled snow.

"Hmm… First to three hits wins?" he suggests, looking up and down the quiet one-way street.

"Do we each get a home base?" My hand trails down the railing, already collecting the snow piled there.

"I don't think we need them, but hiding behind things is fine."

"Okay, and when does time start?"

"Whenever you're ready."

"How about… now!" I ruthlessly pummel him in the face with my fistful of snow, then sprint away as fast as I can.

"You're in trouble," he calls after me, but I'm already ducking behind a nearby car. The make and model are unrecognizable beneath a pillowy layer of perfect snowball snow—just wet enough to stick together, but not too hard to shape. I scoop some into my bare hand then crouch low, hiding as I pat it into a ball. I already regret the lack of gloves, but there's no going back now.

I wait five seconds for Andy to emerge. Then ten. He's nowhere in sight. Listening hard, I can't pick up any hints, so I have no choice but to peek around the side of my car-fortress. To my surprise, the sidewalk is totally abandoned. I look left and right, freezing wind scraping over my cheeks, then start to retrace my steps until I eventually find Andy's bigger footprints in the snow. It looks like he was running straight towards me, until he veered off…

Splat! Splat!

Two snowballs hit my back rapid fire and I shriek, whipping around in time to see Andy disappear behind a dumpster across the street.

"Yeah, you better hide!" I yell, scooping up fresh snow and packing it tight. "Revenge is a dish best served cold, Walsh."

I scurry across the street and duck on the opposite side of the dumpster from Andy. There's no way I'll ever outrun him, so I'll need the element of surprise. My hands are already numb. The time to act is nigh.

Using all of my (admittedly meager) strength, I haul myself onto the top of the dumpster just as Andy curves around the side. I ambush him with a snowball to the top of the head, then jump down on the far side and run for my life, not stopping until I find a new car for cover at least halfway down the block.

"Next hit wins," Andy bellows. He sounds far away, maybe 50 feet, and I'm determined to remain on the offensive.

If he's still down the block, maybe I can creep along the street side of the parked cars until I'm close enough for another sneak attack. The road is unplowed but not unpassable, so I curve around the SUV in front of me and into the street, trying not to let my snow-soaked pant legs distract me from my mission.

I inch along soundlessly, gaining careful ground. It's nearly impossible to see through the cars' windows with the thick layer of snow and ice, but eventually I catch a flicker of motion on the sidewalk and duck low. Target acquired.

Crossing behind the car, I skim snow off the trunk to make my new weapon. But when I leap onto the sidewalk, arm cocked back and poised to strike, Andy is lying in wait.

"Gotcha!" he yells, making me scream. I dodge his snowball as I throw my own, then bolt for cover again. Freezing tears of laughter blur my vision. I beeline for a parked minivan, darting back to the street side blindly.

Then there's a screaming honk.

A sharp jolt of fear.

The sudden bite of snow on my face and the lurch of strong arms around my middle.

A black pickup truck streaks past, not a foot from where I stand locked against Andy's body. It speeds around the corner, blowing the stop sign and disappearing without a trace.

My pulse is pounding. My hands are shaking. I'm not sure I'd even be upright if it weren't for Andy holding me tight against his chest. My breath clouds the air as I clutch his forearms, fingers seeking something stable.

One more second passes. Then two. Then three.

Eventually my heartbeat slows. Andy turns me around in his arms, but doesn't put an inch of space between us yet.

"Are you okay?"

I swallow heavily as my fear and shock turn to embarrassment. "Yeah. Thanks for that."

He doesn't reply, just stares down at me, fists tightening in my coat. The warmth of his body makes me realize how cold I am. I bring my ungloved hands up between us, rubbing them together.

"Should we call it a tie?" I ask, trying to play off how rattled I'm feeling. The last thing I need is to make Andy worried. But then my teeth start chattering, and all bets are off. Andy releases my waist to unzip the front of his coat, and I can't resist. I move into the space he created for me, wind-bitten cheek leaning against his solid chest, frozen fingers curling into his shirt. He wraps the coat as far around me as he can, then rubs his hands up and down over my back.

"No, you clipped me with that last one. You win."

"Then why were you still chasing me?"

"Because I didn't want you to get hit by a car."

"Oh." I pull back just enough to meet his eyes. "Right. Thanks again."

Andy doesn't move, just holds my gaze as he holds my body.

And maybe I'm just caught in the moment—on this day of highs and lows and closeness and almosts—but I forget to look away.

Andy has such nice eyes. Kind eyes. A bottomless dark brown. And so expressive. He's always said more with his eyes than he's ever said with his words.

The fogs of our breath mix in the air. My stare flicks down to his lips for just a second, and I marvel at the curl of steam moving between them.

Sometimes I wish I had a witness to moments like these. Some objective third party who could tell me what I'm seeing. Who knows everything about me and him and our friendship and history, and could tell me if I'm seeing something real or not. Because when I think back on the near-decade of our friendship, I have about a million almost-kisses catalogued there. Moments that were subtle enough to deny. Moments that never would have almost-happened if anyone else had been there. But no one ever was, and we never crossed that line, so the almost-secret was safe with us.

But is any of it real? Or is it just my naively hopeful heart?

Because I did ask him to cross that line once, remember. And he turned me down. It was a long time ago, I know, and people's feelings can change over time. But if Andy's feelings had changed, wouldn't he have said something by now? I've already laid myself on the line— shouldn't he realize the ball's in his court?

Maybe not. He's not exactly socially proactive. But without getting *something* from him, there's no way I can take that risk again.

I pull back, putting a very reasonable foot of space between us. "Should we go back inside?"

"Yeah," he replies, "let's get you warmed up."

10

———— •❦• ————

few hours and one hot shower later, I come out of my
bedroom in a green cotton dress.

"Okay, first date outfit. What do you think?"

I put my hands on my hips, waiting for his review. The dress is knee-length and flowy, maybe a little much for the restaurant I'm going to, but I figure that's okay. My hair is just straight and down, and I put on a little bit of makeup and gold earrings.

Andy puts down his cleaning supplies and gives me his full attention. He scans the outfit from head to toe and back up again. Having two female best friends, he's been asked for outfit feedback before, though this one is taking him longer than usual to form an opinion. I'm actually starting to worry by the time he says, "That's a kind of fancy dress for a first date."

"Andy! You're supposed to say I look great and he's going to love it. Is there something wrong with it? God… I don't know what else I have. I'm going to FaceTime Lia."

I spin on my heel to head back in the bedroom, but he stops me with a stuttered, "No I—I just mean, are you going somewhere fancy?"

"Well, not really." I turn back to face him, leaning against my door frame. "But to be honest I really have to do laundry, and my other date night outfit idea was jeans, so that was an obvious no."

"An obvious no," he deadpans.

"You know, jeans are… logistically difficult."

The quirk in his brow says he's not following.

"I mean, if I don't want to have sex then jeans are fine, because then I don't have to worry about getting them off. But if I do want to have sex a dress is just easier. Not that I even know if he'll want to, but if maybe he decides he does want to, then…" I shrug. "Path of least resistance. Whatever—don't look at me like that! Was that a weird thing to say? Am I making this weird?"

Andy tries to contort his face back into neutrality as he says, "Sorry, yeah, no, yeah, that makes sense."

"Actually, speaking of which, I meant to ask…"

God, this is awkward—it's so painfully awkward—but I have to do it because I have to be a courteous roommate and lordy, maybe this is why women shouldn't room with men.

I look down at my dress as I ask, "What's the apartment policy on bringing dates home?" He doesn't reply right away, so I dare a glance up. And he looks *alarmed.* I rush to backpedal. "I know that this is really your place and I've just been crashing, so if you're not comfortable with me bringing someone back that's totally fine. Really, I want you to be honest. It's totally fine either way."

"Oh, uh, no, it's fine," he stammers. "This—it's your place too. You should, you know, treat it like home."

"You're sure?"

I'm staring at him intently now, but his features are schooled. No tick in his jaw or crease in his forehead to betray an unstated issue. He replies with a collected "I'm sure" and I have no choice but to take him at his word.

"Okay. Thanks." I nod at him—and wow, even that is weird—then head back into my room to finish getting ready.

As I look around for my shoes and bag, I can hear the sounds of Andy opening the refrigerator, sifting through its contents, and pulling out ingredients. A clink of bottles, the crinkle of a wrapper, a tap against the counter. Then the low sound of his voice, asking, "So… you're gonna have sex with this guy?"

"Well," I call towards the open door as I zip up my black boots, "I have to meet him first and then we'll see. I don't even know if he'll want to. But that is kind of the whole point of dating. Okay, well, not the whole point of dating, but it's certainly a major part of rebound dating which is my current vibe." I step back into the kitchen, shoes and coat on, and Andy's wide-eyed expression conveys a clear problem. "You're looking at me like I'm crazy again. Is it the dress?" I smooth down the front nervously. "Tell me now before I leave and it's too late."

"No, no, yeah, totally, yeah," he says. "The dress is fine. Just, you know, be careful."

And it's kind of cute. I don't have brothers, but maybe this is what it would be like to have a brother looking out for me. It's weirdly touching, actually.

"I'll be fine. You helped me pick this guy out, remember? And it looks like you have an equally thrilling night planned with your… pickle, tofu, and grape jelly sandwich?"

He looks down at the counter where he does in fact have the ingredients for a pickle, tofu, and grape jelly sandwich. He shrugs. "The traditional meal of my people."

"And I respect your heritage. Anyway, I have to go. Love you, enjoy your feast!"

His "Love you too" follows me as I shut the door.

11

The date is... fine.

It's not *bad.* He's not a jerk or anything, we just never click. The conversation drags and lulls and I wonder if I'm the boring one or if it's him. Maybe it's both.

By the time I start walking back home, I'm pretty convinced it's a me-problem. Not that I think Patrick was a great catch that I fumbled or something, but I'm realizing I don't actually know how to date anymore. I'm so used to being with the same person for years that I can't remember all the romantic getting-to-know-you social mores. I could even be a bad kisser now, for all I know! And I have no way of assessing it because all I know is what Elliot liked, and any other experience is in the too-far-distant past to recall.

I have a detailed date debrief on the tip of my tongue when I get home, but Andy doesn't seem to be around, so I call Lia instead.

"I very much doubt it was your fault," she insists. Her voice is muffled by the wind—I caught her while taking her sweet bulldog Archie on his night walk.

"Yeah but you already like me. You're biased."

"I like you because you're fun to be around. If you didn't have fun tonight, it's because he wasn't fun."

"I don't know." I belly flop onto my bed, still in my dress but too lazy to change. "Elliot always said I overpower conversations. Maybe that's what happened, and I didn't give the guy a chance to be interesting."

"UGH," Lia yells. "I fucking hate that guy. Sophie, everything Elliot ever said to you, you need to forget. He was just trying to bring you down because he knew you were too good for him."

"Okay, nevermind. Undo. Unsubscribe. I don't want to have this conversation again. Forget I brought him up."

"Can I please just say one last thing, and then we can change the topic?"

I sigh in a completely overdramatic way. "Fine."

"We all know I hated Elliot, and we can joke about that fact all day and night. But I'm not joking when I say that I genuinely think he hurt your self-esteem. He did everything in his power to make you feel undesirable for three years straight, and it's normal that it's taking a little while to build your confidence back after that."

"He wasn't that bad," I say, but there's no heart in it. Suddenly I'm exhausted.

"I just want you to know that you're amazing, and I want you to be open to the right kind of guy when he comes along. Don't settle for some boring guy from the internet just because he's the first one to ask you out."

"I'm not that desperate," I reply.

But aren't I? If Patrick asked me out again, would I say yes? It just seems so entitled, thinking I'm too good for a second date.

When Lia and I hang up, I peek back into the living room for Andy, but he's still not there. In fact, I don't see him at all before I fall asleep. It's not until the following morning, when I stumble out of bed in a glamorous XXL Minnesota State Fair t-shirt, hair in a messy bun and sleep gunk in the corners of my eyes, that I see him again.

It's earlier than I usually get up, but that's what happens when your date ends at 8:30 and you're in bed by 9:00. I walk out of my room mid-yawn, then yelp out loud when I spot something moving in the kitchen.

"Ah! Jesus, Andy, you scared me. I didn't hear you get in. Where'd you go last night?"

He rotates to face me, then freezes stock-still. Only his eyes dart from my face, to my shirt, to the bedroom door.

"Sorry." He hurriedly puts the coffee grinds back into the cabinet, then starts towards the front door. "I'll come back later."

I rush in front of him. "Woah. Slow down there, cowboy. Where are you off to?"

"Just—" His eyes flit down to my sleep shirt again, then back up at my face. "—giving you some space."

He tries to sidestep me, but I block the way again. "Why are you being weird right now?"

"I just don't want to get in the way of your date."

"My date from last night? He's not here."

Andy scratches at the back of his neck. "Oh. He got up early?"

"I wouldn't know. We went our separate ways yesterday after an hour of mind-numbing small talk."

"Oh."

He doesn't try to move towards the door again, so I relax my defense and head back into the kitchen. "Yeah, it was bad. I used to think I was good at small talk, but last night it was not working. It was excruciating, like I could feel our conversation sucking the life force out of me." I pull the orange juice out of the fridge, then pour myself a glass.

"So, he didn't spend the night?" Andy asks, clearly still buffering. "I thought... with the shirt..."

"Oh this?" I glance down at myself. "This is my very own horrifically ratty sleep shirt. He definitely did not spend the night. He didn't even walk me home from the restaurant."

"Seriously?" Andy comes to join me in the kitchen, immediately assuming his role as breakfast chef. "Did this guy not have a dad? You know what, I didn't have a dad, and even I know you have to walk the girl home."

I laugh. "I know you do, Andy. You're the guy who once came like a mile across campus in the middle of the night just to walk me home."

"Don't remind me about V&S guy right now. It'll give me visceral rage."

I snort at the forgotten nickname. "I think his real name was Ashton. Or Ash…ford?"

"Asshole," he mutters.

"You know, I don't even remember why we called him V&S guy anymore." I take my seat at the kitchen table, swigging from my orange juice.

"You don't?"

I shake my head. "I just remember we hooked up and then he told me I couldn't spend the night, but I was scared to walk home alone so I texted NASA." I shrug. "Everything else is a blur."

"Well, I remember." Andy pulls a cutting board and knife out of their respective drawers. "When I got to his building you were sitting on a bench in the lobby because you felt sick. And I asked how much you'd had to drink and if you ate dinner. And you said—"

Realization dawns. "Oh my god, no—"

I stand and rush towards him, trying to cover his mouth before he can pull my humiliation into the light of day, but I'm too slow. He twists out of reach, laughing as he recalls, "You said, 'All I have in my stomach is vodka and semen.'"

And then I'm melting into laughter, collapsing against the countertop as my cheeks flame. "Oh god, vodka and semen—V&S! I do remember that. Oh, that's horrible. That's a really embarrassing story."

"It's embarrassing for him, not you." He calmly lays the vegetables out on the cutting board, then starts to chop.

"It's kind of embarrassing for me."

I grab a mushroom from his pile, popping it into my mouth. When

I reach for a second he swats my hand away. "Would you let me cook? We both know what happens when you don't have any food in your system."

"Low blow, Walsh," I chuckle. "Very low blow."

So I hop up onto the counter and watch him work. Andy places a skillet on the stovetop, then starts chopping the onions and bell peppers, biting his lip with unconscious focus. Once the aromatics are in the pan, he turns to the spice rack, hand running through his hair as he considers his options.

I like this version of Andy—lazy weekend morning Andy. He's usually so polished, but this morning he's wearing a gray sweatsuit that's at least as old as our friendship, with the sweater unzipped halfway to reveal a navy blue t-shirt from some race he ran ages ago.

For a man who's so often tense and hard on himself, he's relaxed while he cooks. He cracks four eggs into the skillet with one hand, then adds the mushrooms, spinach, and spices. I watch him nod down at the pan while it simmers, then turn to pull out plates and silverware.

"Oh, let me do that."

I hop down from the counter to set the table, and by the time the meal is served, any awkwardness from earlier this morning has totally dissipated.

"So," I say around a mouthful of omelet, "our third weekend as roommates. What should we do to celebrate?"

"Well, it has to be special. You know how important week-based anniversaries have always been to me."

"Do you want to get out of the house? We could go somewhere really messy like White Horse or TITS." The two bars aren't so different from each other, but that's the Allston neighborhood for you. Either way we're guaranteed a night of sweaty 21-year-olds, early 2000's dance hits, and bottom-shelf liquor.

"Yeah sure," he says. "An homage to our friendship's humble beginnings. College kids and strong drinks."

"I'll text NASA." I take out my phone and scroll for the group chat as I ask, "What are your plans for the day until then?"

Andy shrugs. "Making my schedule for the week, maybe meal prep, or reading. Nothing special."

"That sounds great. Let's be lazy. Oh, but… I forgot, I finished my book yesterday."

"Did you want to borrow one?"

"Can I?"

"Yeah, come on," he says, rising from the table. "You can pick."

He crosses towards the closed door of his bedroom, and here's the crazy thing: I've never actually been in his room before.

I mean, I went in his college bedroom a bunch because it was a dorm and they threw all kinds of parties there, but that was different. Since he moved here after college, I have never, ever been in his room.

It's hard to explain just how weird that is, but let me try:

NASA is *close*. We are very, very close. Definitely not the type of friend group to keep things off limits. Nolan is the first person I text every month when my period starts, so he can make me his special chicken noodle soup. One time I flossed Lia's teeth for her because her nail polish was wet. I have *often* peed while on the phone with any/all of them and not even bothered to mute. We know each other to our bones. So I should know every inch of Andy's room already, and shouldn't be surprised by the contents. But I don't, and I am.

Andy's bedroom is just off of the living room. He opens the door now, revealing two tall windows on the far wall—same as my room. Between his windows is a queen-sized bed, tidily made with light blue sheets and a dark blue comforter. That's not the part that surprises me. It's the rest.

Dark wood shelves cover all of the remaining walls, floor to ceiling. Brightly colored paperbacks, hardcovers, dictionaries, grammaticals, novellas, anthologies, and manuscripts peek around each other like curious children. There are books stacked in towers on the floor, and more lying face down with creased spines. Even the ones on the shelves are in disarray—some in horizontal rows, others piled atop each other. Four books sit on his nightstand, each with a different item as a makeshift bookmark: a dollar, a blue pen, a receipt, a phone charger.

"This is your room." I don't know if it's a statement or a question, as I rotate to take in the full effect.

"Sorry," he cringes. "I should have cleaned up. Just tell me what series you're reading and I'll see if I have it."

"Oh, no way, buddy. You're not kicking me out yet. I just got here."

I can't help but compare this to his bedroom in college, which had been perfectly tidy except for one university-issued bookshelf that was always overflowing. In many ways, this is its natural evolution.

I start with the shelf on my left, scanning for familiar titles. "Am I in *Beauty and the Beast* or something? Are you going to tell me you can't actually read and all of this is for me?"

"Yes," he says, fingers running through his hair. "It's true, I'm illiterate. You have to give me credit for fooling everyone, though."

"An Oscar-worthy performance, to be sure. I don't know a single other literary editor who can't read." I curve around to the next wall, asking absently, "Do I know your favorite? I can't remember."

"Book?"

"Yeah." I reach up and pluck one from the shelf. I don't recognize the title, but it looks like a special edition. I flip through it gently before putting it back.

"That depends," he says, coming up next to me but keeping his eyes on the shelves. "Do you mean my most recent favorite, or my all-time favorite, or the book I think is technically the best, or my first—"

"All of them," I interrupt. "Any of them. It doesn't even have to be your number one favorite really, just tell me the first... I don't know... three that come to mind."

"Some of them are embarrassing."

"Your secret's safe with me."

He rotates to face the shelves on the adjoining wall, affording himself a bit more privacy as he admits, "Okay. Well, my first favorite when I was a kid was *The Very Hungry Caterpillar...*"

I give him a gentle shove. He stumbles forward a step, chuckling, then glances at me over his shoulder, but doesn't continue his explanation until we're both looking back at the shelves. "My favorite classic… maybe *All Quiet on the Western Front*, if you consider that a classic. A recent favorite… I just read *The Boys in the Boat* and really enjoyed it. I don't know, I feel like a bad parent choosing their favorite kid."

I spot a copy of *All Quiet on the Western Front* right in front of me and pick it up.

"If you weren't so obviously illiterate," I ask, opening to a dog-eared page in the middle, "would you ever want to write something?"

I'm consciously not turning to look at Andy. If I'm going to get a real answer from him, I can't make him feel pressured or observed. And I really, really want a real answer from him.

"I don't know what I'd write about."

I force my voice into nonchalance as I say, "I think I do. You clearly love stories about boys growing up together, friendship, trials that bring people closer. You could write about that."

Out of the corner of my eye, I see him take a step farther away. He doesn't say anything, but the chaos in his mind is unbearably loud, and I know exactly where his thoughts have drifted.

"Have you talked to Owen since the brewery?"

"No."

"Do you want to?"

"I don't know."

I make my way to his nightstand now. The top book, with a dollar bill about 30% of the way through, is Stephen King's *It*.

"I want to want to," he says eventually, "if that makes sense."

We're facing opposite walls now. I can't see him, even from the corner of my eye, and it has my other senses sharpening to a point. The sound of his voice, the pressure in the air. Everything feels intimate and combustible.

"It's like," he continues, "I feel guilty for not wanting to reach out to him. I wish I wanted to, but I don't."

"Maybe someday you will," I reply, just above a whisper, "and I think if that day comes, he'll be there. But you don't have to do anything you don't want to do."

Traffic whirs outside the window. A dog barks. The shelf in front of me is buckling in the middle, curved to bear the weight of old stories.

"We were close as kids, you know?" he says. "It used to be easy. Like how being with you is easy."

I press my eyelids shut, torn between wanting to hug him and wanting to hear more.

"We just got messed up when our dad left. It was like no one knew how to talk to each other anymore. I still don't even know why he left. My mom knows, obviously, and I swear Owen knows too, but no one ever wanted to talk to me about it." I hear the muted *bump, shh* of Andy sliding a book back into place. "I know it's stupid to talk about this stuff that happened when I was a kid. I don't know why I brought it up."

"It's okay."

"It's not, though." Suddenly his voice is firmer, almost angry. "I don't want to be like this. I don't want this hanging over me every time I see him. It was like 16 years ago. I just want to have a normal relationship and not feel like we're walking on eggshells all the time. I don't understand how we got here."

With that, I can't stop myself anymore. I move across the room until my arms are wrapped around his middle and my cheek is pressed between his shoulder blades.

He inhales sharply, then goes still.

"Sometimes when I feel like my emotions are running away with me," I say into the worn cotton of his old sweatshirt, "or when I'm having a big reaction to a small thing and I don't know why, I tell myself that it's just one cloud in a big blue sky. Like, this thing I'm feeling is real, it's here, but it's not everything. I can watch it go by if I want to."

He doesn't respond, but I don't need him to. I just want to stay here, listening to his heartbeat slow, and feeling his hands eventually close around mine. And I think about just how *perfect* this room is for him. So polished and reserved from the outside, but a hurricane of stories and emotions and mess inside.

"Anyway," I continue, "if you ever think of something you want to say, I hope you'll say it, in a book or otherwise. You're so thoughtful and smart and I'm sure anything you wrote would be beautiful."

He doesn't reply, and after a few more beats he lets go of my hands. I take his cue, stepping back to put a few inches of space between us. But he doesn't turn around, and I don't know what that means. Is he upset? With me? Did I make it worse?

He clears his throat. "What book did you say you're looking for?"

"Oh, book three of *The Shape of the Serpent* series, if you have it."

"Uh, yeah," he stammers, turning to the right and crouching down to pick a book off the bottom shelf—the exact one I need. Clearly everything has its place, even if the system is indecipherable to anyone else.

Then finally—*finally*—he turns to face me. "Tell me what you think when you finish. It's a long journey, but the ending is worth it."

I smile and I reach for the story in his hands. "I'm sure it will be."

12

Andy

The night I first fell in love with Sophie, she had a yellow ribbon in her hair.

I remember it exactly, tied in a neat bow around her ponytail. I saw it, and even before she turned around I thought it must be her. Even though it had been months since we'd seen each other last, and months more since that first night on the fire escape.

I saw the ribbon in her hair and knew it had to be her, but I wasn't in love with her yet, so I wasn't yet paralyzed by fear and feeling. I just said, "Excuse me," and she turned around and saw me there.

"Andy, hi! I didn't know you were on campus this summer."

"Yeah, hey. Good to see you."

"Can I help you find something?" There was a library cart in front of her, from which she'd been shelving books. She pushed it to the side to walk towards me.

"*One Hundred Years of Solitude.* I couldn't find it in general fiction."

"Oh yeah, we're setting up a whole magical realism section. Here, come with me." She motioned for me to follow, glancing back over her shoulder as she asked, "Have you read it before?"

"No," I admitted as we moved through the shelves. "And it's not for me. I'm assisting a professor this summer."

"Oh, but it's fantastic. You have to read it and text me your reactions."

"I don't think I have your number."

"You don't?" She stopped in her tracks, turned around, and said, a little too loud for a library, "Oh, hold on. We have to solve that problem right now."

It was amazing, how effortless she was. Her ability to draw people out, make them feel comfortable. She wasn't even trying, she just was this way. A phenomenal contrast to every effortful, ineffective thing I seemed to do—constantly fighting to find the right thing to do or say and usually coming up empty.

I reached into my pocket and placed my phone into her palm. She created a contact for herself, confident as ever, and said, "There. Now you *have* to text me later, so I can have your number too. It's only fair."

I couldn't seem to tuck my smile away, even as I followed her through the stacks to the correct shelf.

"You're an English major, right?" she asked as we searched for the title.

"Yeah. You're not though… Science Ed?"

"Good memory. Yeah no, I'm just a recreational reader slash person with no social life."

"Right," I scoffed, spotting the book and pulling it from the shelf.

"Are you scoffing at me, Andy Walsh?"

"I mean, I don't doubt you like reading, but come on." I gestured to her vaguely. "I doubt you're available on short notice."

She put a stubborn hand on her hip. "Well, would you believe that today is my birthday and my only plan is to watch *Moana* alone in bed?"

"No."

"It's true!" she shouted, again too loud.

But I didn't believe it. It was June on campus, sure, but even during the lows of summer break, if it was really her birthday there was no doubt in my mind people would be clamoring to celebrate with her.

"Ok then," I replied, overcompensating for her loudness with a low whisper. "Prove it. Show me your ID. If it's really your birthday, I will… I don't know, buy you dinner."

"And if it's not, do I have to buy you dinner?"

I shrugged. "Seems fair."

Wordlessly, even smugly, she reached into her purse and pulled out a piece of shiny plastic proof.

I frowned down at the card, then pulled out my phone to double check the date. June 1st. Shit. And there was nothing I could do but hand it back to her with a stammered, "Oh. Sorry, I… happy birthday."

"Thanks." She smiled a little as she took it back and tucked it into her purse, but the gesture was hollow. It fucking bothered me.

"So," I said, "dinner's on me."

And the way her face brightened when she asked "Really?" made me feel like a goddamn superhero. She was so full of brightness, so easy to please. Certainly everyone felt that way around her, but to experience it… it felt like she reacted that way just for me. Like I was worthy of it.

By the time Sophie clocked out of her shift, I'd put together a list of restaurants for her to pick from, since I had no idea what she liked yet. She picked a pub nearby because she heard from a friend that they never carded there. And so it began.

We walked a few blocks, then down narrow stairs into a dark basement. Green Day played over the speakers and my shoes stuck to the floor. The server didn't blink an eye when newly 19-year-old Sophie ordered an absinthe cocktail, and I—no more legal than she at 20— decided to get the same. Neither of us had ever tried it before, but it was a special night.

The drinks arrived, and it was so *easy*. Listening to her, talking to her, even just existing across the table from her. She grasped the helm of the conversation with both hands and guided it expertly, offering up so much of herself that it tempted me to do the same.

The absinthe reminded her of the Lost Generation, and that was a full hour of conversation alone. I told her that I've always liked Hemingway's straightforward language. When she laughed and said she hated him—because "who wants to read boring prose about loathsome people?"—I wasn't even embarrassed to disagree. We ordered another round of drinks to help settle the debate, along with our food orders.

Sophie, I learned, believed that birthdays were for ordering "weird food" you didn't let yourself order on other days. So, instead of a main dish, she ordered three different types of fries: straight, curly, and waffle. We split the three orders between us, and were in perfect agreement that absinthe and fried potatoes paired perfectly. We ordered another drink for the consensus.

Then, when the fries were too cold to eat, Sophie built little houses out of what remained. Waffle fry floors, straight fry walls, waffle fry roofs, and curly fry chimneys. She said we absolutely had to get another drink to celebrate her architectural genius. I really didn't need another, but when she reached across the table—squeezing one of my hands in both of hers and pouting that bottom lip that I suddenly wanted to feel between my own—I found I couldn't refuse.

The hours passed quickly, and then it was last call. She tried to split the bill but that wasn't happening, both because it was her birthday and because I'd lost the bet. Fair was fair.

She rocketed out of the bar like a champagne cork, all sparkles and momentum, then looped her arm through mine. Her summer dorm wasn't in the same direction as mine, but drunk as we were I could hardly let her walk home alone.

"I'm glad I ran into you today," she said, slurring the slightest bit. "I was gonna be really depressed."

"I'm glad, too."

"Sometimes I just feel so lonely, yanno?"

"Yeah," I said, knowing exactly.

"I thought college would be better," she continued, leaning most of her body weight on me by then. "And I mean okay yeah *I guess* I have friends here, but they suck. I mean, they don't suck. Lia is great. But everyone else, pfft. They don't care about me."

She was a rambling kind of drunk, I realized, but it was cute.

"Or it's just a bunch of guys who only want to hook up. And I'm sorry, but I'm not about to have my first time with a random dude I barely know who doesn't care about me."

Her shoe snagged on a crack and suddenly she was tumbling forwards. I barely caught her around the middle before she could hit the ground, then pulled her up to standing.

"I might be drunk," she giggled, folding forward until her face was pressed over my heart. There was no way she was making it home unassisted.

"Okay, come here," I said, hoisting her up into my arms. Her ensuing shriek of laughter was lightning bright in the darkness. Several passers-by turned their heads, and I walked more quickly to clear their stares.

"You're my friend, right Andy?" she asked from my arms. "Like my real friend who actually cares about me?"

"If you're mine."

She flashed her fluorescent grin up at me—guileless and toothy and real—and it felt like my ribs were inflating. "It's a deal."

By the time I set her down in front of her building, I was somehow already missing the night that wasn't yet over.

Then she raised her gaze to mine and asked, "Would you maybe wanna… come in? With me?"

At first I thought I'd misunderstood. But she took a step closer, trailing her fingers along my arm, and the invitation couldn't have been more clear.

She was a perfect temptation, crafted just for me. Her full lips. Her hair in that yellow ribbon. The freckles across her nose. She was soft and natural and captivating. Cute and pretty. Sweet and wild. The devil on my shoulder screamed, "Yes! Go inside with her! She's the one who asked." But then she stumbled as she waited for my answer, and she'd just said it would be her first time…

I wanted her. Of course I did. I wanted her so badly. I just didn't want her to regret it. Or just as bad, forget it.

I still hadn't answered. Her offer hung in the air between us as I excavated a string of words from the annals of my mind, ultimately landing on, "I should head home."

Her face fell. I felt like an asshole.

"But hey," I tried, pulling her back against my chest, if only to hide myself from the sadness in her eyes, "thanks for spending your birthday with me. I'm… glad we're friends."

I don't know if Sophie remembers the end of that night. After all this time, I've never been brave enough to ask.

But I remember it.

That night is a well-loved paperback—spine creased, pages dog-eared, annotations in the margins.

Because I fell in love with her that night, and in all the years since I've never been able to move on.

I fell in love with Sophie in the library, confident and kind. Sophie in the bar, opinionated and teasing. Sophie outside her dorm, bold and beautiful.

I've reread those chapters in my mind a hundred times. Two hundred. Trying to convince myself I made the right choice. That summer especially, I thought of her every day, trying to seem cool in my texts, wondering if there was a sober part of Sophie that really wanted me, too scared to ask, thankful for anything she'd give.

From the very start, Sophie didn't just make me feel accepted. She made me feel *needed*. I don't think I'd ever felt needed before I met her. And as our friendship grew, that year and in the years to follow, I promised myself I would always be someone she could rely on.

I've never let her down since.

I won't start now.

13

Me: Andy and I are going to white horse tonight if you want to come! Like 9ish?

Lia: YES BITCH. im gonna bring rayna, she lives like a block away

Nolan: Can I bring Jaiden

Lia: are you dating jaiden? if so then yes

Nolan: So you automatically get to bring Rayna just because you're dating but I don't get to bring anhond

Nolan: anyone*

Lia: no nolan, you dont get to bring anhond

Me: I've never met Anhond, are they nice?

Andy: Oh, Anhond is coming? That's awesome.

Nolan: I hate you guys

Me: Tell Anhond I'm excited to meet them and tell Rayna she has to do my eyeliner <3

Nolan: I'm bringing Jaiden

The White Horse bar bathroom is a 5 out of 10 on the dinginess scale. Two small stalls, two small sinks, and a moderate amount of graffiti, plus a vaguely *bathroom* smell about it, like it's perpetually a little wet. Lia leads the way in, staking out one of the sinks for our makeover station. Rayna spreads a paper towel on the counter and starts unpacking her lavender makeup bag while Lia drags me under the overhead light.

"You're in grad school right?" Rayna asks, sifting through her products.

"Not yet," I reply. "I'm hoping to start my PhD next year though."

"What's your field?" She pulls out a black eyeliner from the bunch.

"Science education."

"Use the brown on her," Lia interjects. "She's such a soft autumn."

"Can I ask," Rayna continues, shuffling through her bag once more, "I hope this doesn't sound bad, but do you need a PhD for that?"

"No," I laugh. "You don't need one to teach, but I actually want to do research."

"Oh?"

"Yeah, I'm really interested in experiential learning. I grew up on a farm and that's what really got me interested in science in the first place. The plant cycles and the ecosystems, you know. And now I work at a museum that's all about hands-on—ooh, is that liquid?"

"Yeah, it goes on so smooth." She pulls off the lid. "Just stay still for a moment."

"Sorry." I tilt my chin up toward the light and close my eyes.

"But you were saying?"

"Yeah, so my research will focus on kids who don't thrive in traditional classroom experiences, and seeing what kinds of experiential or project-based learning models help grow their interest in science."

"Sophie, Rayna's too nice to tell you to stop moving so much, but I'm not."

"Sorry!"

"You should've brought a stamp for her. She's a fidgeter."

"You're good," Rayna assures me. "But okay, how do you even

research that? Like how do you get kids to test on?"

I let out another laugh, then realize I'm not supposed to be moving and snap my posture back to attention. "Well, we don't really *get* kids to test on. And it depends on the project. Sometimes you can partner with schools or other educational institutions like museums or park districts to evaluate programs they're running. Other times it's more like conducting surveys, like some researchers at Ashmore partner with College Board to survey kids right after the SAT. There's lots of options. And then once we have the data we can do whatever analysis we want."

"Turn to the right a little," Rayna says as two more women enter the bathroom.

"I've only had two drinks but they're hitting me so hard," said the first new girl, her voice low and smooth as she closes a stall door behind her.

"I love a heavy pour," says the other girl, voice high and bright. "Save me money and fuck me up."

"Do you do content creation full time?" I ask Rayna, eyes closed again.

"I'm also an entrepreneur, actually. I have my own makeup line."

"No way!"

"Yeah. Mostly foundation but I've started branching into some other products too."

"Can I get at the sink for a second?" Lia scoots behind me and turns on the faucet, then starts wetting the ends of her hair to coax the curls into shape.

"Is that a hard market to break into?" I ask.

One of the new girls flushes her toilet.

"Well, the market for foundation has big gaps," Rayna says. "Most major brands are not shade inclusive at all, and even when dark shades are available they don't have nearly as many undertones as the light shades."

The low-voiced bathroom girl shouts "So true!" from her stall, making all of us laugh.

"So anyway, it's a specific hole in the market that I'm trying to fill."

"That's amazing. Do you do your own marketing and everything?"

She lifts her fingers from where they were anchored on my cheeks. "That's how I got into content creation, yeah. You're done by the way."

I open my eyes and turn towards the mirror. "Oh my god, I love it! Thank you." I move my head from side to side to see all of the angles as Rayna and Lia start clearing the sink.

"So Soph," Lia adds, "see how it's basically straight? You do yours too curved up, but you can just go straight out with it."

"I see that. It looks so good. Thank you, Rayna."

"No worries," she smiles. "Happy to help."

"You have to send me a link to your brand. I don't use foundation that much but I'll share it everywhere."

"That would be amazing," Rayna says before pulling out her own dark red lipstick and applying it liberally.

"I can't believe you run a business and make content *and* have time to date."

"Lucky me." Lia grabs her around the waist and kisses her cheek.

"Well," Rayna laughs, "Lia's as busy as I am so it kind of works out. Are you seeing anyone?"

"Recent breakup actually."

"Oh, sorry." Rayna cringes like she's not sure if the topic is forbidden

"Don't be. He was an asshole."

"Lia!" Rayna scolds.

"She's kind of right," I admit.

"Well, then I'm sorry about that too," Rayna says.

Then the high-voiced girl in the second stall yells "Fuck him!" and we're all laughing again.

"You know," Rayna starts again, "I don't want to ask a question that I'm not supposed to ask, but... has Andy ever made a move on you?"

I let out a staccato laugh that's way too loud. "No, definitely not."

"Really?"

"Yeah!" I feel myself start to sweat. "He's not into me like that."

"Come *on*," Lia says, but when I snap my head in her direction I see she's talking to her wayward curls.

"Well, are you getting back out there with anyone yet?" Rayna asks.

"I don't know. I haven't been feeling super confident lately. I tried going on a date last weekend but it was horrible. At least one of us was extremely boring and I couldn't tell if it was me or him. I might just try celibacy. Or get back with my ex. Who knows."

"Fuck that," Lia spits, still wrapping her damp strands into finger curls. "Your confidence is just low right now because Elliot sucked it out of you and you haven't rebounded yet. I think you should go out there tonight, pick a hot guy, and just dance with him. Don't overthink it."

"I agree!" chimes the high-voiced girl again before flushing her toilet. "Get back out there!"

Then the low-voiced girl, now washing her hands at the other sink, adds, "Yeah, you look hot. You should do it."

Their encouragement is sweet but I can feel myself blushing already at just the thought. "Oh my god, I am not going to walk up to a stranger and ask him to dance."

"Well no, don't *ask him to dance*. This isn't the eighth-grade formal," Lia gibes. "Just make eye contact, vibe check, and then grab on for the ride."

"Lia, my love, that only works for people who look like you. And honestly I'm kind of tired of always being the person taking initiative and trying so hard."

"She doesn't have to do anything she's not ready for," Rayna tells her girlfriend.

"Yes, she does," Lia insists, then turns to me. "Yes, you do. Trust me."

Both bathroom ladies agree with a hearty "Yes, you do!" Then the low-voiced one leans towards Rayna, asking, "Did you say you have a foundation line?"

14

olan and his roommate Jaiden are standing next to our table, engrossed in making some kind of secret handshake like the children they are. Andy is sitting in the booth, boxed in by a curvy brunette woman with a hand resting on his bicep. She's chattering away and he's barely nodding. From anyone else it would be a pitiful approximation of politeness, but for him it's pretty good.

Lia, Rayna, and I approach and Andy seems to sense us coming, straightening up and catching my eye immediately. I shake my head at him with a teasing smile. (This isn't my first experience watching women flirt with Andy, as you know.)

The brunette follows his gaze, then her eyes dart between us—to Andy, then me, then Andy again. But Andy doesn't even seem to notice. He's cracking a genuine one-dimple smile as I approach—a smile I doubt the other girl got even a hint of. The surety of it sparkles in my chest.

"Oh, I'm sorry," she says to me, rising from the booth. "I didn't realize…" Then she slinks off towards the dancefloor, not even

125

finishing her thought.

There's a beat of processing between the group before Lia bellows, "Damn, Soph! Effortless cockblock!"

Jaiden roars in laughter as Lia slides into the booth, but Nolan looks serious as he says, "Lia, can you not?"

"What?" she returns. "I'm not allowed to point out when they're doing *that* anymore?" She waves her hand in a vague circle at us.

"No," Nolan replies sternly, expression unreadable.

Mercifully, the opening notes of "Get Low" shatter the bizarre moment, and our entire group runs to the dance floor, abandoning our first round of empty glasses on the table. (Andy tries to stay behind, but I don't give him the chance because his hand is already in mine.)

We order drink number two.

Lia and Rayna disappear almost immediately, recognizing some art friend in the crowd.

We order drink number three.

Nolan convinces Jaiden to be his wingman—a role that's more strategy-heavy than any of us foresaw. They spend a full ten minutes huddled together like football players until Jaiden stands upright, pats Nolan's shoulder twice, and the pair heads off towards the bar.

That leaves Andy and me to our own devices along the edge of the dancefloor. Lights strobe and bass blares and the average age in the room is about five years our junior. I'm starting to think about drink number four, so I lean towards him and ask, "Should we get absinthe?"

He leans in towards my ear to be heard over the music. "Why absinthe?"

"You said we're doing college nostalgia tonight, right? I think that's what we drank the first night we hung out, just the two of us." I pull back just far enough to check his face for recognition. "Remember?"

He watches my mouth, lipreading over the boom of the crowded bar. He seems to understand the question, but his expression remains locked, almost uncannily neutral.

Only then does it occur to me that he *really might not remember*. That the night that's seared into my memory might have been utterly forgettable to the person I shared it with.

I mean, that makes sense. There's always some woman throwing herself at Andy. Why would the night I did it stand out? Especially since he wasn't interested. But even so—even just as friends—my heart sinks at the realization that our first night out wasn't as special in his mind.

I'm about ready to open my mouth and brush it off with a friendly *You probably don't remember, but trust me we drank absinthe and it was great!* but then he nods, and takes one step closer, and bends until his lips just barely graze the shell of my ear.

"It was a great night," he says, just loud enough for me to hear over the music. One hand rests on my waist, but it's light, tentative. "Do you—" He hesitates, and I feel his fingers curl more ardently against my ribs. "Do you remember all of it?"

Embarrassment heats my face, but I know he can't see it with his cheek pressed to mine. So I nod.

"Even… the end?"

I should feel humiliated, dragging the memory of his rejection into the spotlight like this. But under the pulsing lights, surrounded by strangers, three drinks deep and nearly a decade past, it almost doesn't feel real. I shrug, playing it off like it's no big deal. But Andy places a hand under my chin, tilting my face up until I'm looking into his eyes.

I read his lips as he asks: "Do you?"

He reads mine as I say: "I do."

Andy takes a breath, and I think he's going to reply—and say what, I have no idea—when someone dances into my back, shoving me forward onto him. He catches me around the waist, and I brace both hands on his chest to keep myself upright. I regain my balance fairly quickly, but even as I try to stand on my own again, Andy doesn't loosen his hold. If anything, his hands wrap farther around my body, keeping me there against him.

I could try to step away, but I don't. Instead I stay close, letting my arms slide slowly up over his shoulders and around his neck.

Suddenly I couldn't tell you what song is playing. I couldn't tell you the color of the walls or the number of people in the room or even what bar we're even in. All I know is that my body is pressed against Andy's and his hands are on my waist and we're starting to move together, dancing to who knows what song in who knows what bar and he feels warm and solid against my chest. Then his hands begin to move, traveling up my back, over the sides of my body, and I don't know what's happening but I never want it to end.

The crowd hides us from view in this liminal pocket of closeness. His breath skims over my neck. My fingers wind into his hair. And this could be a thing friends do, right? Friends could dance together at a bar. But the way our bodies fit together feels like more, and I want it. I want it so badly as his thumb traces the edge of my hipbone and his body moves with mine.

I don't know when I closed my eyes, but suddenly I want to see him. I want to read his face and know what he's thinking and see if this means anything for him the way it does for me. But when I open my eyes, what I see over Andy's shoulder makes my whole body tense. He feels the change in me, and turns to follow my gaze. Then he sees it too.

Elliot.

My ex is standing at the bar, maybe ten feet away. There's a full beer in his hand and a scowl on his face. He's been watching.

Andy pulls me tight against him again, asking, "Do you want to go? We can go right now."

But Elliot is still staring. And after three years together, I suppose I owe him more than running away.

"I should talk to him." I pull back from Andy, my hand lingering on his shoulder as his lingers on my hip. "Give us a minute?"

And he's a good friend, so he nods and steps back, giving me the space I asked for even though there's a tiny (medium-sized) part of me that wishes he wouldn't.

Every step I take brings Elliot into sharper focus. His clothes look rumpled, and that's unusual for him. He's always been perfectly polished, especially in public. The bags under his eyes are deeper, and he's white-knuckling the bar with his free hand. I stop about a foot away, as far as I can stay and expect to hear him over the music. Immediately, he barks, "You're here with him?"

No greeting. So that's how this is going to go.

"With Andy? Yes, we're just—"

"I knew it, Sophie. I fucking knew it." He points a finger at me in accusation. "You always said there was nothing going on between the two of you."

"There wasn't…" My voice is meek, pathetic, but I'm too stunned by his anger to do anything else.

"Oh really? Then what was that?"

"We were just dancing, but it's—"

"You think I never noticed the way he is with you? He looks at you like he's starving and you're the fucking main course. And you were always finding some excuse to be around him. Whenever you needed something, you called him first. Never me. Always him. I spent so long trying to convince myself it was nothing just for you to go fuck him the minute we break up? Are you serious right now?"

He's furious, and clearly drunk, and I'm wondering if maybe I should've taken Andy's offer to leave when I had the chance.

"It's… it's not like that."

"And now you're gonna lie to my face. You really are a piece of work." His face is red with emotion. "What does he have that I don't, huh? The guy's an idiot, he can barely hold a conversation."

The words feel like a slap. I can take him criticizing me, because I'm used to it and I know what he means, but I can't stand to hear him criticize Andy who he barely knows and doesn't understand at all.

"Don't talk about him like that," I say, taking one step closer to him. "If you want to believe there was something going on between me and Andy while we were together then by all means, be my guest. But I'm not going to stand here and listen to you insult him when he had *nothing* to do with our breakup. We broke up because of *you*. You didn't support my dreams, and you didn't value my opinions, and I wasn't going to spend the rest of my life playing out some patriarchal fantasy with you."

Elliot closes the distance between us, taking hold of my face in a plea. "Sophie, you don't get it. I want you back. I'll be better. We can go wherever you want. Please—I love you. Say you'll come back to me."

"Elliot—" I try to pull away but he shifts his grip to my upper arms.

"I haven't even told my family we broke up. I couldn't do it. We've been together for *three years*, Soph. You really want to throw all that away? They expect me to marry you. They expect grandkids. I thought you wanted kids!"

"I do—"

"Just stop this, Sophie." His fingers are bruising, but his expression is longing, and it's tearing my self-restraint in two. "Please. You don't belong with someone like him. You're supposed to be with me."

Then his lips crash against mine, and my adrenaline spikes. I didn't ask for this. I don't want this. I shove at his chest but it's no use. I can't be here. But I can't break free. So I do the only thing I can think of and bite his lip, hard enough to draw blood.

"Ow! The fuck?"

He releases me more forcefully than he means to and I stumble back, slamming against the bar and shattering a glass before hitting the ground, the taste of iron in my mouth. Then someone else's hands are on my arms, but these hands are gentle, coaxing me up and setting me on a barstool. It's Andy—his palm cupping the side of my face and eyes flitting over my body.

"Sophie, are you okay? Are you hurt?"

"I... uh... I don't know."

Andy spins to face Elliot. "What did you just do to her? What the fuck did you just do?" He crosses a protective arm in front of me—my seatbelt. I'm safe.

Elliot rises to the challenge, taking a step towards Andy with rage in his eyes. "Get the hell away from my girl, man. I'm not playing around."

But Andy has a solid three inches on him and isn't backing down.

He steps in closer still, glaring down like death and speaking low enough that I'm not sure whether I really hear him say, "She's not your girl anymore. And even when she was yours, she's always been mine."

"Fuck you," Elliot spits, reaching around him to grab for me again.

And that's when Andy punches him—clean across the face.

I have never, *ever* seen Andy do anything violent in his life. He'd always protected me and helped me in his own ways. But it's like a caveman part of his brain came to life for the first time: all instinct, no remorse, just to defend me.

The room is a crush of bodies and sound, yet somehow the bouncer finds us in an instant—thick arms shoving them apart, booming voice yelling *step away*. Elliot is bent over, hand clutching his jaw. Andy raises his arms in a sign of peace as he turns to me.

"We're leaving, right Soph?"

But something he sees has his face falling. He rushes up, one hand on my cheek, the other gently cupping my right elbow. I look down and see there's blood on his fingers, blood on the broken glass across the bar. I can't even feel it, my adrenaline is so high, but my lip is starting to tremble with the shock of it all.

"It's okay. You're okay," he assures.

Then Andy lifts me into his arms, storming out of the bar and not looking back.

15

"I'm just going to get the first aid kit and I'll be right back, okay?"

I nod from my seat in the kitchen as wayward tears streak down my face. I'm not even in pain with the shock of it all, but emotions are crashing over me all at once and I can't make it stop.

"I'm so embarrassed." There's a catch in my voice I can't conceal. "It's just a cut, I'm sure I'll be fine."

Andy reemerges from the bathroom carrying a blue and white bin labeled First Aid, as well as a washcloth and a bowl of soapy water. He pulls out the chair next to me, positioning us face-to-face and setting the supplies beside us on the kitchen table. "There's nothing to be embarrassed about. I'm just going to take a look and then we can decide if you need stitches, okay?"

"No stitches," I insist. "My insurance sucks. And I don't think it's that bad, really. I'm sorry I'm crying." I wipe more tears away, laughing a little. "I'm even ruining the eyeliner Rayna did. This is so silly."

"It's not silly." His voice is firm, calm. "But Soph, I need you to take off your shirt so I can see the cut. Do you want a blanket or something?"

I shake my head. "No, that's okay, just give me a second."

He politely looks away as I pull my turtleneck up and over my head, then drop the ruined garment on the table.

"There, all set."

Andy turns back to me and very pointedly does *not* look at my chest. Instead, he leans in to look at the gash in my right tricep.

"Alright," he says, gently turning my arm in his hands, "it looks pretty deep, which explains the bleeding, but it's not very long. I think we can skip the stitches if we need to."

"Thanks."

"First, I'm going to wipe off the blood," he explains, "then I'll check if there's glass in the cut, and if there isn't we'll just wash the whole area with soap and water and bandage you up. Okay?"

I nod, and he begins.

"You know, I have a scar in almost the same spot," he says in a low, even voice, like I'm an animal he doesn't want to spook. "From when Owen and I were kids. We were playing in the forest by our house when I was probably five or six." His touch is feather light as he slowly wipes the blood from my skin. "I was chasing Owen but he was faster than me, and I was a kind of clumsy little kid, so I tripped on a stick and it poked right into my arm."

With his attention locked on the task, I can watch him openly. It's not often I get a full, uninterrupted story out of him—especially not a story about Owen—and I'm captivated.

"I threw a real fit about it. But Owen was there and he was so calm." Andy carefully examines the wound for glass, clearing away the drops of red as they well up. "He was only seven or eight, but he was so confident I would be okay that I just believed him. And when I stopped crying, he took my hand and walked me home, and we seemed so normal when we got into the house that our mom wasn't even worried. She just cleaned me up and that was that."

His eyes meet mine, earnest as they've ever been. "There's a piece of glass I have to remove. Is that okay?"

"Yeah," I reply, my voice hoarse.

Andy cleans the tweezers with a sterile wipe, then holds my arm in place with gentle fingers as he goes to remove the shard.

"Ah!" I flinch at the first touch, a cascade of new tears falling.

"I know it hurts, baby—"

Baby. My heart trips on the word.

"—but I need you to stay still for one more second and then it'll be out. On the count of three give me a long exhale. One, two, three."

He's so sure, and I'm grateful he's here to tell me what to do. I obey, taking a deep breath in and out, and he's done before I am.

And he called me *baby.*

"Good job." He catches the tear trailing along my jaw with his index finger. "This next part might sting too, but I'll be quick."

The clean end of the cloth dips into the sudsy water.

"It sounds like you and Owen used to be really close," I say, pleading for distraction again.

"We were," he replies, but doesn't offer more. The cloth touches my arm with tenderness, the gentlest scrape over my raw skin and rawer nerves. Then he looks up again. "Just have to bandage it up. You doing alright?"

I force a smile. "You're really good at this. It's like you were a battlefield surgeon in a past life or something."

"Nah," he says as he pulls ointment, cotton pads, and gauze from the kit. "I'm not great under pressure."

"Don't do that."

He instantly pulls his hands back.

"You're always putting yourself down. Clearly tonight proves you're great under pressure."

Andy exhales, but doesn't argue, just silently treats and wraps the wound.

"There. All done. How does it feel?"

I test out moving my arm a bit. "Honestly? Horrible." I smile up at him so he knows I'm okay. "But you did an amazing job. Thank you."

"I'll get some ibuprofen."

"Okay. I guess I should put on a shirt anyway," I laugh.

And it's like Andy forgot I was sitting here in my bra until that moment. I thought he just wasn't interested, but now…

The full weight of his attention drags down, from my face, to my neck, then lower. His dark eyes are blown black, his chest lifting and falling with each controlled breath.

Every inch of my skin feels flushed, but trapped as I am in the lock of his gaze, I don't want to cover up. I want him to see me.

I want him to want me.

He lowers to his knees before me, and it feels like anything could happen. The calm before the storm, the stillness before the dive. His eyes fix on my ribs, where a smudge of blood remains. Holding the washcloth, he raises a hand and drags it over the mark, featherlight, just skimming the underside of my bra as he wipes away the stain.

I inhale sharply at his touch—I can't help it. And that seems to break the trance.

Andy stands abruptly, clearing his throat. "I'll uh—I'll go get that ibuprofen." He takes a few stumbling steps backwards towards the bathroom before finally looking away.

As soon as the bathroom door shuts behind him, I bolt up and into my room.

Pajamas. I need pajamas. I need extremely unsexy pajamas. I don't know what's happening right now but I'm too exhausted and tipsy to figure it out.

I find a pair of oversized Ashmore sweats and a long sleeve NPR t-shirt. Perfectly schlubby. And as I work to pull them on—which is not easy with a tender new arm injury—I convince myself that what just happened was not weird. It doesn't mean Andy has figured out I'm into him, and it also doesn't mean he's into me. It means emotions are high and we're drunk and not in our right minds.

It takes ten—ten!—anchoring breaths before I'm ready to open my bedroom door again.

"Wow," I say as I enter the living room, declaring my presence, "getting dressed is not easy like this."

Andy is sitting on the couch. He pats the seat beside him, where he's thoughtfully laid out painkillers and a glass of water. I take a seat and take the pills, and only once I've swallowed them down does he say, "Sophie, I have to know. What happened back there? With Elliot?"

His question hits me like a tidal wave, pulling the events of the night over my head to drown me. I feel my chin start to quiver, and bury my face behind my hands before Andy can see me cry.

Immediately he's there, wrapping his arms around me and tucking me against his chest. "Shit, I'm sorry. We don't have to talk about it."

And then he just holds me. He holds me there against his chest for I don't know how long, letting me cry, stroking my hair, rubbing circles across my back.

Poor Andy. I never cry in front of other people—really, I hate feeling like the one other people have to take care of—but somehow I always end up crying in front of *him*.

As soon as I can gather myself a bit, I sit up and wipe my palms over my cheeks. "I guess this is what I get for ignoring our problems for so long." My feeble laughter doesn't stick. "This is what I get for just... wanting someone to love me."

There's a pause, then Andy says quietly, "I love you, Soph."

"I know," I say, letting myself curl back towards his chest. "But I want someone to be *in love* with me. I want..." But I don't know how to explain it in a non-pathetic way, so I just let it drop.

"Elliot was in love with you for a long time," Andy offers. "He probably still is. You're... very easy to love."

"You know what's really sad? I honestly don't think he was. If he loved me..." I trail off again.

"What?"

"You want to know why we broke up?" I ask. "It's not even dramatic or interesting. It wasn't his comment about not dating hot girls at the karaoke bar—though that did make me want to jump off a bridge. And it wasn't the fact that we hardly saw each other anymore because he was always at work or with his friends or doing something else that didn't include me. We were talking about my grad school applications, and I mentioned that if I don't get into Ashmore again we might have to move to California. Which he knew! He was there when I decided what schools to apply to. We talked all about it and he said my list sounded great to him. But that day he just scoffed and said we weren't going to uproot our lives and move to California for—and I quote—my hobby."

"Your hobby?"

"He basically said that a PhD was nice if I wanted it, but that my first priority was going to have to be our kids in a few years, so it wasn't worth moving for. Like, even though I had never said *anything* about being a stay-at-home mom, he just assumed I would do it because that's what he wanted. And he was so condescending and horrible about it. He was like, 'well it's not like you have a serious career anyway.' And it was like… oh my god, who have I been with for three years? Do we even know each other? Like I suddenly realized I had spent all this time with a guy who didn't share my values or my interests. He didn't even like how I *looked*. He just thought I was easy. An easy option to get to the life he envisioned for himself." More tears are falling now, but they're angry tears, so I angrily wipe one away. "Maybe I should just accept that people only like the easy part of me. The part that always makes jokes and diffuses tension and is okay with everything. Maybe I'm just this superficial, party trick of a person."

"Sophie…"

"That's how it was with my parents after their divorce. They were so mad all the time that there was no room for me to be anything but alright. And I love them and wanted to make things better, so that was fine. I could play that role. I could be happy no matter what. But somehow it feels worse when it happens in my relationships. I love so hard and try so hard and they just… don't. They just think I'll be fun and fine and an easy lay until something better comes along."

I feel him squeeze me tighter to his chest, and I know he doesn't know what to say when I get like this but I can't stop.

"Then tonight Elliot said some things that I just… I couldn't take it anymore. I'd spent so long trying to be what he wanted, trying to make him really love me, and he just *didn't*. I'm not the one who was emotionally unavailable in that relationship. Or maybe he's not emotionally unavailable, but I just wasn't good enough. I just...." I take a deep breath. "I'm so tired. I'm tired of pretending to be okay. I'm tired of caring so much, and always being the one who loves more. I want someone to know everything about me, even the sad things and the dark things and the dumb things, and still choose me. Still love me. I know it's stupid, but it's the truth."

Andy leans his head against my hair, holding me tight. The radiator clangs, my sniffles slow, and eventually he asks, "Do you remember the party where we met, my sophomore year?"

I nod into his chest.

"You know I've always hated parties. Especially at college. They just felt like loud rooms full of people I didn't care about. And when my roommates hosted they were always worried I'd ruin things by being too quiet or sullen or whatever... they literally had to supervise me. It felt like I was bringing them down just by being there."

I start tracing slow swirls across Andy's forearm, not wanting to interrupt his story, but reminding him I'm listening.

"All of freshman year I dreaded those parties, so for our first party of sophomore year I promised I would stay for an hour, then leave before I could mess things up. But then you were there. You barged into my room and surprised me and I..." He shakes his head against the top of mine, gathering his thoughts.

"You said people only like the easy parts of you. Well, let me tell you, that night when I met you—yes, it felt easy. For maybe the first time ever, it felt easy to be with someone. I didn't feel anxious, I just felt like a—a person. I don't know if that makes sense, but..." He squeezes me tighter against him, taking time to find his words. "What I'm trying to say is—you are not a party trick, Sophie. You are this rare, amazing person. You're smart without making other people feel dumb, and you're loud without making other people feel too quiet. And you *are* easy to be around, but that's just the start. You bring out the best in people. At least, I feel like the best version of myself when I'm around you."

A new tear traces the corner of my lip. Andy reaches up to stop its path with the pad of his thumb, and the whole world narrows into that touch.

It would be so simple, to fall into each other. Sitting together on this couch with a decade behind us and two inches between us. My face tilted up towards his, a familiar longing whispering there.

And I know he's just my friend. I do. But then why is there a pull under my skin and an ache in my chest?

Just show me you feel it too, Andy. I've been shot down before, but I'm still right here. If you want this too, you have to show me.

But he doesn't. And when I've held his gaze long enough that I feel the stinging behind my eyes change from Elliot-tears to Andy-tears, I know I'm torturing myself for nothing.

I shift away—still next to Andy, but supporting my own weight.

"Well." I clear my throat. "You *were* a pretty great version of yourself in the bar today. Coming for Elliot like that? I'm very impressed, Walsh."

"This is the brave new me." He cocks a one-dimple smile. "Get used to it."

I break our eye contact, but grant myself permission to rest my head on his shoulder, one last time.

"I really do love you, Soph," he says, almost a whisper.

And I know he does. So I say, "I love you, too."

But I can't go on like this. I can't languish in hope for another nine years. Something has to change.

16

Lia: where are you? did you guys leave without us?

Nolan: I think they left like two hours ago

Lia: why didnt you say bye?????????

Nolan: Did you guys see Elliot was here?

Lia: elliot wAS AT THE BAR??

Lia: s are you ok? did you talk to him??

Lia: HELLOOOO????

Lia: n should we show up at their apartment for a wellness
check

Nolan: I'm in bed leave me alone

Lia: TELL ME WHAT HAPPENED

Lia emphasized a message

Lia emphasized a message

Lia emphasized a message

Lia emphasized a message

Andy: We did talk to Elliot and it sucked, but everything is
> fine now. We're sleeping. Goodnight.

Lia: details!!! tomorrow!!!!!!

Nolan: Ya

Nolan: I'm coming over in the morning. 9:30?

Andy: Don't show up here at 9:30. I won't be back from my
> run yet.

Nolan: 10:30??

Lia: i cant do 10:30 i have to go to a cafe show!

Lia: ill be there at noon dont gossip without me

Andy's pulling pancakes off the griddle when I trudge into the kitchen, still in my pajamas, idly scrolling through the texts that came in from NASA after I fell asleep.

Am I embarrassed about last night? Yes. Does my arm still hurt? Absolutely. Do I feel renewed determination to move on from my infatuation with Andy? One thousand percent. And I think I've even come around on a plan.

"Good morning. That smells good. Make any extra?"

"Of course I did." Andy says with a bluntness that's a bit extreme, even for him. He loads a stack of pancakes onto each plate and brings them over to the table. I reach across the table for the maple syrup, then pour on a generous amount.

"Did you sleep well?"

"Not really."

"Worried about me?" I tease.

He responds with a flat, "Yes."

All of a sudden, this conversation feels like more than I can handle before breakfast and caffeine, but I try one more time. "Did you… still go on a run this morning?"

"Yup."

Okay fine. Eating in silence it is.

Our silence is usually comfortable, but this one decidedly *isn't*, and

I'm trying to figure out why. Either he's just tired and grumpy in general, or he's specifically mad at me for something that happened last night. Honestly, it could be almost anything. Last night wasn't exactly a sparkling gem in the crown of my mid-20's. And oh God... he punched Elliot last night. Like he actually *punched him in the face*. Maybe he's just stressed about that? But it's not like Elliot is going to press charges or come looking for him or something. Even still, drunk actions always feel worse in the sharp and horrible light of day, so I move in that direction.

"I'm sorry about last night."

"What are you sorry for," he says—no question mark at the end.

"I just feel like I overreacted to everything, and made you get in a literal fight and then take care of me. So I guess I'm sorry for being such a mess."

"It's fine."

"Andy, come on." I toss my arms up in a helpless gesture. "Why are you being grumpy right now? Are you mad because I overreacted? Or is it something else?"

"Overreacted to what?"

"The whole Elliot thing."

He isn't even looking at me, eyes fixed on his plate like it's the horizon and the sway of our conversation is making him seasick. "I still don't actually know what you and Elliot said to each other last night, so I have no idea."

I shove a bite of pancake into my mouth, buying a few more seconds to figure out how to explain the revelations from my largely sleepless night.

"Well, he definitely said some jerky things, but in hindsight it wasn't that big of a deal. And he also said some kind of... sweet things."

Andy puts his fork down with a *thwack*. "You're shitting me, right?"

"I mean..." I swallow my food, then continue. "He's not perfect, but I don't know."

"Why don't you just tell me what you talked about?"

"Well, he saw us dancing." I feel myself blushing—*hard*—at the memory, but I push through, dissecting my pancake into smaller and smaller bits. "So he accused me of being involved with you behind his back and basically tried to blame you for our breakup. And I said you had nothing to do with it, and we broke up because of him. Then he said that he wanted me back, and that he would be better this time and that he loves me. And then he kissed me, which was bad because we're broken up, but I also get it because he was caught up in the moment. So anyway, I bit him so I could break away from the kiss, and that's when I hurt my arm. It's not like he intentionally tried to hurt me. And I kind of hurt him first."

Andy is silent, and I know that means he's pissed. So I look up and say, "You're pissed."

He exhales. "Yes, I'm pissed."

"Don't be. He really didn't mean any harm."

"Why are you defending him?"

"Because I don't know!" I rub my palms over my eyes, realizing this will be harder than I thought.

Andy's voice is ice cold as he asks, "You're thinking about getting back together with him, aren't you?"

"You don't get it." I push syrup around my plate, appetite gone. "It's hard out there. I know people hit on you out in the wild all the time, but it's not like that for the rest of us. I don't have infinite options, and it's not like grad school is a great time to start a relationship. And anyway, he really did sound sorry. I just don't think it's realistic to wait around forever for some hypothetically perfect person."

"That's bullshit," he bites. "Anyone would be better than him."

"Andy, with all due respect, you don't know what our relationship was like." I stand from the table in a huff, bringing my dish to the sink and starting to scrub at it forcefully. "Things got bad at the end, but we had some great years before that. His family is great. He wants kids. And besides, even if I wanted to date other people, I have no idea how to even do it anymore."

I plop my plate onto the drying rack, then cross the kitchen towards the front door, putting more space between myself and Andy. His chair scrapes loudly against the floor and then he's standing, affronted.

"What are you *talking about?*"

I try to verbalize the intangible. "It's like… all I know is what Elliot likes. That's all I've done for three years, and I don't know if it's going to translate with other people." I'm pacing now, wearing a hole into Andy's pristine hardwood floor. "I don't know how to, like, signal interest in someone I meet, or make conversation on a date. I don't even know how to *kiss* someone who's not him anymore! I haven't kissed someone else in *years*. How does it even work? I don't remember! You know what I mean? It's a safer bet to stay with the guy I already know."

"Don't say that." Andy squeezes his eyes shut, hand gripping the edge of the table like this conversation physically pains him.

"Look, I know you don't like Elliot and don't want us back together, and I get that. But I'm also serious." My gestures grow more animated as I speak. "The kissing thing is a perfect example: I've only kissed one person for almost half a decade. What if I developed bad habits? What if I misinterpret their body language, or do weird things with my tongue, or—"

Andy is a blur as he rushes towards me, grabbing both sides of my face.

"Sophie," he says, and the word is a command.

"Yes?"

His dark eyes bore into mine. "Stop talking."

And then he kisses me.

He *kisses* me.

And it's a tidal wave.

Andy crushes his lips to mine. There's a wildness to his touch, a recklessness in the press of his fingertips against my scalp. And for a moment I can't move—paralyzed by the soul-shaking novelty of being someone who's shared everything with him before, but never this.

Then I give in, holding want and need and have together in my hands for the first time. I want to memorize the taste of him, the heat of his body against mine, the texture of his hair as I slide my fingers into it.

I wrap both arms around him, fisting my hands into the fabric of his shirt to pull him closer, and he takes it as the encouragement it is. His tongue plunges into my mouth and it feels like he's claiming me. Consuming me and leaving no trace for anyone else.

I have never been kissed like this.

Ever.

His hands are hungry and tender and everywhere, tracing my back, my hips, my waist. He follows every curve with savoring pressure and I've never been more aware of my body or my skin. His warm palm tucks under my shirt, splaying across my lower back, and the press of each fingertip is a flame. His chest is hard and his lips are soft and it feels so right that I can't believe it's real.

This is *Andy*. I'm kissing *Andy*.

The friction is perfect and nowhere near enough, and I catch my body moving against his. One of his hands twines into my hair, tilting my head to the side with a dominance that sparkles low in my belly. And when his mouth leaves mine I'm prepared to beg for it back. Beg him to keep touching me and taking whatever he wants. But then his lips are on my skin again, this time trailing wet kisses down my neck, each spot of contact bringing me to life until I'm vibrating with need.

My fingers find his jawline, then demandingly pull his mouth back to mine. He moans against my lips and I realize he's hard—the length of him pressed firm against my hip, his thigh shifting between mine exactly where I need it.

"Andy, mmh—"

I can't help it. It feels too good. And he must not mind the sounds I'm making as he starts to grind against me, harder, until the final restraints on his control snap. He pushes me up against the door and—

"Ow! Mother—"

"What?" Andy leaps backward, breaking our connection completely. "What happened? Are you okay?" He's panting as he scans my face and body. "God, did I hurt you?"

It feels like surfacing from the water, disorienting and orienting all at once.

"It's nothing. Ow. Sorry." I try to laugh it off. "I just hit my arm on the door. But it's fine." I'm rubbing my injured arm from last night, and Andy's already taken another step away from me.

"Fuck, Soph, I'm so sorry. Are you sure you're okay?"

"Yeah, yeah, I'm really fine. Just a little startled."

There's alarm in his eyes that I'm sure mirrors my own, and a million questions balloon between us: What just happened? Why did he do that? Why now? What does it mean?

Where do we go from here?

We can't take it back. It happened. So now we have to figure out what's next. Was he just proving a point? It didn't seem like it. It seemed like he liked it—*a lot*. So then does he… want to be together?

For a moment, a shard of hope shines in my chest.

Then I smash that shard to bits, because Andy is looking at me with uncertainty that borders on panic. No—what we need right now is damage control. Hope can come later.

I open my mouth to say something comforting, but I don't know what.

It didn't mean anything wouldn't be true.

I've wanted to do that for years would be *too* true.

Do it again is what I'm really thinking, and I think it over and over, praying the thought is somehow loud enough to hear.

His chest rises and falls with his own unsaid words, and the silence feels interminable.

Do it again, I beg. *Do it again. Do it again.*

But then he repeats "I'm sorry" as he backs away from me. "That shouldn't have happened. I should just… I should just go. I should… yeah. I'll be back later. I… sorry, again."

He grabs his keys off the front table, then opens the door and disappears. I'm alone and shattered.

17

About thirty minutes after Andy's abrupt departure, there's a knock on the apartment door.

My eyes snap up. Reruns of *Law & Order* have been playing on the TV in front of me, but I've been too lost in my thoughts to follow the plot. The knock jolts me out of the labyrinth of my brain and back to reality.

I take a deep breath, then stand and walk to the door. With each step, I thank God that Andy is both courteous and prescient enough to give me a warning knock, instead of just using his key to barge in on me freaking out. As the door inches closer, I remind myself of the plan: play it down, laugh it off, don't make it weird and get kicked out of this apartment.

Thirty minutes has been plenty of time to imagine what Andy would say when he gets back. Something along the lines of, *I don't know what came over me. I've told you before that I just want to be friends.*

Or maybe, *It was one kiss—we don't have to make it a big deal.*

Or worse, *Yes, that kiss was amazing and soul-shattering and I can't deny it was the best kiss of my life but that doesn't change anything. You shouldn't have gotten your hopes up, silly girl.*

Okay, maybe he won't put it that way exactly, but the underlying message likely stands.

Mid-spiral, I'm absolutely shocked when I open the door to find Nolan's sunny grin beaming back at me.

"Hey, Soph! I brought the goods." He's carrying a four-pack of iced coffees in one hand and a paper Market Basket bag in the other. "How's it going, babes?"

He kisses the top of my head and walks in like he owns the place. Which, to be fair, is normal for NASA—what's mine is yours and all that. But today it feels like an avalanche.

"You have to tell me everything that happened last night. I can't believe Elliot was there." His burly man arms grab a large plastic bowl out of the kitchen cabinet, tear open a family sized bag of chips, and dump them out to share. "I didn't even see him. Not that I wanted to. I'm mostly just curious if he's figured out what Lia did to his pants while we were there getting your stuff."

Nolan has this way of occupying all the space in a room. I usually love it. It's sweet—like innocent himbo Hercules barreling into the town square full-steam ahead. But today, right now, his cheer is just disorienting. I spent the last half hour burrowing into a sullen self-doubt hole that felt like a perfectly suitable permanent residence. Then in comes my own personal Kronk, pulling levers at random and shaking me awake.

He doesn't even notice that I haven't responded until the snacks are all laid out and he's taken the first sip of his coffee. He holds a second bottle out towards me, asking, "You want one?" but all I can do is weakly shake my head.

"Hey, are you alright?" His thick eyebrows furrow as he urges me into a kitchen chair, then takes the seat next to me. "Where's Andy anyway?"

My face feels like an open flame and I'm stammering, not quite sure how to say what I'm about to say. "Uh… Nolan, right before you got here… Andy and I… we… kissed."

I watch the gears turn in his head. His eyes slowly widen, then a grin bursts across his face and he rockets up from the chair. "WOO! YES!" His arms are raised, punching the air like he's just won some sportsball world championship.

"Well, I'm glad you're so happy about it," I yell, "but I'm freaking out!"

That sobers him quickly. He sits back down. "Wait, so you're not together now?"

"No, we're not *together* now! Nolan, it was a kiss. He—I—we just…" I pinch the bridge of my nose and try to unearth something that resembles a sentence. "We kissed. We kissed just now." I gesture helplessly toward the spot where it happened. "And I don't know why or what to do about it."

I explain everything. The fight with Elliot last night, Andy taking care of me, then this morning when he was in such an awful mood until all of a sudden…

By the time my story ends, Nolan is up and pacing. He looks about as stressed out as I feel.

"And he just bolted?" Nolan asks. "No explanation, no… declaration?"

"No. What? Nolan, I swear I told you literally every word we said to each other, and then he was gone."

He sits back down, elbows on the table as he cradles his head in his hands. I can't help but roll my eyes at the dramatics. When he finally looks up at me again, he asks, "If he had stayed, what would you have done?"

I feel the blush that scorches across my cheeks. The memory of his lips on mine, his grip on the side of my neck, his hardness pressing against me. I shake my head to clear the fog of it all. "I don't know," I lie. If we hadn't been interrupted, I know exactly what I would've done. "I just wish I knew what he was thinking. I'm so nervous he's going to come back any second and tell me he needs space, and that I have to move out because things are irrevocably weird between us."

"Well, he's never going to do that, so you can let that one go right now. Even if he wasn't in—" Nolan cuts himself off, a look on his face like his brain short circuited.

"Even if he wasn't in what?"

"Nothing," he says quickly. "I just... he's a really good guy, Sophie."

"Why are you being weird right now? I know that. He's my best friend, you think I don't know he's one of the best people on Earth?"

"Maybe you should give him a chance." Nolan's expression is painfully sweet, and it's so like him to assume things are that simple.

"He doesn't..." I start to explain, but then back up. "He was just upset. He didn't mean it. He doesn't see me that way." I glance down at my hands as I say it, trying not to remember how they felt running through his hair, pulling him against me.

"What do you mean? He just kissed you. Of course he sees you that way."

"I know! I mean... for a second I thought..." I shake my head to reorder my warring thoughts. "Look, one kiss doesn't have to mean anything. I think emotions were high after last night and we were both confused and possibly generally horny. I mean, the *second* we stopped kissing and actually had to face each other again... you should have seen the way he ran out of here. He literally told me it shouldn't have happened and then he *left*. I don't think I can deal with another rejection like that, especially from him."

He sighs. "Okay, but you don't know—"

A buzzing sound cuts him off, and I pull my phone out of my back pocket.

"Hang on, Lia's calling." I answer and throw her on speaker. "Hey Li—"

"ANDY KISSED YOU? WHAT THE FUCK!"

Andy's voice immediately follows, like he's yelling from somewhere in the background. "Lia, stop! Jesus—Sophie, I'm so sorry about this."

"You're together?" I ask, my face burning at about a billion degrees.

Nolan pulls my outstretched palm towards him, leaning directly over the phone. "Andy, man, I'm so happy for—"

"Nolan, shut the fuck up right now," Andy barks, cutting him off. "I'm serious. Shut up."

"He's at my café show," Lia explains. "He just showed up. So does this mean you're dating now?"

"For fuck's sake," Andy says in the distance. "No, we're not dating now."

"Then you two can't just start kissing each other! It's going to mess up the NASA dynamic."

"Guys—" I try to cut in, but I'm bulldozed as Nolan fully snatches the phone from my hand.

"Lia, grow up. This isn't about you."

"Grow up? GROW UP? Andy and Sophie just frenched like horny 16-year-olds and you're telling *me* to grow up?"

"Can we *please* not make this a group discussion?" I beg, but no one is listening.

"I'm going to murder you," Andy's voice threatens. "You're dead in the ground."

"You murder me and you'll have the Italian mob on your ass."

"Stop saying that. Our family isn't in the mob."

"What did it mean?" Lia screams into the receiver. "What does it mean for NASA? Will things ever be normal again?"

"It didn't mean anything," Andy insists.

"Bro, come on, you don't mean that—"

"NOLAN," he shouts. "I'm fucking serious, man."

I grab the phone back from Nolan. "Guys! Can Andy and I please talk about this alone before we present our case to the Supreme Court?"

"Sure," Lia says, all bite. "You talk about it. But I will not have you two messing up my friend group. Keep it in your pants unless you're gonna fucking marry each other. Got it?"

I sigh. "Yeah. Got it."

"If you think you're still my friend after this, Lia, you're out of your fu—"

Then the call cuts off.

———— •♦• ————

Two *Law & Order* episodes later, the jury is about to return their verdict when I hear the sound of a key in the lock. Nolan and I jolt up to attention, partially spilling the bowl of chips on the cushion between us as we look towards the sound, then back to each other.

The door slides open. Andy takes one step in before looking up, right at me.

"Hi," he says quietly.

"Hi," I return.

Then nothing. We're frozen in place, eyes locked. Nolan's gaze darts between us like we've gone insane. The jury foreman declares, "We find the defendant... guilty," before anyone in the room remembers how to speak.

"Okay..." Nolan drawls. "I'm just going to see myself out."

He stands, grabs his jacket and shoes, and mutters something under his breath as the apartment door shuts. It might be in Italian. I can't even tell at this point.

Once he's gone, Andy reanimates. His eyes leave mine as he hangs up his jacket, hastily, clumsily. "I forgot Nolan was coming over," he says, pulling off his boots and placing them in their spot on the shoe rack. "I kind of thought he was joking."

"He never jokes about inviting himself somewhere." My smile feels forced, but it doesn't matter because Andy isn't looking at me. "So... how was Lia's show?"

"Uh... it was good."

"That's good."

"Yeah."

Andy hesitates, then finally joins me in the living room. He sits stiffly in the corner armchair as I send up a prayer: *God, please don't let this ruin our friendship. Please let things go back to normal. If Andy lets me keep living here, I swear I'll never do something that reckless again. I'll go to church. I'll be good forever. Whatever you want.*

Lia's phone call ambush—while possibly the most annoying thing she's ever done—was a blessing in the end, because at least Andy's contributions gave me a preview of the conversation to come: We're not together now. We're not dating. We won't be doing it again.

(But what I wouldn't give to skip over the verbalization of those facts straight into pretending it never happened.)

Andy leans back, running a hand through his hair. "I don't know what to say."

"Me either," I admit. Then, "Are you okay?"

"Yeah, yeah. Are you okay?"

"Yeah."

"So…"

I take a deep breath in. "So… you kissed me."

"Jesus Christ." Andy falls forward, elbows on knees, clearly ready to die.

"What! I'm sorry! But we have to get it out in the open."

"No, I'm sorry," he says to the floor. "I shouldn't have… God."

"I mean, don't apologize. It was…" I start to laugh because I can't believe what's coming out of my mouth. "It was really good."

Andy's head pops up. He doesn't say a word but his gaze is frantic—flicking from my eyes to my hands to my lips and back, the two curved lines between his brows deepening as he obviously starts to spiral.

"Don't look at me like that." I wave a hand through the air between us. "I know it doesn't mean we're together now or anything. I'm just saying, I think we can acknowledge it was a really good kiss. Right? Or am I wrong? Oh no—did you think it was *bad?*"

Andy's face lands in his hands, palms rubbing forceful circles over his eyes. "No, it wasn't bad."

When he doesn't say more, I reach forward to squeeze his knee. "Hey, stop worrying so much. Lia's not actually gonna make you marry me or something. We're friends and we're roommates. That's all. But it happened, right? Whatever was going through our heads at the time, it happened."

"Yeah," he mutters, face still buried. "It happened."

"And… you're not going to kick me out?" A bit of genuine nervousness creeps into my tone. "Because I really can't afford rent on my own. I'm so sorry if this whole thing is making you uncomfortable, but I really need this apartment, Andy, and I'm not afraid to beg."

"No, of course not. See this is why I shouldn't…" He takes a centering breath, then meets my eyes. "I'm sorry you were worried about that. I would never kick you out. You live here now. I didn't mean to stress you out."

I want to put a period at the end of this interaction. Start a new paragraph, a new page. Draw dark lines under it in red and black, then lose track of it in the massive tome of our history. So I paste on a neutral smile and ask, "Friends?"

He almost-smiles, no dimple in sight. "Friends."

But then, as I stand and head towards my room, Andy calls, "Wait—Soph?"

My heart shifts into second gear as I turn back. "Yeah?"

"Don't get back together with him."

I study him—the hard set of his jaw, the almost sorrowful tilt to his brow—then ask, "Why?"

He whispers, "Just don't."

His expression is layered and pained and it makes me wish I could reach into his chest and rip out his heart, looking for brutal honesty next to my name in all the pulsing atria. But I can't. So I just say, "Okay."

18

I did not plan on going to the Garment District tonight, but it's my last hope. This morning I realized I have *nothing* to wear to the exhibit launch event tomorrow, but it's not like I could take the day off work to go shopping, and now that I'm free the mall is already closed so… here we go.

This whole week has been a blur, to be honest. It feels like I've been hungover from the weekend for five days. But not literally, physically hungover. More like… emotionally hungover? I swear, I'm only 26 but I'm already too old for this level of drama. Seeing Elliot, messing up my arm, *kissing Andy*, then having to talk to Andy *about* kissing Andy… it's enough to knock my brain straight into next week.

And my reward for surviving it all? The Garment District.

If you've never heard of the Garment District, just know it's best known for selling rumpled clothing by the pound instead of by the item—a real Boston gem.

My anxiety ratchets up with each step of the walk there.

Fortunately, Lia's already waiting by the door when I arrive.

Together, we beeline through the hot pink walls, past the racks of faux fur coats and cut-off jorts, beneath the oversized cut-out of Dolly Parton's head and a tenuously mounted motorcycle, and into the so-called 'professional women's apparel' section.

"It has to be at least knee-length, and ideally I want something that totally covers my arm bandage, so no cap sleeves or sleeveless."

"What about this?" Lia pulls out a fitted red dress with a pencil skirt and a sweetheart neckline.

"Oh wow, yes! That's perfect for my Jessica Rabbit cosplay. That's why we're here, right?"

"Point taken." She returns the dress to the rack. "Do you know what your work friends are wearing?"

"No, I should have asked. I've felt so frazzled all week that it didn't cross my mind." I start sifting through a line of heinous gingham frocks as I add, "Oh but actually, speaking of the event, I can bring a guest if you're free. It's tomorrow at 7:30 and there's an open bar. I will have to schmooze for some percent of the time, but after my remarks are done we'd be free to drink champagne on the company's dime."

"Ooh, I'm sorry Soph, I can't." Lia pulls out a green dress with long, puffy sleeves and holds it up in front of me. I shake my head and she puts it back. "I'm supposed to go live with my embroidery classes at the same time every week so that the algorithm will pick it up. I've been doing Fridays at 7."

"That's okay," I shrug. "I'll be brave and go stag."

"Why don't you ask Andy to go with you?"

Hearing his name feels like a glass breaking in my chest. "I don't know if that's a good idea."

"Why not?"

"Things have just been kind of weird since the whole kiss thing."

"*The whole kiss thing*," Lia mocks. "You mean when your long-time best friend mauled your face out of nowhere?"

"I told you it wasn't like that."

"Then what was it like?" Lia pushes.

"It was just weird!" I reply in grave mischaracterization. The kiss wasn't weird at all. Even just mentioning it now has my temperature rising—the memory of his body trapping mine, the firm press of his lips, the moans he pulled from me…

"So you didn't like it," Lia probes.

"That's not what I said."

"Okay, stop." Lia takes hold of my shoulders and spins me until we're face to face. "Look me in the eye and be honest. Did you want Andy to kiss you, yes or no?"

My eyes dart from left to right, making sure we're totally alone before whispering, "If I tell you this, it goes with you to your grave. Do you understand?"

Lia makes a show of crossing herself piously, then brings her hands together in prayer. "I swear."

"The problem is," I start to explain, lowering my voice even further, "I really *did* want the kiss to happen. I mean, you know I've always kind of had a crush on him."

"Excuse me!" Lia yells, completely breaking the facade of privacy. "Hold that fucking horse right there. No, I did not know that."

"I told you he was cute the night I met him freshman year!"

"Okay sweetie, thinking a man at a party is cute and having an ongoing crush on your best friend are two very different things."

"Did you forget that I literally tried to sleep with him that one time?"

"Honestly, I thought you were just drunk and horny, I didn't realize it was a full-on Andy crush—oh my god!"

"Well, whatever," I hiss. "Now you know. And these last couple of weeks, every time I'm around him I'm like… I don't know. Just something about living with him, and seeing all these intimate parts of his life, and how he's been taking such good care of me. I just can't stop myself from thinking about…" I try to trail off suggestively, but Lia gives me a look that demands I say it out loud. "Thinking about him! Thinking about jumping his bones! Thinking about ripping a manuscript out of his hands, crawling into his lap, and screwing his brains out right on that beige armchair. God, what is wrong with me?"

My face is nine billion degrees as I bury it in my hands.

"Sophie, oh my god," Lia whisper-shouts through a laugh. "That's amazing!"

"Is it amazing though?" I peek through my fingers with desperation. "Because we finally kissed and he was so freaked out he literally ran away. Like immediately evacuated the dance floor. And then he came back and was still freaked out like two hours later, and we decided to just be friends, and now we've been tiptoeing around each other all week and I hate it."

"Sophie, he definitely freaked out because he thought *you* were freaking out. That man has been in love with you for years."

"What?" I shriek, grabbing her arm. "Did he tell you that?"

"No, but he didn't have to. It's obvious from literally everything he does."

I drop her arm and turn away, trying to hide the emotions I'm wearing like makeup. "That's not true. We just have a very close friendship. Whatever—why am I explaining this to *you* of all people? You know what we're like."

"Yes, I do," she insists. "I know what you're like together, and I know what he's like when you're not there, and I know what he's like when he's watching you and thinking about you and talking about—"

"Stop!" I shove her shoulder. "It's not like that."

"I'm not going to stop until you admit he's in love with you."

"If he was in love with me, why wouldn't he just ask me out? Ever? Even once in the last nine-plus years?"

Lia turns towards me, hands on her hips. "Do you really want to know what I think, or are you going to dismiss it out of hand?"

I mirror her pose, feigning bravery. "I really want to know what you think."

"I think, at first, it was just Andy being Andy. The boy is indecisive and nervous as all hell and too used to dates just appearing from thin air. And then I think as time went on, it just became too much pressure. He loves you too much, even as a friend, to risk messing it up."

"But he *knows* I'm interested in him!" A woman at the adjoining rack shoots eye daggers at me and I realize I'm shouting again. I lower my voice, leaning in towards Lia. "He's always known, ever since that first summer. Why—why wouldn't—I mean, if he really—"

"There's no use looking for logic," she interrupts. "Andy's a gold medalist in mental gymnastics." She turns back to the rack, continuing to browse like this conversation isn't shattering my whole worldview. "I think you should invite him to the museum event with you. It can be as friends, low pressure. But hey, if you happen to look stunning in a new dress with your hair and makeup done, and he happens to end the night by confessing his undying love, then all the better."

I'm a pesky little bird, flitting at her shoulder. "I thought you didn't want us together? Don't I recall you saying something about me staying away from him unless we're going to get married like… four days ago?"

"I was trying to protect him, Soph." She hits me with a genuinely somber expression, and I realize she's telling the God's honest truth. "And you. I was picturing the two of you starting some half-assed friends-with-benefits thing, and it's all fun and games until it's not. One of you is in love, and the other is just there for a good time, and suddenly our friendships are all fucked."

I exhale, and it's an echo of the fears she just voiced. "Yeah, that would be awful."

"But if you are serious about starting something with him…" Lia slowly pulls a black dress out from the bunch before her. It has a structured top with half-sleeves and a collared V-neck, almost like a blazer. The bottom is a sensible knee-length skirt. She holds it in front of herself with an eyebrow raised like *what do you think?*

A tinny announcement sounds through the loudspeakers. "The Garment District will be closing in ten minutes. All customers please make your way to check out."

I grab the dress out of Lia's hands. "Time to make a choice, I guess."

"———— •♦• ————"

The living room is empty when I get home. I kick off my shoes, toss my purse over the back of the couch, and—finding uninspiring options in the fridge—decide on a well-rounded dinner of chips and salsa.

Just when I shove the first chip in my mouth, Andy surprises me by walking out of his room. He obviously didn't hear me come in, and now stands frozen in his doorway, blinking.

His posture is tense. He looks nervous. I *feel* nervous. Everything sucks.

I swallow my chip, then say, "Hi."

He replies, "Hi."

"How was your day?"

"Okay."

With no idea what to say next, I dip a fresh chip in the jar of salsa and extend it towards him. He looks like he has to gear himself up just to come accept it, but then crosses over to me, sitting down across the table and popping it into his mouth.

How did this get so weird between us? Maybe Lia's suggestion has some merit.

We both chew through a few more seconds of silence before Andy asks, "How about your day?"

"It was busy, but good. I think we're ready for the event, but I'm still nervous."

"Don't be. Everything's already done, right?"

"Well, almost," I say. "I actually have to give some remarks at the launch. But once that's done I'm planning to chug at least three glasses of complementary champagne immediately."

"You're speaking at the event?"

"Yeah." This is my opening and I'm going for it. "By the way, I'm allowed to bring a guest with me if you're free tomorrow at 7:30. No pressure, I know it's last minute." I look away from him, dipping another chip to give him time to think.

"You're inviting me?"

"Yes, but if you don't want to come you don't have to. Really, it's fine."

"No, yes, I—I'd love to come. I'll be there." He sounds genuinely excited and I can feel my self-consciousness evaporating. "Thanks for the invitation."

"Thanks for saying yes." Our eyes meet across the table, and it feels like we're halfway back to normal again.

Progress.

19

The apartment door slams open as I barrel in, snow boots pounding salt into the hardwood floor.

"I'm late! I have to change! Gosh darn it!" I throw down my purse and charge straight into my room. "The fricking train... I swear every train except the B came in like ten times before a single B showed up." I dump a basket of beauty supplies out onto my bed, then frantically rummage through them. "I was doing mental calculus like should I take the C to Coolidge Corner and walk? Should I take the Red Line to Harvard and transfer to a bus? But every time I thought about getting on a different train I was like no, surely the next one will be a B. And look at where it got me! Now I just got here and we have to leave in like 20 minutes and I haven't even started doing my hair. Why is life this way?"

Andy comes up to my open door and says, with uncanny calm, "We can take an Uber. You have time."

"I still don't know what I'm even doing with my hair." I whip around—where the heck did I put my curling iron?—and catch a glimpse of Andy in the doorway. I'd been in such a rush on my way in that I barely glanced at him, but now…

He takes up nearly the whole door frame with a casual lean, tall as he is. His black suit jacket is unbuttoned, revealing the sharp white shirt and black tie underneath. Simple. Classic. Painfully hot. (Ugh!) He gives me a one-dimple smile, and I realize inviting him to this event was tantamount to self-torture.

"I think you could go as you are," he offers coolly.

"Ha. Right," I deadpan, forcing myself to look away from him and continue scavenging through my mess. "If you're going to look like *that* next to me, I barely stand a chance. Do we think the pope is available to perform a miracle on short notice? And can he do them over the phone or is that strictly an in-person service?"

"I don't think that's how being the pope works."

"Well then how useless is he!" Giving up on the curling iron for now, I spin around to face my friend. "Okay Andy, I love you, but can you leave so I can change?"

He does, and once the door is shut behind him, I bend down to fish my new dress out of the hot pink Garment District bag. Thank God it doesn't need ironing—at least I have one win for the day. Though suddenly, as I'm faced with the imminent prospect of putting it on my body, does it look smaller? And the fabric really has no stretch at all… but at this point it's the eleventh hour, so there's nothing for it but to cram myself inside somehow. After three failed attempts to zip up, I realize I'm going to have to make myself smaller by any means necessary, including removing my bra. Normally I would be worried about being unprofessional, but the fabric is actually quite thick, so I think it should be fine.

Ultimately, with a held breath and a firm grip, I succeed in fully closing the zipper under the left arm. (Why wasn't the zipper on the back like a normal dress? Who made this death trap? Fricking Garment District…) Then, in another small mercy, I spot the end of my curling iron sticking out of my nightstand drawer. Success!

Quickly checking my phone, I have *maybe* ten minutes left to curl my hair and throw on some makeup. So much for Lia's grand vision of me looking amazing enough to make Andy "confess his love" tonight. It's not like that's how anything works, anyway.

When I finally emerge from my bedroom, Andy is pacing in the kitchen. "Ready?" I ask, giving my dress a final smooth-down. Andy halts and looks up at the sound of my voice.

He doesn't answer the question. In fact, he doesn't say anything at all. Instead, his eyes track a path down my body, over the fitted bodice of the black dress, down to where it flares out at the hips, to my semi-opaque tights and plain black heels, then back up, slowly.

Eventually, his dark eyes meet mine as he says, "You look great."

That man has been in love with you for years, Lia's traitorous voice echoes. And I guess I'm still breathing despite it all, because I manage to say, "Thanks. You're not half bad yourself."

His gaze drops to my mouth. There's at least ten feet and a table between us, but he might as well be dragging his thumb across my lip for how intimately I feel his attention. Then his eyes shift, just a few inches, to the small red jewels hanging from my ears. "You've been wearing those a lot recently," he says, tapping his own lobe.

"Have I?" I ask, and hope he understands everything I can't say out loud when I add, "They're my favorites."

Another charged beat pulses. Then Andy seems to remember himself enough to glance down at his watch. And he's right, we really don't have time for all this.

"Here," he says, reaching for my coat on the hook and holding it out to me. "Can't have you late for your big day."

"———— ◆ ————"

One Uber ride through relatively light traffic later, Andy and I walk into the new *Unlocking the Universe* exhibit wing at the Boston Museum of Science.

Every inch of the space has been meticulously and creatively envisioned. No thanks to me—to be clear. I just sent some emails and told people when they were going over budget. But the designers did a really amazing job. Interactive screens transport visitors through time and space. There are colorful LEDs along the walls that create a feeling of motion. Giant planets hang from the ceiling, and invisible projectors trace patterns along the floor to guide our guests' eyes and footsteps. Every sense has a sensation. I feel almost giddy as I watch groups of adult patrons in formal attire start letting their inner children play and explore. Even stoic Andy reaches out to turn a hand crank model of the Milky Way.

Slowly, we wind our way towards one of the bars. We only get soda water—I don't want to drink before my remarks, and Andy is too courteous to leave me behind. Plus I'm *way* too keyed up to eat any of the hors d'oeuvres being passed on silver trays.

I force small talk with a number of slightly familiar faces in the crowd: colleagues, donors, trustees. All the while, my arm is looped through Andy's, who says nothing to anyone. But I wouldn't expect him to; that's not why I brought him. I brought him to anchor me as my nerves soar, and at that, he's doing a phenomenal job.

Eventually, an intern lets me know the program is about to start. I turn to Andy with a smile and a bounce. "Wish me luck!"

His mouth says, "You've got this."

His eyes say, *I see through that bounce. I know you're nervous out of your mind, but don't be.*

I try to listen to both.

Mariane is waiting for me in the long backstage hallway. "Hey," she whispers. "You ready? You look great!"

Our Board Chair, Adira, takes the stage, and the room hushes as her remarks begin.

"I think so," I squeak back to Mariane, soto voce.

"The mic on the podium is adjustable," she tells me. "Feel free to raise or lower it when you get up there."

"Got it."

I watch Adira speak from the wings, my palms growing clammier with each passing sentence. I wipe them on the skirt of my dress in an extremely unsubtle way that has Mariane asking, "Nervous?"

"Not really," I insist. "We rehearsed so much. I'm sure it'll be fine."

But Mari knows me well enough to know I'm lying, and benevolently offers a topic for distraction. "Did I see you with a date earlier? Who is he?"

"Oh that's just Andy. He's the friend I told you about, the one I'm living with now."

Mariane's eyes visibly widen. "Friend? Okay then…"

"What?" I hiss.

"I get it." She raises her hands in surrender. "I'm your coworker. This is a job and stuff. You don't have to tell me what goes on at home…" The suspicious look she gives me out of the corner of her eye completely belies her words.

"Mari!"

"Honey, good for you! If I was single and that man offered to take me home, I would crawl there on my hands and knees."

"Oh my god." Now my palms are sweating for a completely different reason, and it takes all of my willpower to keep my volume down. "We are just friends. And platonic roommates. Nothing is happening there." I shake my head and look away, hoping the hallway lights are too dim for her to read my expression.

"Now I could stand up here and gab all night," says the voice onstage, "but I know you all want to hear about the real impact of your support. So, without further ado, it is my great pleasure to introduce Program Manager Sophie Lindell, who will share more about what this new exhibit means for the future of the Museum of Science."

And that's my cue. I walk onto the stage, nervous as a minnow on a hook, trying to remind myself that most of the people in this room don't really care what I say. Rational thinking, however, cannot stop the heavy pounding in my chest.

"Thank you for that warm introduction, Adira," I say into the podium mic. "And hello everyone. As Adira said, my name is Sophie Lindell and I am the Program Manager for the new *Unlocking the Universe* exhibit here at the Museum of Science."

My voice is shaky—darn it. And now that I'm focusing on that fact, I'm sure it'll just get shakier. I consciously take a steadying breath. In through the nose, out through the mouth.

Then I spot Andy in the crowd. Him and his two-dimple smile, just a few rows away, shaking his head like he can't believe I'm speaking to this huge crowd at this fancy gala. And he looks so inexplicably *proud* of me, even though I've barely done anything yet, that my nerves melt with the rest of me into a puddle on the floor.

I say my next line directly to him, like we're rehearsing in our kitchen and no one else can hear.

"The initial idea for this exhibit came from an icebreaker at a staff retreat a few years ago." My voice sounds steadier already, so I continue. "We asked our staff, 'What is the first science concept you learned as a child that amazed you?' Then we asked, 'What's a science concept you never learned as a child, but you wish you had?'…"

Every time I look up from my notes, I look for Andy's face in the crowd first. He's like my charging station—when my battery gets low I find him and build up the will to engage the crowd.

"…Fortunately, as technology advances, and science education forges new frontiers, museums have a new opportunity to put the universe in the palm of a child's hand…"

I feel the rhythm of it now, and you know what? This isn't so bad. I say one of my scripted jokes—cheesy as it is—and the crowd actually *laughs* with me. It's not a roar, but it's a titter, and that's enough.

"…Through a combination of tactile models, cutting-edge visualization screens, and even 3D projections, *Unlocking the Universe* provides developmentally appropriate and interactive experiences for learners in a wide range of ages…"

When my remarks conclude, the audience is generous with their applause. (What was I worried about? I should've known they would be nice to me!) Then the program finishes with a few quick video clips from our pilot test group. I've seen them a million times, so although I'm still standing at the side of the stage, I look away from the screen and glance around the room.

When my eyes find Andy now, his expression has changed. It's yet another look I don't know how to interpret. The only way I can describe it is *sincere*. Almost Nolan-esque in its openness. The corner of his mouth thinks about a smile, but his eyes look... determined? wistful? somewhere in between? And I could tell myself, sure, that's a look one friend could give another friend. But the evidence is mounting that it's more than that. He *kissed* me! And yes, he freaked out afterwards—but so did I, and lord knows that doesn't mean I don't want him.

Caught in the spell of his attention, I almost feel brave enough to do something about it. To go home tonight and demand he tell me his feelings, and demand of myself that I do the same.

Almost.

When the video ends and I step back out into the wings, Mari greets me with a feline grin.

"Were you looking at him?" she asks—no longer forced to whisper with the remarks finally behind us.

"Who?"

"Your 'platonic roommate.'"

I hedge. "A little bit... Why?"

"He was staring at you like you hung the Moon."

I roll my eyes, because what else could I possibly do—here, now, away from him. "He was not. That's just how handsome people look when they're listening."

Mariane pokes me in the arm like a child. "So, you admit he's handsome?"

"Mari!" I chide for the second time tonight—a feeble comeback.

"Here's what I think," she continues. "You remember when you told me the reason you love sticky notes? Because it's easier to think clearly when something is right in front of you? Well, this man is right in front of you, Soph, so it's time to start thinking clearly about what you want from him. Because I would bet anything he's yours for the taking."

She squeezes my arm once, then walks away. And it's for the best, because I can barely remember how to speak. I need champagne. And I need Andy.

I walk back into the main event space to find the guests eating, drinking, and socializing much more boisterously than before. The room feels loud and full. It's a sea of men in dark suits and women in colorful satin, with one human life raft floating in the middle.

My best friend is leaning against a pillar with his arms crossed, waiting for me.

"Hey," I say, walking straight into his arms.

"You were amazing," he says into my hair.

"Thanks." I pull back to look at him. "Can we drink now, please?"

He laughs and follows my lead towards the bar. He's a half-step behind me, and I feel a broad palm touch my lower back—feather light, only the slightest warmth pressing through my dress, down to the skin that wants more.

We order champagne as I silently remind myself I am at work right now, and I do not have the bandwidth to ask Andy *what are we and what is happening and what if what if what if?* Proving this point, I feel a tap on my shoulder and turn to find our Board Chair behind me.

"Adira, hi!"

"I won't keep you from celebrating," Adira says, nodding down towards my glass. (I'm allowed to be drinking, I'll have you know. But even so I feel *mortified*.) "I just wanted to personally congratulate you on an amazing launch." Adira's in her mid-70's, with peachy skin, curly silver hair, and an air of subdued confidence. She shakes my free hand as she says, "Of course, I hope you'll stay with the museum forever, but if you ever need a reference in the future I hope you will use my name."

"Wow." I shake her hand more rapidly, going for grateful but landing on crazy. "Thank you, that means so much. I honestly wasn't sure how the trustees felt about this exhibit from the preview a few weeks ago."

"You mean Jeff, right?" she asks with a scoff. "He's an idiot."

Andy turns his bark of laughter into a cough—unsubtly.

"But who cares about him?" Adira continues, handing me her business card. "Reach out to me directly if you ever need anything."

20

Andy

If anyone asked me what happened after Sophie's gala, I would say I barely remember. We got home tipsy, everything was a blur, then we fell asleep.

But that's not true. I'll remember every moment of it until I die.

It took Sophie a full minute to get the apartment door unlocked, due to the combination of three glasses of champagne and sheer giddiness. Watching her struggle with the key, I realized she'd barely eaten anything at the event.

"Do you want food, Soph?" I suggested as the door finally opened. "It didn't seem like you had anything earlier."

"Oh my god, do you know what I want so bad?" Sophie asked, rhetorically of course, because she was about to tell me. "Bread."

"What kind of bread? We've got rye and I think some bagels, though they might be stale."

I was heading towards the fridge when Sophie said, "No! You know what I really want?"

I looked back at her indulgently. "What?"

"Scallion. Pancakes." She punctuated each word. "Please, Andy! If you love me at all please, please make me scallion pancakes."

"Do we have scallions?"

"Yes, but they're not in the fridge. I put them in a cup of water on the window."

I looked to where she was giddily pointing. "So you did. Alright then, as you wish."

Sophie squealed. "You are perfect! I'm going to put on pajamas while you cook, and then I'll eat, and then I'm planning to pass out very full and very happy."

She skipped into her room to change, leaving me to work. I started by chopping up the scallions, then put the water on the stove to boil before measuring out the flour. I pulled out my phone to Google which steps of the recipe I could plausibly skip to save time and get us both some carbs ASAP.

Minutes ticked by, and I was just placing the first pancake onto the pan when I heard a plaintive voice from the next room call, "Andy?"

"Yeah?"

"I think I need your help with this."

"With what?" I turned the stove to its lowest setting and went to open Sophie's door. Inside, she had taken off her shoes and tights but was still in her formal black dress. The zipper under one arm was undone, though it revealed nothing more than a tame sliver of skin.

"Okay, it's not because I'm drunk, because I'm not that drunk, but I literally cannot get this dress off. It's—" She fell into giggles as she tried to explain. "It's super tight around the shoulders, and I can barely raise my arms in it, which would be fine except for I have to get it up over my head in order to take it off. And I still have the bandage on. And I can't even, like, cross my…" She tried to pantomime crossing her arms to lift a garment over her head, but she gave up and fell further into hysterics. "Whatever, you get the point, I can't get this off over my head by myself. It's just too hard with an injured arm and a dress that's too tight and okay, yes, I'm a little drunk! Sue me!"

At first, I was so entertained by her ranting and miming that I didn't get it. "So what do you want me to do?"

"Can you please help me get this dress off? I literally can't do it."

Can you please help me get this dress off.

Help me get this dress off.

Dress off.

"Hello? Earth to Andy…" She snapped her fingers in front of my face. "Come on, slowpoke. It doesn't have to be weird. You just have to lift from the bottom hem, and I can't do it by myself."

"Um. Alright. Yeah. Okay."

I reached for the bottom of the dress, figuring I could get it over with quickly and then it wouldn't be a big deal. I mean, we'd certainly been to the beach together before, and underwear was basically a bathing suit. Just a private bathing suit. A private, personal bathing suit that other people weren't meant to see but I was about to see on her because she asked me to, and—

"Wait, hang on. I have to turn around first." She rotated to give me her back.

"Does that… make it easier to… remove?" I asked articulately.

"Not really, I'm just not wearing a bra."

I'm just not wearing a bra.

Not wearing a bra.

No bra.

"Okay, ready when you are," she chirped. "This is as high as I can raise my arms so it'll have to do." The arms in question were barely three inches away from her ribcage, but I didn't give a shit about that at a time like this. I funneled all of my focus into two things: keeping my breathing slow and calm, and keeping my dick under control.

I reached for the knee-length hem of Sophie's dress, telling myself it really didn't have to be a big deal. I really had been to the beach with her before. And it really was just a body. I'd seen women's bodies. Several. Many, even. So this would all be fine. Nothing new.

Sophie, meanwhile, didn't seem nearly as concerned. If anything, she was in a rush to get it over with.

"You can move faster. You've got to get it up to my shoulders before we even get to the hard part so just go for it."

I told myself: yeah, this will be fine.

Then I calmly lifted the hem of her dress up, reaching the height of her chest before things started getting tricky.

"Hang on here," Sophie said. "It's like… caught on my boobs I think? I think I can just…" She started adjusting the material at the bust of her dress to inch it up. Standing behind her, there was nothing I could do to help. So I waited, holding her dress up and exposing her underwear and lower body which I was definitely not going to look at. Not. Even. A little.

"Is it caught on itself back there? Can you see if you can scootch it up?"

She wanted me to look. I had to look. I had to look down and see if it was caught on something. But that would be fine. Just a body. Just a body.

I looked down through the scant inches of space between us, to the dress rolled and scrunched at her ribcage. Then lower, to her underwear—light pink, with lace along the top and bottom edges.

And fuck me, I'm not a saint, alright? I gave in and enjoyed the view.

Sophie's body curved in all the right places. The generous swell of her ass, the smooth skin of her back, the softness of her thighs. I had a desperate, virulent impulse to sink my teeth into each of those places and watch her body respond.

"Andy?"

"Ah! I mean… uh, yeah. I mean no! No. No, it's not caught on anything, I think I just have to um… pull it harder."

"Alright but please go slow now because I'm nervous about my arm."

"Okay," I exhaled. Determined to keep my hands steady, I changed my grip from the bottom hem of the dress to the fabric at her ribs, which snagged just under her breasts and around her shoulders. Gently,

I urged it upwards until her chest was free and only her shoulders remained confined. I slowly brought the dress up her arms, listening and watching for any sign of pain. When it finally slipped off over her hands, I tossed it aside onto the bed.

The dress was off.

I could have moved, but I didn't.

Instead, we stayed frozen in place. Me, fully clothed. Her, in almost nothing. I wasn't even touching her—was barely allowing myself to *look* at her—and yet my whole body felt alert. Mere inches apart, her back to my front, our breaths shallow.

I reached for my self-restraint, and found the well completely dry.

Slowly, I placed a hand on her bare waist.

She took in a shaky breath, and I felt the rise and fall of it in her abdomen.

I wished I could see her face. Wished more than anything that I could hear her thoughts. Did she want this? Did she want this the way I wanted it, with every molecule of myself for as long as I could remember?

I had to know.

"Sophie?" I asked from behind her back, frozen still.

"Yeah?"

"Can I tell you something?"

"Yeah," she said, quieter this time.

I knew this was my chance to get the truth out. It had to be now, before I left her room and my courage behind. So I took a deep breath, closed my eyes, and said, "I don't think that kiss was a mistake."

"Yeah?"

"Yeah. I think it was the best thing I've done in a long time." My voice was a low scrape, the words barely daring to cross the threshold of my lips. "And then tonight, at the gala, you were so… so beautiful and so smart and now you're here and…" The fingertips of my free hand trailed up her side. She shivered in response, and it felt like victory and possibility. "…and I want to do a lot more than kiss you."

"Yeah?" she asked.

"Yeah," I answered.

"Then why don't you."

It was not a question. It was a request.

Slowly, I placed both hands on her waist, letting my thumbs trace a sloping path across her ribs. My blood was thrumming in my ears, part of me eager to rush, to take and to have, another part wanting to discover her slowly, take her apart piece by piece.

That had to be the way. Slow and steady. I wouldn't mess this up again.

I traced a freckle on her side, noting its exact location, right where her hip began to bloom. The space between our bodies was a whisper, faint and fading, but still there. My fingers pressed deeper into her soft flesh, and the only thought in my head was: *This is Sophie.*

With everything else in life, I'd learned how to rein myself in. No laundry unfolded, no run skipped, no comma misplaced, no temptation insurmountable—except her. She was a temptation made just for me. She was safe and she was terrifying. She was all of my wildest impulses. And most days I thought I knew her better than I knew myself—except in this. Her body. Where she liked to be touched. How soft, how slow, how she would respond to me, the sounds she would make, the way she would move. In this, I didn't know her at all. Yet.

Damned if I didn't want to learn every last thing.

This was the thought that had my hands starting to trail over all the parts of her I'd never touched before. Her stomach, her spine, her hipbones. I skimmed over the top edge of her underwear, reminding myself to take it slow—not yet. Every move felt reverent. She was the sweetest wine and I was drunk on the closeness of her.

"I don't know what to do with you, Soph," I admitted, placing a kiss against the side of her neck, tender and testing, all instinct, no plan. "Is this okay?"

"Andy, I..." My knuckles brushed beneath her breast and her speech stammered. "Y—yes."

Thank God.

Her head dropped back against my shoulder as I tasted the place where her pulse beat.

"But I…"

She trailed off and I froze, needing to hear the end of that sentence more than I needed air. Did I mess up again? She had been drinking. So had I. Was this crazy? Was she in a position to consent? She only had a few, but without food…

Her breathy voice continued, "I don't want you to feel pressured to do anything you don't want to do. I just want to be sure you want this too. I know I'm the one who called you in my room tonight and—"

Maybe the alcohol was making me bold. Or maybe enough was just enough. If she was still doubting that I wanted her—if *that* was the thing getting in our way—it ended now.

I cut her off with a tug of her body to mine. She gasped—the evidence of my desire obvious between us.

"I want this, Soph," I murmured into her ear. "I know you can feel how much I want this."

Before she could reply, my hands moved to cup her breasts. Her soft, full, perfect breasts. Time slowed as I touched her, as I felt her pebble under the attention. A moan slipped from her lips and I couldn't believe what was happening—touching her, watching her react to my touch. Logic and consequences were long gone as I let my hand wander farther down the front of her body.

"If I touch you here…" My fingertips teased the lace at the front of her underwear. "Will I find out that you want this too?"

"There's only one way to know for sure," she breathed, placing her hand over mine and guiding it lower.

Slowly, my fingers pushed beneath her waistband. I leaned over her shoulder, both of us watching my hand disappear under the pink silk.

"Fuck, Soph." She felt like heaven, so wet, so ready. "I need to—"

Like a shockwave, an alarm blared through the apartment.

We screamed "Jesus Christ!" and "What the fuck!" and Sophie cried, "Is that your building's fire alarm?"

I raced out of the bedroom. In the kitchen, Sophie's highly coveted scallion pancake was not only burned but fully on fire on the stove. My cries of "Shit! Shit! Shit!" mixed with Sophie's shriek of "Where is the fire extinguisher? Please tell me you have a fire extinguisher!"

I did not, but I had a backup plan. I threw on oven mitts, grabbed the pan handle, and thrust the entire thing into the sink, covering it with a dish towel to smother the flame before turning the water on. A huge plume of steam rose up around it, which seemed to further anger the fire alarm which sounded even louder now. How was that possible?

"Come on Andy, we're supposed to leave the building! It's literally a fire drill! Or like, a real fire! I don't know what it is but hurry up!"

"We just put out the fire—it's fine!"

"Andy, if I don't get out of this building and away from this sound right now I'm going to lose my mind!"

"Sophie, you're still naked!"

She looked down at herself—chest fully out in the middle of the kitchen—then back up at me with panic.

"Come on, get some clothes and let's go," I insisted, halting her mid-spiral. There'd be time to lose it later when she was dressed and everything was much quieter.

She ran back into her room, threw on her robe, then took my outstretched hand as we raced away from the most horrendous noise we'd ever had the displeasure of hearing.

"I don't understand how it could possibly take this long," Sophie mused from where we sat on the steps of the restaurant around the corner. "I feel like each peal is burrowing deeper inside my psyche."

"It's an old building. I think the firefighters have to use a physical key on each alarm to turn it off."

"This is because I don't go to church, isn't it?" she asked, looking skyward. "I'm sorry that I have a busy life! Can you cut me some slack?"

I chuckled as her head found a spot on my shoulder.

It was comfortable, like nothing had changed. Except it wasn't, because it had. I was reeling and terrified and hopeful and totally unsure how to behave or what to say. Last week, I couldn't even act normal after kissing her—I *certainly* wasn't equipped to act normal now.

I forced myself to ask, "Hey, are you okay? With what we just did, I mean?"

"Yeah," she said, not quite nervous, but not confident either. "I am."

She placed a tentative hand on my knee, and it felt like a question. The night was dark and her eyes were fixed on the shop ahead and I clawed through the dirt in my soul, digging for the courage to keep going.

"What do you want, Soph?"

"What do you mean?"

"From me? What do you want from me? I hope that doesn't sound rude. I really just need to know. Because if what you need is a friend then I will get it together and be a better friend, but these past few—"

"Be a better friend? Andy, you're one of the best friends I've ever had. You couldn't possibly be a better friend. You're literally letting me live in your apartment and not pay rent, for God's sake. I love you."

"I know. I just feel like I'm ruining everything. First with the kiss. And then, God, tonight..." I scrubbed my hands over my eyes, unable to look at her as I explained, "Look, I love being your friend. But since you moved in I've felt so confused about where we stand and what you want, and then I let myself do this crazy shit and I worry I'm ruining the best part. The part where we feel safe with each other. Because I don't feel safe with other people the way I feel with you. Even Nolan and Lia. I love them too, but with you everything's just better."

Sophie waited a beat, then shocked me by asking, "Would you ever... maybe... want to see if we could do both? Like maybe we can still be friends, still be us, but also see if we could be... more?" In the time it took me to inhale and open my mouth, she was already walking it back. "Only if you want to though, of course. No pressure. It's fine if you don't think it's a good idea. I'm not trying to mess everything up between us with an ill-fated relationship, especially if you're not into it."

Her laugh was forced, her heart on the line.

I turned to face her, not laughing at all. "Do you really want to?"

Sophie swallowed, then said, "Yeah? I mean, I'd give it a try if you would."

I reached up to cup one side of her face, then the other, enjoying the simple feeling of my palms against her jaw. She placed her hands over mine. Then she kissed me.

This kiss was different from our first. It was chaste, soft, slow. There was no rush of momentum, just her lips on mine, tender and real.

Eventually, Sophie pulled back gingerly and said, "The alarm is off."

"So it is," I replied, trying and failing to keep a lid on my smile. I stood from the stoop and extended a hand. She took it, and we walked back to the apartment.

By the time we got inside, the reality of the day was starting to hit me—the gala, the alcohol, the almost-sex, the conversation, the kiss. I was still reeling from it all when Sophie said, "I think we should go on a date. A real date. If you'd be into that."

A date. Shit—I should've thought of that. "Yes. A date. Yes. Makes sense." It felt like I'd never done this before. "Are you free tomorrow?"

"Yeah, sure. I'm free all day."

"Okay… I have an idea. How about after dinner, around 8:00?"

"Okay."

Our uncertainty was a physical presence in the room. There were a million things I wanted to say to her, but none of them connected to words in my brain. After a too-long moment, it was Sophie who said, "Goodnight, Andy." Then she leaned forward on her tiptoes, kissed my cheek, and walked into her room.

I barely slept a wink, my mind whirling through the future and the past. The memory of Sophie's body pressed against mine, the taste of her, all of the almosts, the missed opportunities, the opportunity in front of me.

A date. We were going on a date.

It had to be perfect.

21

"**I** did ice skating as a kid, you know."

Andy's mouth actually gapes open. "You did?"

"Yup," I say smugly as I tie up my laces. "Not much else to do in rural Minnesota in the winter. That and cross-country skiing, which I hated."

"So you're saying you actually did a sport?"

I shove his shoulder harder than usual. "What are you implying? That I'm not athletic?"

"That's exactly what I'm implying," he replies with two dimples.

"Well then why don't you put your money where your mouth is?"

"What money where what mouth is?" Andy asks, standing and testing out his skates.

I stand too, rolling my shoulders as an intimidation tactic. "I bet you I can do… three skating moves you can't do."

Andy opens the gate to the rink and lets me step out first. "Well that hardly seems fair. Will you give me a lesson at least?"

"I will, and I'll even let you decide what you get if you win." I glide

182

out onto the rink, arcing around to face him with my hands lazily on my hips. (I may be showing off the tiniest bit.)

He follows, stepping onto the ice with caution and sticking to the side boards.

"Hmm, okay…" he muses. "If I can do at least two out of three, you have to text Nolan and tell him you wrote an original poem that you want his constructive feedback on. And you have to actually send a poem."

This has me doubling over in a full belly laugh. "Oh my god, you are deranged. Poor Nolan is going to take it so seriously."

"What if you win? What do you get?"

"Okay, you've inspired me." I start skating backwards as we chat (still showing off). "If you can't do at least two out of three of the moves, you have to text Lia a list of your top 10 favorite things about me. No context, just 'hey I wanted you to know my top 10 favorite things about Sophie.'"

"Easy."

I stop against the side board next to him, looking down at our skates as I dare to ask, "Did you tell them about this, by the way? That we're on a date?"

He shakes his head. "Did you?"

I shake my head, too.

Then we both start talking at once. "I just didn't want to put pressure—" "They always overreact—"

Andy laughs, but it sounds nervous. "Yeah, exactly."

"Come on," I say, taking his hand. "It's time for your lesson."

⸻ •◦• ⸻

"The score is now tied, Walsh." I drift in taunting circles around him. "I admit your backwards skating was passable, but you horribly failed at the toe loop."

"Way to protect my ego there, Soph."

"It's now time for your final test." I make a little trumpet sound through my cupped hands and Andy rolls his eyes, but the twitch of his lips says he loves it. "Based on your undeniable mediocrity, we're going to take it down a notch. This trick is called the bunny hop."

Andy rolls his neck and shoulders, then rubs his hands together. "Bunny hop. Let's do this."

I take my time explaining the trick to Andy: start by skating forward, then push off with your left foot and lift the right to make an "h" shape with your legs. Land on the toe pick of the right and continue forward on the left. I demonstrate a few times too, as slowly as I can. Andy watches me with a deep crease between his brows, nodding along. He's so serious that it almost makes me laugh.

Finally, he tells me he's ready. He moves back about 10 feet, takes a deep breath, and goes for it. And he's got gumption, if not technique. He's right next to me when he jumps, but instead of landing on the toe pick, his right foot lands flat on the blade. Before he can stop his momentum, his foot slides out from under him and catapults his body backwards. His arms flail, grabbing desperately for support and catching the edge of my jacket before he backflops onto the cold, hard ice. I come barreling down too—shrieking as we hit the ground with a *splat*, Andy taking the worst of the blow. My body is cushioned by his, our limbs a mad tangle.

"Fuuuck," he laughs out through the pain.

"Oh my god." I'm laughing too, forehead collapsed onto his shoulder. "Are you okay?"

"Yeah," he says, closing his eyes and letting his head rest back on the ice. "Ow. But yeah."

"Okay good, because Andy?"

"Yeah?" He peeks an eye open.

"That was the worst bunny hop I've ever seen." I pinch his cheek in a tease, then start to push up to stand.

"Not yet." Andy wraps his arms tighter around my waist, trapping me there. "I'm not ready to face the public."

"Okay," I laugh, "but I think I'm flashing everyone in this dress."

"Fine." He takes one more long breath before loosening his hold. I help him to his feet as a biting gust of wind slices past us.

"Alright hot shot, I think we're done for the day." I adjust his jacket and give him a consoling pat on the chest.

"Why do I feel like this wasn't the way to impress you on our first date?"

"I hate to break it to you, Walsh, but the time for impressions has come and gone. My image of you is set in stone."

"Oh yeah?" he asks, following me out of the rink onto safe ground. "And what image is that?"

"Wouldn't you like to know?"

"I would."

"Well, I guess you should've won the bet and made that your prize. Here, sit down."

I lead us to a bench by the side boards where we can take off our skates. There's a tree above us, sparkling with bright white string lights, the snow glistening in reflection.

"You know," Andy says, struggling with his laces, "despite the evidence, I still can't imagine you actually going out onto a frozen pond to skate."

"Why not?" I pull off my first skate and reach for the second.

"I don't know. It's hard to believe you did stuff before you met me."

I give him a look that I hope conveys extreme incredulity.

"Okay, that sounded bad."

I laugh. "Ya think?"

"I—I meant—" He stutters, nervous now, and I feel bad for giving him a hard time. "I guess I forget there was ever a time before we knew each other. It feels like we've always been on the same path, even though we haven't."

And that was actually really sweet. Sweeter than I know what to do with. So I shoot him a wink as I say, "I promise to never stop surprising you."

I meant it to be teasing, but it comes out sincere. His eyes catch mine, and suddenly my palms are sweaty. I reach down to pull off my second skate, but my hand slips and I elbow him in the side. "Ope, sorry."

He laughs. "That's okay."

I feel like I'm a teenager again, fumbling and hopeful and trying ridiculously hard.

"I think I know what you mean though," I offer. "Sometimes when it's just the two of us it feels like we're the same person, but then we go out in the world and I'm reminded how different we are."

"Like at karaoke."

"Okay, you love karaoke exactly as much as I do. You just hide it well."

"I'll come, but I have never wanted to get up and sing." We stand and walk to the skate return, reclaiming our boots from the rink employee.

"I never want to get up and sing either," I protest, "but it's part of the experience. Maybe the difference is I'm more susceptible to peer pressure than you."

"Maybe," he shrugs. "We also don't like any of the same books."

"Okay well there's no accounting for taste." I knock my shoulder into his and he rolls his eyes. "I still think we're more similar than we are different. The differences are just the obvious stuff."

"Yeah, the obvious stuff like one of us likes people and one of us doesn't."

"Okay," I allow, "but we both like cats more than dogs."

"I like cooking and you hate it."

"That's true... Oh! We're both bad at keeping succulents alive."

"Yeah, but I overwater them and you under-water them."

"Whatever. Still counts."

We leave the rink area and head into the surrounding park. Andy's hand tentatively reaches for mine and our fingers lace together as we wander down the path, aimless, surrounded by evergreens and strangers and the yellowy light of the park lanterns.

Tonight has been disorienting and exhilarating and perfect. I keep oscillating between the feeling that I'm just out somewhere with

Andy—my best friend Andy—and everything is normal, but then he takes my hand, or touches my cheek, and I'm hit with the chest-clenching, sweat-inducing, horrible, wonderful realization that we're on a date. A romantic date. It feels like the edge of something that could either make me whole or break me into pieces.

"How do you feel about soft pretzels?" Andy asks.

"That depends…" I hedge, reminding myself to breathe and behave like a person. "Do you like them or hate them? I'm still trying to prove a point over here."

"I do like them," he chuckles, casually brushing a piece of hair behind my ear. Goosebumps explode across my neck. "But also, there's a stand over there if you're hungry."

"Oh, yes please."

The pretzel stand is small and dingy, operated by a gruff man in a Patriots hat who says nothing as he hands over two pretzels and about ten thousand napkins. There are open benches nearby, but we decided to keep moving to stay warm.

"Have you ever come to see the winter lights in Boston Common before today?" I ask between bites.

Andy nods as he chews. "I came with Carly once." Then he cringes. "Sorry, I just realized I'm not supposed to talk about an ex on a date. I'm not used to censoring that stuff with you."

"Don't. It's okay. That would've been like… four years ago anyway, right?" We walk a few steps more before I ask, "Since you were honest about Elliot before, can I be honest about Carly?" Andy turns towards me, listening. "I don't want to say I didn't like her, but I guess I never really made inroads with her? It seemed like she hated me even though I was trying so hard with her."

"It's not your fault. I think she could tell that…" He trails off and clears his throat. "I mean, I think she was insecure about how close you and I were."

"That's silly," I say dismissively. "It's not like I was single and trying to steal you. Wasn't I with Adrian then anyway?"

"Adrian hated me."

"He did not."

"He did," Andy insists, throwing his pretzel wrapper into a garbage can as we pass. "Remember when we went to the haunted house with Nolan and Lia and Adrian and Carly?"

"Yes! God, I still can't believe Lia talked us into that. We were all scared shitless. I literally cried. Do you remember?"

"Yeah, well afterwards Adrian told me to stay away from you."

I stop dead in my tracks. "What?"

"He thought we were getting too close in the clown room."

"That wasn't your fault! You were just standing next to me when the jumpscare happened. I would've grabbed Adrian if he was there." I picture the scene, the scare that had me clinging to Andy's torso, eyes squeezed shut against him.

"Yeah well he said it in front of Carly too. That was basically the end for us."

I can't help but grimace. "I'm sorry. I guess I owe Carly an apology."

"If you do then so do I, because he was right. I would've used any excuse to hold you back then."

And there it is, the feeling that grabs me and squeezes me and screams *This is your chance! Don't mess it up!*

I take a step closer. "And what about now?"

"Now…" He wraps his arms around me slowly, holding my body tight to his. "Now I just want your leftovers." Fast as lightning he bites into my pretzel, then runs away with it still dangling from his mouth. I scream as I give chase and he benevolently lets me catch him. I grab his coat and spin him around to face me just as he shoves the rest into his mouth. He's so ridiculous and unrestrained that I can't help but pull his face down to mine, planting a laughing kiss on his lips despite his cheeks full of pretzel. He swallows and a smile blooms. I tuck my hand back into his and pull him back to the path.

We fall into step again, and I ask, "Are we bad people? I mean it's probably not great that all our exes were suspicious of us."

"Maybe," Andy says, considering. "I don't know. I don't think we're bad people, I think we were just… trying to figure things out."

We move through the pine trees until we find ourselves in the Public Garden. This side of the Boston Common has a long pond stretching through its middle, and we walk up to the edge. Without any trees overhead, we can just make out a few dim stars in the sky. I ask, "See any constellations you know?"

He follows my gaze skyward. "It's not my forte. I can sometimes find a dipper or two."

I pull his shoulder down until he's eye level with me. "The easiest one is Orion." I take his hand in mine and point. "There. The three bright stars in a line."

"I see it," he says, hand curving around my waist as he tucks himself into the space next to me.

"And once you find Orion," I continue, "he's pointing to Taurus. That's the V right… there." I shift our fingers an inch to the right, tracing a V in the sky.

"Not bad for the city."

I lower our hands. But when I make no move to leave, Andy steps behind me, wrapping both arms around my waist.

After a moment, I ask, "Can I tell you something embarrassing?"

He doesn't reply, just tucks my head beneath his chin.

"Do you remember, in our new exhibit, there's the part about the multiverse? It has a video playing and then there's that long kind of pinkish hallway—"

"I remember."

"It freaks me out a little. Not just our exhibit—the whole idea of a multiverse. There's a theory that for every choice you've ever made in your life, there's a universe where you did the opposite. Maybe in this universe you made the wrong choice and you'll never know. Maybe in that other universe you're so much happier. Maybe you almost had everything you ever wanted, but you didn't realize it, and now you never will. It's sort of paralyzing. Like, how am I supposed to ever make a decision now? There's no way I'm *not* gonna mess it up."

He considers, then says, "I get it. But it's just a theory, right? Fate is a theory too. Maybe this is the universe you're meant to be in."

I focus on the press of his chest against my back, the comfort and strength in the contact. "Yeah, maybe you're right."

A child laughs in the distance. The wind bites at our cheeks. I pull his arms tighter around myself, protecting our fragile warmth from the raw winter air.

"Can I tell you something embarrassing?" he asks in reciprocity, lips skimming the crown of my hair.

I nod.

"I think I do want to be a writer, eventually."

"Yeah?"

"Yeah. I think I've always wanted to, but I was scared to try and be bad at it. But I guess we're being brave now, right?" He squeezes my ribs, playing it off as a joke when it's anything but.

"I'd love to read your writing someday, if you'd let me."

"If there's anyone I'd want to read it, it would be you."

That statement has me turning in his arms, resting my palms on his chest, a little overwhelmed by all these new axes of closeness between us.

"Well," I breathe, "I can confidently say this is the best first date I've ever been on."

"It's not over yet," he says, one hand coming to rest on my jaw. Even in the low light, the expression in his eyes melts me down to nothing. And when he slowly bends to kiss me, I feel him everywhere. His lips on mine, yes. His hand on my cheek—but not just there. I feel him along my spine and beneath my ribs and low in my belly. Everything is Andy. My Andy, here, kissing me because he wants to and I want him to and all our almosts are suddenly something real.

The darkness makes me bold. My hands start to explore in the way they've wanted to for so long, moving up his chest to his shoulders, then drifting back down across the hard plane of his stomach. He pulls me tighter against his body, one hand still clasping the side of my neck as the other holds my lower back. The kiss grows hungry, our tongues tangling together, and I'm pretty sure I could die from how much I want him.

He breathes my name against my mouth, and it's as much as I can take. I pull back to meet his eyes. "It's kind of cold out here," I exhale. "I think we should head home. If you want to."

He blinks once, then seems to understand. "Y—yes," he stammers. "Let's just—uh—yeah. Good idea. Let's head back." But he doesn't move. Not until I grab him by the hand and drag him back down the park path.

22

" ———— •❖• ———— "

The train car is nearly empty when we board.

B LINE TO BOSTO COLL GE

We take seats next to each other. His thigh presses against mine.

Somewhere on the edge of my consciousness, the train screeches mercilessly along its track.

This is almost something. Very, very almost.

This is Arlington, an automated voice says.

This is Copley.

This is Hynes Convention Center.

I place my right hand on Andy's knee, squeezing once.

Andy places his hand atop it, lacing our fingers together.

This is Kenmore.

I let my thumb start to move, tracing small, slow circles across his thigh.

This is Blandford.

I should say something.

This is Boston University East.

I should definitely say something.

This is Boston University Central.

"You know it's funny…" I say, rotating my hand up until my palm is flush with his, then locking our fingers together. "I feel like you know a lot about dates I've been on, but I barely know anything about yours."

"Is there…" He clears his throat. "Is there something you want to know?"

My thumb starts moving again, back and forth over his.

"Yeah…" I reply.

"What?"

"It's not exactly the kind of thing you just ask someone."

"I don't mind."

I look at him out of the corner of my eye, then quickly back down to where our hands are joined.

My pulse is racing. Or is that his? I can't tell anymore.

"I guess I'm just wondering where you see tonight going. Or… how far."

Next to me, Andy stops breathing.

This is Armory Street.

I rush to explain, "Because we live together, so I'm going home with you, obviously, but I don't want you to feel like you have to do anything you don't want to do just because I'm there and I want to. I mean, I've never done the whole 'dating your roommate' thing and I feel like all the signals I would normally give as the green light are just inevitable because I live there, so I guess I just wanted to explicitly give a green light, but also if you don't want to give a green light that's totally fine. Whatever you want. That's all I—"

"Sophie." Andy drops my hand to take hold of both sides of my face. He looks straight into my eyes and says, "Green light."

"Yeah?"

"Yeah."

This is Babcock Street.

I try to control my smile as our hands clasp again, a new energy buzzing there.

This is Packard's Corner.

This is Harvard Avenue.

By the time the train doors opened at our stop, we're already waiting by the door.

23

The walk from the train to the apartment is exquisite torture. I'm acutely aware of the press of our hands, the pace of our steps.

I want to do everything perfectly.

I can't get ahead of myself. It could be nothing; he could change his mind. Or it could be the start of everything.

We unlock the apartment like it's any other day. Remove our shoes. Andy hangs his coat on the coat rack. I put my purse on the kitchen table. We look at each other, and I can feel the blood in my veins.

Andy's gaze drags down my body, and it's another expression I've never seen from him before: hunger that borders on impatience.

We're fifteen feet apart and the distance feels enormous.

Eventually I take the first step towards him, cautiously, then another.

"Andy…"

He's stepping towards me too, first slowly, then picking up speed until he reaches me and locks me in a crushing kiss. I clasp his face with both hands and he's hoisting me in the air, carrying me backwards into the kitchen, placing me on the table's edge and stepping into the space between my legs.

It still feels new—holding him like this, being held by him, pressing my mouth to his and feeling the way our bodies move together. Here in the apartment where we both live, perched on the table where we now eat breakfast together every morning and dinner every night—we've somehow skipped over casual and straight into vital.

My back arches as Andy moves to my neck, biting and sucking his way across my skin. He finds the freckles along my collarbone and kisses one, then another, disintegrating all my remaining brain cells. When his path is intercepted by cotton, he looks to me for approval before carefully lowering the dress from my shoulders. It pools at my waist, leaving me in a black lace bra.

He takes one step back, eyes raking over me. And I know my hair is mussed, my cheeks are red, my clothes are in disarray. I must look a mess. But he whispers, almost to himself, "You are so beautiful."

I reach forward, pulling his face back to mine. One of my hands twines into his hair while the other travels slowly down his body, over the taught plane of his stomach, until I reach the front of his pants. I find the hardness there and let out a small gasp.

"Oh my god." My fingers curve around him, palm tracing an exploring path over the fabric. "Andy—you're so big."

"Fuck, Sophie," he breathes into the next kiss.

Then my hand is gone and we're grinding against each other, the hardness of him pressing right between my legs, my hips bucking up to meet him because I need *more*. I wrap my arms around his neck, pulling him in tighter, pressing him where I need him most. But then his hands are on my hips and he's pushing away, creating distance where there should be none.

"Wait, Soph. Hold on. I don't want to…" His head falls against my shoulder, his breathing heavy.

Already, the inch of space between our bodies is clearing my head. I'm disappointed, yes, but I get it. I hold his face gently to my shoulder as I say, "That's okay. We don't have to."

His head snaps up, eyes finding mine. "No. Sophie. God—I *want to*. I *really* want to." His lips meet mine with hunger again, and between fervent kisses he murmurs, "I meant I don't want to come. Not yet."

And good lord, knowing that what we're doing has him that close is the hottest thing I've ever experienced.

"Let's go to your room," I say, barely sane and not above begging. "Please."

Andy lifts me straight up into his arms. I wrap my legs around his torso and he carries me towards his room, kicking open the door.

From the moment he places my feet on the floor by his bed, he's already pulling at the buttons on his shirt. His hands are shaking, his motions stilted and frenzied. I don't want him to be nervous, so I do the only thing I can think of: I pull my dress over my head and drop it on the floor. When he finally tosses his shirt to the ground and looks back up at me, I'm in nearly nothing—black lace underwear to match the black lace bra—and it's like a hard reset. Time slows, and whatever nervous thoughts were swirling through Andy's head before are forgotten.

"Sophie…" He stalks forward, nearly closing the distance between us but not quite. "You wore these for our date. For me."

It's not really a question, but I breathe out a "Yes." I've never felt more exposed or more secure.

His hands wrap around my waist with urgent slowness, then guide me backwards onto the bed. I lie back, propped on my elbows as Andy's body moves to cage mine. He pauses there, just looking at me, midnight whirlpools in his eyes. With the tips of two fingers, he traces the lightest path over my ribs, then my stomach. His touch is warm, and he lowers himself to kiss the plane of my stomach once. Twice. Then his gaze slides back up to mine.

"Show me," he begs.

And I will do anything he asks.

Eyes never leaving his, I tuck one arm beneath myself, unfastening my bra and tossing it to the side. When my hands move to the fabric at my hips, Andy takes over, replacing my hands with his own. He slowly pulls the black lace over my thighs, then lower, until it's tossed aside.

Andy doesn't touch me yet. He comes to kneel on the bed between my legs, gaze ravenous, flitting across me in a way that I *know* means he's memorizing every inch. His hands hover between us, like they can't quite decide where to go first. Slowly, his expression glazes over.

"I've dreamed of this," he says. "I've... tortured myself."

His hands find my thighs, fingers kneading the flesh in a way that's somehow too light for the intensity of his grip, the obvious tension of his muscles.

"Being so close to you, just on the other side of that wall. Imagining you, like this, with some other guy. Some stranger."

His palms slide up to my hips, fingertips pressing ardently into the soft flesh as my body becomes his confessional, and I want to hear every sin.

"Even before that. Fucking other women with my eyes closed. Wishing they were you. And now..."

He moves reverently up my stomach, cupping my breasts, teasing each nipple with a thumb, and I'm losing my mind.

"Andy." His eyes snap up to mine and he's back, haze clearing from his expression. "Take off your pants."

He obeys, pulling away to undo his belt buckle. What remains of his clothes falls to the floor and I stare unrepentantly. I feel like an animal—a biological need begging to have him inside me.

I realize we're about to cross a line that can never be uncrossed. That we can *never* just be friends again after this.

I wouldn't want to, anyway.

I drag my teeth across my bottom lip. "What are you waiting for?"

His responding smirk reminds me that this is still my best friend, and somehow that makes it even better. He chuckles as he crawls over me, every hard edge of his body finding its corresponding curve on mine. He centers himself between my legs and the sensation has me sighing, lifting my hips, grinding against him, showing him just how much I want this.

"Soph," he pants, kissing behind my ear, "I swear I'm usually better at foreplay than this, but I just—"

"I've had like nine years of foreplay, Andy. I just want you. Now. Please."

He groans like it's the best thing he's ever heard, then reaches towards his nightstand to pull out a condom, tearing it open and rolling it on.

Our eyes lock as he positions himself between my thighs again.

I nod, hand cupping the side of his face. Then finally, slowly, he pushes inside me.

I moan as I take him in, I can't help it. He's so big and my body is a livewire, and even without moving another inch it's the best sex I've ever had.

Then he captures my lips again as he starts to shift forward, gradually, savoring every inch of pressure. And it's incomparable.

"Andy." His name feels heavy on my lips. "God."

My body rolls into his, nails pressing half moons into the back of his neck. My eyes flutter closed and I know he's watching me, but I love it, need it.

"You are—" he says as his mouth moves to the hollow of my throat "—so perfect." He's thrusting in and out at a languid pace, teasing us both. "You feel so fucking perfect, Soph. Like you were made for me."

My hands roam over his shoulders and back. "Maybe I was."

His groan is anguished as he starts to kiss farther down my body, reaching my breast, dragging his tongue over my nipple with torturously light contact that has me writing under him. When I beg for more, harder, he only switches to the other side, repeating the same torment until my moans are loud enough to wake the dead.

With every sound we make, every kiss we place on each other's bodies, it's like we forget ourselves a little more, until we're nothing but sensation and raw, searing emotion.

"In my wildest dreams," he's saying, "I never believed I could really have you." His breath traces the pulse in my neck. "I still can't believe it."

Then he's finally thrusting faster, giving us both what we so desperately need. His rhythm is punishing as I pull his body deeper into mine.

"God, Andy, I love you. I love you so much."

Then he's coming, pulsing inside me as he presses his fingers where I need them most, and I'm gone too, falling over that edge with him. We kiss through each wave, coming down together until we're both gasping for breath.

Our hearts begin to slow, and we meet each other's eyes with tentative smiles. Then it turns into full-fledged grins, and suddenly we're both laughing. A relieved, contented, intimate laugh.

It feels so good—to know we're still ourselves.

Andy is still inside me as his forehead comes to rest against mine. He brushes the hair from my face, then kisses me once more before pulling out. He offers to grab something to clean us up and I thank him.

Only once he's left the room do I realize what I said. I said *I love him*. Which, to be clear, I do. And he knows that. We say it all the time. But it definitely feels different to say it *while we're having sex...*

Oh my god. We had sex. And it was amazing, life-ruining sex. The kind of sex where everything else will just be downhill from here on out.

He walks back in the room with a washcloth for me and a stupid happy grin on his face. It makes my chest squeeze. I love his dimples. *I love him.*

The thought terrifies me, but I make the active choice to put a pin in it. Today, I just get to be happy.

Once we're both cleaned up, Andy crawls back into bed and pulls me into him, tucking us both under the top sheet. I rest my head on his chest and he kisses my hair.

"Andy, that was... oh my god." He chuckles, and I feel the resonance against my cheek. "I mean, I'm retroactively jealous of your exes."

He trails his thumb over my bottom lip. "I was actively jealous of all of your exes while you were together. I think I win."

Warmth spreads across my cheeks as I nestle back into him. I want to burrow into this moment and never leave. But even reeling from his words, a little sliver of doubt makes me say, "Okay, but can I ask you something?"

"Anything."

I try to bend my voice away from accusation. "If you were jealous… I mean, if you wanted to sleep with me for so long… why didn't you ever take me up on my offer?"

"What are you talking about?" he asks without a trace of malice, peeking down to find my eyes.

"I just mean, I'm the one who wanted to do this from the beginning. And it was a pretty hard road to get you here eight years later. And that's fine," I insist, leaning up on my forearm to look at him fully. "I wouldn't have wanted you to do anything you didn't want to do at the time. I just mean, you know, wanting to be with me now is good enough, even if it's new."

"Sophie. Just to anchor us in the reality of this situation. Are you talking about the night when you were browned out on absinthe, asked me to be your friend, told me you were a virgin, and then had to be physically carried home? That's the night when you 'wanted to do this'?"

"Well, when you put it like that…"

He laughs and kisses me softly. "I wanted you then too. I've never stopped."

I roll onto him, straddling his torso and grabbing his face to pull him into a rougher kiss. He reciprocates enthusiastically, his hands traveling up my body, then back down to rest on my hips.

But then another thought bursts through my mind and I pull back. "Oh God. We're going to have to tell Lia and Nolan. They're gonna lose their minds."

"They…" he hesitates before confessing "…may have been helping me out."

"Helping you out?"

"Helping me with you. Helping me figure out how to tell you how I felt, these last couple weeks."

"Oh yeah?" I say with a note of mischief. "And how do you feel?"

"Like I'm obsessed with you," he says before rolling on top of me and attacking kisses down my face and neck. I erupt into laughter.

"I can't believe they didn't tell me. I've been freaking out for weeks thinking I was being a creep for checking you out and wanting to…" I trail off.

"Wanting to?"

"Well, do what we just did! I don't know if I should be mad at them or impressed that they kept a secret for the first time in their lives."

"Don't be mad," he says. "I was really losing it there, and they screwed my head back on. Especially Lia."

"I still kind of want revenge."

"What are you thinking?" he asks, curiosity piqued.

"What if instead of telling them about us the normal way, with words, we just send a picture of us right now with no explanation? And then refuse to answer them for like a full day?"

"You're evil," he laughs, pulling me back into another smiling kiss.

"Here, lie down next to me."

He does as I ask, handing over his phone. I position my head so that it's resting on his bare shoulder, with his arm holding me in place. I raise the phone up in front of us, take a picture, then flip it around so we can review our work. And it's absolutely perfect.

I'm beaming up at the camera with a thousand-watt, over-satisfied smile. Andy is looking away from the camera, nose nuzzled against my hair, eyes closed, wearing an absolutely dopey grin. Only one of his dimples is visible from that angle, but everything about it screams two-dimple smile. And even though it only captured from our shoulders up, we are *very clearly* unclothed, together, in a bed.

I hit send and we burst into laughter.

"I think that was the single trolliest thing I've ever done in my life," I say, tears streaking down my face.

"We're going to regret that when they break down the door," Andy says, pulling me tighter into his chest.

"Put your phone on silent. We'll deal with them tomorrow. Tonight, I just want this."

He agrees, flipping the phone to silent then kissing the top of my head. We curl into each other and gradually drift off to sleep.

24

I wake up slowly, floating back into consciousness. There's a bright streak of sun across my face, and a warm chest pressed against my own. Even in sleep, our bodies demand to be intertwined. Andy's arm is wrapped under my waist, holding me tight. The other cradles the back of my neck with the gentlest touch, letting my cheek rest on his chest. Our legs twist together like vines, trapping me exactly where I want to be.

It crosses my mind to check the time, but the moment I start to roll over Andy pulls me back with a low, "Mmm not yet." I'm powerless to argue, nestling back into him and raising a hand to his jaw, feeling the slight prickles of morning stubble there for the first time.

Andy's eyes crack open, with an expression that's half dream and half awake. "Good morning."

My smile bursts out of me. "Good morning."

"How'd you sleep?" he asks, brushing a piece of hair from my face.

"Amazing." My hand trails from his jaw down to his shoulder, ultimately resting against his chest. He feels warm and strong and I've never felt safer than I do lying here wrapped up in him. "How'd you sleep?"

"Amazing," he replies, then dips his head to kiss me softly.

I pull back half-heartedly. "I haven't brushed my teeth yet."

"I don't care," he says as he brings my lips back to his. The kiss deepens until he starts to move down my neck, then farther, pulling the sheet back to cherish every curve and freckle I've ever questioned on myself with his lips and tongue.

A prickle of shyness emerges in the back of my mind, watching him slowly move down my body in the warm light of day. But Andy's touch is worshipful, and I can't help but give in to it. He makes me feel beautiful and powerful and infinite and so turned on I can barely see straight.

When his kisses reach my stomach, he looks up at me with heady desire in his eyes.

"Can I taste you?"

I feel the tension thrumming in my core.

"Andy, I—"

"I won't if you don't want me to. But God, Soph, I want to."

Every nerve in my body begs me to say yes, but even so I find myself stammering "I... I..."

Andy immediately shifts back up my body, catching my lips with his. "We don't have to."

"No, I want to. I do. I just... I've never done that before."

Andy's gaze goes blank, like his brain is buffering too slowly to respond. Flickers of emotion pass behind his eyes—confusion, realization, disbelief—until he says, "Sophie, are you telling me that none of your exes ever... Elliot never...?"

I shake my head.

"Or Adrian...?"

"Nope."

"Holy shit... I knew I hated those guys."

I laugh, and his shock is the perfect antidote to my nerves. "Andy, are you going to talk about my exes all morning or are you going to eat me out?"

He laughs too, but it's a raw, almost desperate sound. He drags his teeth over his lip. "You're sure you want to?"

Now that the idea is in my head, I can't think of anything else. "Yes."

He kisses me deeply, then starts to move down my body again, savoring every taste. When he reaches his destination, he pauses to look back up at me again—a final confirmation. Then, with a burning fire in his half-lidded eyes, he slowly lowers his mouth to me—*just* as a frantic pounding starts sounding at the front door.

KNOCK. KNOCK. KNOCK. KNOCK.

"Sophie! Andy! Are you home?"

Lia's voice is shrill and shrieking and I swear to God I'm never speaking to her again after this.

Andy, however, seems like he hasn't even noticed. His fingers press into the soft flesh of my thighs as his tongue moves over me, once, twice, and lord it feels so unbelievably good that I, too, have almost forgotten about Lia until her demonic fist pounds on the door again.

"Sophie! You better let me in right now! I'm not joking!"

"Andy—" I moan, barely able to breathe. "We have to stop."

"Mm mm," he dissents, not breaking his rhythm for even a moment. And you know what? That's actually a really good point. My fingers twine into his hair as I hold him in place, needing more, aching and climbing higher.

"ANDY!" Satan screams from the hallway. "Open up right now or I'm calling the police!"

Lia would definitely not be calling the police, but the neighbors *thinking* she's going to call the police would be suboptimal.

Summoning all of my willpower and then some, I gently push Andy's shoulders back. "We have to get her."

His mouth lingers along the inside of my thigh. "I don't want to."

"I know." I shift back, putting a torturous amount of space between us before pulling his face up to mine. I can taste myself on his lips, and it's so unexpectedly hot that I almost forget what I was doing. But the pounding starts up again and it has me pulling back, pressing our foreheads together as I sigh, "Will you go get her?"

Andy growls—like a literal growl sound comes out of his mouth. It makes me burst into loud laughter.

"I can hear you in there! Open up right this second!"

Glowing with white hot frustration, Andy stands from the bed and hauls on a pair of sweatpants, then heads out into the living room. He's completely unpresentable—shirtless, hair sticking in every direction, smoke coming out of his ears—and the sight makes me laugh even harder.

I tuck my naked body under the covers and listen for the start of his confrontation with Lia. There's the sound of the front door opening, then a gritted, "Hello, Amelia."

(Oooh, full name. She's really in trouble.)

"Andrew Motherfucking Walsh," she says at an unfathomably loud volume, "if you don't let me in this apartment right this second—"

He must pull her inside, because I hear the door click closed before Lia continues.

"Are you shitting me, Andy? This is the thanks I get for talking you off the ledge all week? You just send a fucking crazy picture and then ignore my texts and calls? If I find out that picture was a joke I'm going to have your balls in a jar. I swear to God. I will pluck them off you myself."

Footsteps pound inside the apartment. Another door opens—maybe the door to my room?—followed by some shuffling sounds.

"Where is she?"

Andy doesn't reply, pissed off as he is, and I can hear Lia starting to get frantic, so I call out, "I'm in here!"

There's a pause—no sound at all. Then someone is stomping towards Andy's room and flinging the door open.

"Oh my god, it's real!"

Lia is—comically—dressed for combat. Her hair is in a slickback ponytail and she's wearing black Doc Martens, wide-leg khaki pants, and an oversized army jacket. I would stake my life on a bet that she intentionally dressed for battle today.

"Sophieeee!" she squeals, launching herself onto the bed and grappling me. "I'm so happy for you. You have to tell me everything. Start immediately after the kiss and hit me with excruciating detail. Pretend he's not here." She gestures half-heartedly in Andy's direction—Andy who's standing with one arm propped against the doorframe, eyes locked on me, and that same dopey smile back on his face.

He shakes his head. "I think our friendship has crossed some important lines."

"Shut up," Lia barks over her shoulder. "Men don't get it."

"Sophie is literally naked, and you're sitting on the sheets we had sex in."

Lia explodes backwards off the bed like a landmine. "Ah! God! Jesus! Fuck!" She starts rubbing at her clothes like she can shake off the cooties with enough determination. Her expletives continue as she shoves past Andy back into the living room, voice traveling with her. "Okay well I have to go take a million showers and then jump into the Sun, but I am truly so happy for you guys. Really." I hear the front door open before Lia adds, "And you better be good to her, Andy. I'm serious. I love you, but she's out of your league and I'll kill you if you hurt her."

He replies, "I know, Lia. Believe me, I know."

And I would love to pause there and unpack that at length. What does he know? That Lia will kill him if he's mean to me? Or that I'm out of his league? I mean, we all know I'm not actually out of his league—I'd like to paint myself generously and say we're pretty evenly matched—but is he saying he *thinks* I'm out of his league? Or is he just saying he knows he has to be nice to me or Lia will be mad? I really hope it's the former—if only because it'll make me feel a little better about my mid-sex "I love you" if he's as into this as I am.

I consider just asking him. For a few seconds I really consider it. But when I go to open my mouth I just can't let myself be *that* needy this early on.

(And honestly, I'm a little scared of his answer.)

I know I always rush things, always push my partners to want too much too soon. There is no way I'm going to let myself make that mistake with Andy. No matter what happens, I won't let myself take more than he's ready to give.

After seeing Lia out, Andy comes back to bed, the portrait of temptation as he crawls over the covers towards me. And I feel every emotion at once—lust curling low in my belly, hope stretching its wings in my brain, nervousness sparkling like pop rocks in my chest.

"What should we do for the rest of the day?" he asks, trapping me beneath him.

"Hear me out," I reply, twining my fingers in his hair as he starts to kiss my neck. "What if we just don't leave the bed? We can order take out. Have a lot more sex. Maybe read our books. But the floor is lava. Everywhere but the bed is lava. We have to stay here."

"Is there a bathroom break clause?" he mutters against my skin. "It won't change my answer, just trying to make a hydration plan."

"Bathroom breaks are negotiable."

"You're a generous overlord," he says, then picks up right where he left off.

25

My Ashmore interview is tomorrow, and I can't focus for the life of me. I spend half the workday imagining catastrophic interview scenarios—they'll quiz me on organic chemistry, or ask me why I didn't have a summer internship between sophomore and junior years, or tell me the Principal Investigator of the lab I'm interested in is moving to Portugal—and the other half of the day lost in memories of my weekend with Andy—the positions he put me in, the sounds we made, then the way he made me laugh until real tears were streaming down my cheeks.

I text him for support.

> Me: Can we go out tonight? My brain is mush and I think I'll go crazy sitting in the house
>
> Andy: Yes. I will make a dinner reservation.

After a thorough and systematic review of online ratings, menus, and photos, Andy makes a reservation for us at a new speakeasy across the river in Cambridge. We enter through a black door in an alley, marked only with a crescent moon. Hand-in-hand, we descend a flight of stairs, following the sounds of airy female vocals, then duck through a night blue curtain into a dimly lit single room. There's a long bar against the back wall, soft blue and purple uplighting illuminating the herringbone wallpaper, and mismatched velvet chairs around mismatched wooden tables.

We're given a table in the corner. I sit in a red armchair, and Andy takes the long wooden bench against the wall. The menus are leather bound books with ink illustrations, and I am absolutely delighted by them. When our cocktails and food arrive, my drink is garnished with some kind of dried fruit that looks like a tongue, and I can't resist doing bits with it. Every time Andy reaches for his fork I use it to lick his hand until he's hanging onto his sanity by a thread and I'm cracking up.

"If you lick me with that thing one more time you're gonna regret it," he says, batting my fingers away before finally taking a successful bite of his meal.

"Oh yeah? What are you gonna do about it?"

He puts his fork down, gaze searing me from across the table. "Maybe I'll just have to lick you back."

Suddenly I'm not just hungry for the food on my plate.

I lean forward, dragging my lower lip between my teeth. "Don't threaten me with a good time, Walsh."

Then he breaks our eye contact with a laugh, scrubbing his hands over his eyes and shaking his head. "Yeah, that's not good."

"What!" I shriek. "You started it. You—" I point at him across the table "—are not allowed to make fun of me for trying to be sexy while we're on a date. That's like... a low blow, dude."

"It's not... you're not..." He sighs the world's biggest sigh, then leans across the table towards me, voice dropping to a whisper. "You're making me hard in public, *Sophia*." He says my name like it committed a crime. "Biting your lip like that, when I spent the whole day imagining things I want to do to your mouth. Fuck." He tears his gaze away, looking to the left and up and right and anywhere but at me. "Say something really unsexy," he begs. "Please."

I'm fighting a losing battle with a grin. "Mmmmmm….. Okay, I've got it! When I was a kid we had a bunch of chickens on the farm, and they used to lay eggs that we could sell or use in our own cooking or whatever. And one time I was baking a cake—I don't remember why—and I needed eggs, so I went out to the yard to get some, and there were plenty to choose from, and when I got them inside they all looked perfectly normal. So, I started cracking them into my batter, and I was adding the very last one, but when it cracked open it was bloody. Like—have you ever seen a bloody egg? It was like mucus-y streaks of red and purple instead of a normal yolk… absolutely disgusting. I almost vomited into my cake batter. And it wouldn't have even mattered if I had, because I had to throw the whole thing out anyway. And that was the day I decided I hate cooking."

Andy stares at me in horror, blinking slowly. "Okay… That was pretty good. I think it got me down to a semi."

My laugh shoots out like a bullet, ricocheting off the walls until it hits Andy in the chest and he starts laughing too. We're almost hysterical when we realize the tables on either side of us are glaring. But honestly, it's hard to care when everything else is perfect. Even Andy, who's usually so desperate to fade into the background of everyone's attention, offers me a beaming two-dimple smile from across the table, like these strangers' glares are simply less important than the moment we're sharing.

It's such a small thing—for anyone else it would be nothing—but with him it means the world.

"Do you ever miss living on the farm?" he asks.

I shrug. "I miss some things."

"Like what?"

"Like the chickens and the ducks. They always had a really chaotic energy, and they each had their own personality, which I loved. And we had a pond with a whole ecosystem that evolved every year. I think I've told you that's what got me interested in biology originally—

watching the plants and animals in the pond change over time. I just miss the little things like that. But I could never see myself going back."

"Why not?"

I push some food around on my plate. "I guess I'm a city girl like my mom. The farm just felt… claustrophobic somehow? Which doesn't really make sense because on a farm there's nothing but space. But like… emotionally claustrophobic?" I take a bite, then say around it, "I probably sound insane right now."

Andy doesn't reply, but the look in his eyes says he finds my explanation both reasonable and interesting. Though maybe that's my wishful thinking. I am in love with the guy, after all.

Before I can start spiraling about *that* particular fact, I start rambling again.

"That was a big part of why my parents got a divorce. My mom moved to the farm because she loved my dad and wanted him to have the life he was dreaming of—'cause he inherited the land from his dad and on and on for a few generations—but it was never right for her. She was going for the 'love conquers all' thing, but in the end it just wasn't enough. I know she resented my dad for it, even though it was her own choice."

"Your mom's happier in Minneapolis now?"

"Much. And I'm happy for her. But my dad… I don't know if he'll ever get over it. It seems like he regrets everything about the last 30 years of his life."

With that, I look up at the man across the table from me, the one I know I could never get over—have never gotten over in all of these years of trying.

I notice the small things that have changed in the time I've known him. The crease in his brow that's a bit deeper, the tiniest number of gray hairs starting to appear at his temples—though you wouldn't notice them unless you were really looking. The same soft intensity he's always had, though. The same rare, genuine smile that cracks my chest wide open.

"That can't be true," Andy says. "You've been around for 26 of those years, and I don't think anyone could regret you."

It's not elaborate or poetic or effusive. It's such a simple statement. But in that moment, the love I feel for him is so intense that it aches. My happiness is so wild that it defies itself and leaves me devastated. Because I love him, I really do. But I'm not naive. If life has taught me anything, it's that I'm better at loving others than being loved.

My parents love me, but it wasn't enough to keep them together. My exes loved me—at least they claimed to—but never enough to make it work. And Andy… well, I know he loves me too. He certainly loves me as a friend. He's a great friend. And I can't deny he seems to like having sex with me…

Does it make me ungrateful to want more?

My traitorous brain pulls forward all the things I've done that he hasn't. I asked to move in with him. I asked if we could be more than friends. I suggested we go on a date, and sleep together. I told him I love him while he was inside me, and the absence of his response throbs like a phantom limb.

I could beg him to explain what he's thinking now—about me, about us—but I can't quite face the present yet. It's easier to start with the past.

"Can I ask you something?"

"Sure."

I reach up to touch my earlobe, the red gem hanging there. "Why did you give me these earrings?"

Andy cocks his head to the side, obviously confused by the question. "For graduation…?"

I already know that much, obviously, but it's not what I'm asking. Since the day I got them, I've always wondered if the gesture meant as much to Andy as it did to me.

He gave them to me during my and Lia's last week of college, the night of our senior formal. We invited the other half of NASA as our "dates" so we could all enjoy the event together, since Andy and Nolan graduated the year prior. Of course, I brought Nolan and Lia brought Andy—there was no way Lia was bringing her brother as a date, even in the most nominal way. And I was mid-prep, mascara wand in hand, when I heard a knock on my dorm room door.

"Come in!"

Andy poked his head around the door. "Hi."

"Hi! I didn't hear you guys arrive." I gestured for him to enter. "Make yourself at home, I still have to do my makeup."

"You're wearing red."

"Yes…" I quirked a brow in his direction. "Is that okay with you?"

"Yeah, no it's good," Andy replied, seeming distracted or maybe nervous. "I… um… got you a graduation present."

"Really?" I asked, putting the mascara wand back in its tube and turning to face him. "You didn't have to do that."

"I know," he shrugged. "And moreover, I didn't get anything for Lia so don't tell her."

I laughed, then covered my mouth, realizing I had to be quiet with Lia in the next room. "Okay, what is it?"

"Don't get excited, it's not as fancy as it seems."

Andy pulled a small square package out from his pants pocket. I walked over, then took it from him as I joined him on the edge of the bed. The gift was immaculately wrapped, every corner crisp and neat—such a perfectionist, even back then.

He seemed tense, anxiously running his fingers through his hair as I tore through the paper and hinged open the small gray box. Inside was a pair of tear-shaped red gems on gold posts.

"Earrings?" I asked, emotion evident in my voice.

"I should tell you—I didn't buy them or anything. They're old. They were my grandma's, and then they were my mom's, but she doesn't have a daughter, obviously, so she just gave them to me and told me I should give them to someone I care about."

He must have seen something change in my expression then, because he jumped to add, "I—I figure my best friend qualifies."

"Andy, I don't know what to say." I cradled the box in my palm, tracing the velvet exterior with my fingertip.

"Is that okay?" he asked.

"I didn't get you anything for your graduation last year."

"Sure you did. You used my extra ticket when Owen didn't show up, and you made conversation with my mom all day—that's a gift money can't buy. And you cheered embarrassingly loud," he said as he bumped my shoulder, "so now I get to embarrass you a little."

I slapped his arm. "Well, you've succeeded. This is way too nice, I don't think I can take these."

"Yes, you can," he said. And that was that.

I stood and rushed back to my mirror to try them on. I could feel tears welling at the corners of my eyes. "I really love them. I've never had anything like this. Thank you."

Then I ran back across the room, tackling Andy backwards onto the mattress and squeezing him tight. He laughed as he hugged me back, until he felt the wetness of my tears on his neck.

"Hey, hey, don't cry," he said, pushing me back just far enough to swipe the apple of my cheek with his thumb. "I'm never going to give you a gift again if you can't keep it together."

I tried to laugh but the tears kept falling.

"And hey, this is a secret, remember?" he whispered, catching another tear as it fell. "You can't go out there crying and give me away to Lia."

"You're right, you're right" I said, finally standing up and drying my face. "I just really love them. Thank you."

That whole night, it felt like we were sharing a secret. When I looked up and caught him smiling at me across the dancefloor, or when I squeezed his hand as he walked past. It almost felt like the start of something more.

But a week later, Andy had a new girlfriend—a girlfriend who wasn't me—and that was the death of my fledgling hope.

Yet even so, a little part of me has always wondered why. Why bother with such a thoughtful gift, if it really meant nothing? After everything that's happened between us in the last month, I'd kind of hoped I'd finally get an answer, but Andy's still looking confused from across the table as he says, "I gave them to you the night of senior formal, remember?"

"Yeah, no, yeah, I remember. But I mean… they're really nice," I push. "You didn't have to do that."

"I know," he shrugs. "I wanted to."

The server drops our check on the table and it pulls Andy's attention away. I feel like I'm deflating, so disappointed in his non-answer. I'm certainly not going to ask him to put a label on our relationship now.

Just as Andy places his card in the check envelope, a voice calls from his left, "No way! Andy?"

We look up to find Owen approaching from across the room.

Andy's eyes flash to me, slightly panicked. I offer my calmest smile and try to wordlessly communicate, *This is fine. I like Owen, remember?*

"Hey, man. What are the odds we would both be across the river tonight?"

"Hey, Owen," he replies, trying not to visibly grimace.

And the surprises aren't over.

"You're not going to believe it," Owen says as he pulls a tiny blonde woman into his side. "This is my brother."

"Meeting the family already?" she replies. "You must be really into me, huh?"

She's absolutely lovely in a short silver dress, and has the dewy youthfulness of someone far below Owen's years. They paint quite the picture: her delicate frame next to Owen's bulky build, tailored suit, and beard.

"I'll show you what I'm into," Owen says as he grabs her jaw and pulls her into a messy kiss right there in the middle of the restaurant. Andy and I scream volumes through our eyes.

After several uncomfortable beats, Andy clears his throat. "Anyway, we're just paying the check, but have a good night."

"What's with the rush to get rid of me?" Owen asks, taking a seat on the bench next to Andy and pulling the tiny blonde onto his lap. "Wait, you two aren't on a date or something are you?"

"Owen," he deadpans.

"Babe, you're so mean," the blonde says from Owen's lap. "Stop teasing your brother."

"I'm just kidding around. He can take it. Sophie, great to see you as always."

"You too, Owen." I offer the warmest smile I can muster, then extend a hand towards his date. "And hi, I don't think we've met. I'm Sophie."

"Bella. Oh my god, you're so cute." She places her hand atop mine, more like I'm going to kiss it than shake it.

"Um… you too?" I give our weirdly joined hands a shake.

"What are you doing here?" Andy asks with increasing annoyance.

"I, little brother, am on a date." Owen turns to Bella and bites her lip in another grotesque kiss. Then he adds, with the slightly condescending tone of someone bestowing much-needed advice, "I think the two of you might be the only platonic pair here. It's kind of a romantic spot, you know."

"Aw, you're really not together?" Bella whines. "That's so sad."

I catch Andy's eye across the table and attempt a new round of telepathy: *You can tell them about us, if you want to!*

(And I really hope he does, if only because I, too, might gain some clarity from the explanation.)

Andy says nothing.

"Don't worry about them, princess," Owen says, eliciting a horny giggle from Bella. "Why don't you head to our table and I'll be right there."

Bella stands from Owen's lap with a flirty look. He winks and taps her ass—(barf)—sending her on her way.

Once she's gone, Owen's body language immediately takes one step back towards normal. "Anyway," he says, "it really is fun to run into you guys. You should come by my place sometime. There's lots of great bars and restaurants by me if you're into this kind of scene."

"That would be nice," I manage. "Thanks."

Andy, still, says nothing.

The silence stretches. Owen looks from Andy to me to Andy again.

I watch Andy for any sign that he wants to tell Owen the truth about us. Andy stares blankly at his hands.

"Alright, well." Owen finally stands to go, clasping one big palm on his brother's shoulder, "I won't crash your night. Have fun, kids."

But before walking away, he bends to whisper something in Andy's ear. It's hard to hear with the noise of the restaurant around us, but it sounds something like, "Make your move, man. I'm rooting for you."

⸺ •●• ⸺

It would be a short walk to the nearest T stop, but the night is young and the air is unseasonably warm, so we decide to walk along the river instead—hand-in-hand, lost in our own thoughts.

Mine go a little something like this:

Why didn't Andy correct Owen about the dating jokes? Did he not want Owen to know? Or did he think I don't want Owen to know? Or is there nothing *to* know? It certainly feels like there is *something* to know, even if it's just a friends-with-benefits situation. That's a significant update! And also… we went on a date! And tonight was a date too, right? Is it still considered friends-with-benefits if you also go on dates? I've never done this before, so I'm admittedly fuzzy on the rules.

Maybe Andy doesn't want to tell people until I figure out my grad school situation. My interview is tomorrow, so we're kind of in the home stretch. And it would be reasonable for him to want to keep things under wraps until we know if I'm even staying in Boston. In fact, it would be *unreasonable* if not downright *stupid* to call ourselves a couple when I might be mere weeks away from the decision that will end it all.

And you know what? Speaking of grad school, now seems like a great time to stress about my interview, too!

Tomorrow could go badly. Tomorrow could very easily go badly. I'm not great under pressure. I'm always a little nervous speaking to people in a formal setting. I feel like I ramble and go off topic and have a hard time presenting myself in a professional light. If tomorrow's interview goes badly then that's it—I'm shipping off to San Diego and Andy and I will just have a weird long-distance friendship where we know we went crazy one week and had a bunch of sex and then called it off. Yeah… we can't go telling people that. We would sound like idiots. Horny, ridiculous idiots.

And speaking of horny, ridiculous idiots… What the heck was up with Owen tonight? Why does he adopt this weird casanova persona around women he's interested in? He's such a nice guy when he's just being normal. I don't get it. And *Bella*! The most ridiculous and horny of all the idiots! I try hard to think highly of all women I meet, but some people simply push the bounds.

I glance at Andy on my left, and he's visibly tense. It's been several minutes since we've said anything. Something about that Owen interaction set us back, and it feels like the ice needs to be re-broken. I take a swing.

"So I have to ask…"

Andy flinches at the sudden sound of my voice, then tries to cover it by clearing his throat. "Yeah?"

What did I do? Why is he so tense? Unsure how to fix it, I proceed with my stupid joke.

"Do you think Bella was born before or after the *Twilight* books came out?"

Andy lets out a small bark of laughter. (Thank God.)

"I know. When they walked up all I could think about was whether she's legally old enough to date my brother."

"Price is Right rules to guess her age? I'm going 19 and 10 months."

"I'll give Owen the benefit of the doubt with a solid 21."

"That's generous of you." I shake my head. "God, Owen, what are you doing? He really is an enigma isn't he."

"I never know what to do with him," Andy says. "One minute he's an obnoxious asshole and the next he's a nice guy who wants to be best friends."

"Well either way, I certainly don't think Bella Swan of Forks, Washington brings out the best in him."

We lapse into silence again as we step onto the footbridge, crossing over the Charles River from Cambridge into Boston proper. My mind cycles through the unhelpful thoughts, snagging on the same ones over and over: What are we? What are we doing? What does he want? What can I do to not mess this up?

"Hey, where are you right now?"

His words bring me back. "Sorry. I'm here."

Andy takes a guess at my thoughts. "How are you feeling about the interview?"

I exhale. "Well, nervous." We crest the top of the bridge, and I pause to lean against the stone wall. Andy leans next to me. Lights from the downtown high rises flicker across the dark water.

"They didn't tell me much about what to expect, just the time and place. I guess it can look pretty different depending on the department and the research you want to do, so I've been trying to prepare but I still feel like I'm going in blind."

Andy moves behind me, wrapping his arms around my waist and resting his chin on my head. I lean back into him.

"I just want it to go well. I want it so much. I don't want to have to move across the country and leave my whole life here."

"I would come with you."

I spin around to face him.

"What?"

"I'll move. I'll come with you. If you want."

And I'm at a loss for words, almost unable to understand. I meet the eyes of my best friend—my obstinate, regimented best friend—as he offers to uproot his entire life for me, and I don't know how to react.

"Wow… really?"

"Of course," he says, like it's that simple.

Without any words to offer in response, I take his face in both hands and kiss him.

He leans us back against the footbridge's stone barrier, his fingers threading into my hair as I cherish the warmth of each place our bodies touch. Traffic whirs, the river flows, and for a few minutes I let myself forget that tomorrow will come.

But later, when my nerves will rob me of precious hours of sleep, I will think back on that moment and deem the conversation incomplete.

Andy can't commit to such a big change without taking time to think it through. Three weeks ago I was still dating Elliot, and now Andy's offering to move across the country with me? It's crazy.

(It *is* crazy, right?)

You can't move across the country just because your friend is moving. Although we aren't just friends anymore. Suddenly we're something else. But that's just the thing. It *is* sudden. And Andy never does anything without thinking it through. No matter what happens, I don't want him to make a choice he'll regret.

I don't want him to regret choosing me.

26

I'm a panicker by nature. I can admit that about myself. Every year during finals I swore up and down that I would have to drop out because I'd failed all my exams, ruined my career before it began, brought shame on my family name, et cetera. And every year it was actually fine. So I get it, I have a history of overreacting. But this is not one of those times.

"Well, that's it," I exclaim as I burst through the apartment door. "I screwed up. I completely screwed it up. It truly and genuinely could not have gone worse."

I throw my purse and coat on the floor, kick my shoes off haphazardly, and head straight for the fridge. There's half a bottle of white wine in the door that I pop open, tossing the cork over my shoulder towards the kitchen sink. "Don't mind me, I'm just going to drink this straight from the bottle and wait for death to come."

From his vantage point in the corner armchair, I can tell Andy doesn't believe me. His expression is completely unbothered, and frankly it's a little annoying!

"What happened?" he asks, standing and coming over to wrap his arms around me.

"Andy, I'm not joking. I can tell you think I'm exaggerating and I'm not. I did a bad job." I spin out of his arms like a petulant child, but he's too mature to take the bait.

"It's okay. Bring your bottle to the couch and come tell me about it."

I stomp over to the couch, plop down as hard as I can, and take a big swig from the bottle.

"What happened?" he asks again, taking the seat next to me.

"God, it's so stupid. I can't look at you while I tell this story."

"Here," he says, pulling our bodies together so that he's leaning against the arm of the couch and I'm nestled between his legs.

I take a deep breath, then start to explain. "You know how I told you I wasn't sure what to expect really?" He nods into my hair. "Well, it ended up being a panel of three, which wasn't that surprising, that seems like a pretty standard scenario. One was the professor I want to work with, one was a department administrator, and one was—get this—Jeff."

"Jeff? That old jerk from the museum board?"

"Yeah, well apparently he's a busybody old jerk because he's on the Ashmore board too."

"Fuck that guy," Andy says automatically, squeezing me a little tighter.

I take another swig of wine, then continue. "When I saw him in the room I was a little panicked, but I tried really hard to remind myself that he actually likes me. I just don't like *him*. But I felt pretty confident I could pretend during the interview and it wouldn't be a problem."

Andy's thumb starts tracing a figure-eight along my ribs, calming and anchoring.

"I thought maybe he would ask me a question about why I made this career choice or something comparably asinine, but I was prepared for that kind of question anyway, so I figured I could handle it. But he didn't ask any questions. Like at all. What he did instead was at the very start of the interview, after I was in the room but before anyone had started asking questions, he turns to the panel and says, 'I think this one's wasted her potential, but you'll probably love her.'"

Andy noticeably tenses behind me. "He said that? Verbatim?"

"Verbatim. And intentionally loud enough for me to hear."

"What the fuck."

"And then he didn't say a single other thing the entire hour. And every question that was asked felt like… like I knew the answer a minute ago. I knew it yesterday. But here and now, with him in front of me calling me 'wasted potential' I have no idea what the answer is." Emotion wells up in my voice, and I quiet to a whisper. "I really screwed it up, Andy. I'm sorry."

Andy places a kiss behind my ear, squeezing me tighter. "I'm really sorry, Soph. I… I wish there was something I could do to change it."

"Me too." I let a tear fall, but I don't wipe it away. I don't want Andy to realize I'm crying yet.

When the tear has dried on my cheek, Andy offers to cook whatever I want for dinner. I don't have the energy to choose, so he just makes something "simple"—pasta and veggies—and it's delicious, but there's a heaviness in the air as we eat. I feel like such a failure. Everything was so good, and all I had to do was this *one thing* and I just couldn't get it right. And now what? Where do we even go from here?

"What are you thinking about, Soph?"

I poke at my meal without looking up.

"Andy, is this crazy?"

"What?"

"Us."

He immediately puts down his fork and comes around to the seat next to me, grabbing both my hands in his. "What are you talking about?"

"I know last night you said you would move to California with me, but I feel like you haven't really had time to think it through. I don't want you to make that choice lightly." My eyes are watery as I try to avoid his.

"Hey, we don't have to figure it all out now, right?" He reaches up to touch my cheek. "It'll take time for Ashmore to make a decision, and then we can take it from there."

"One week. They said they'd tell me in one week."

"Okay."

"Andy." I look up at him now, gently removing his hand from my face. "I can tell you're holding onto hope for Ashmore and I wish you wouldn't. I think we have to confront the very real possibility that I am leaving Boston."

"It doesn't matter to me," he says simply.

"It doesn't matter to you?"

"No."

"Well, it matters to me!" My voice rises as I do, standing from my chair to cross away from him. "I don't want to mess up our whole lives so I can do some random program."

Andy follows me into the living room. "It's not some random program. Don't let Elliot's bullshit live in your head. This is important."

He means it to be comforting, but the reminder of Elliot feels like a slap to the face. Elliot wasn't willing to move with me after three *years* together. It's crazy to ask it of Andy now.

I sit on the couch, shaking my head. "I can't make you move to San Diego."

He follows again, kneeling on the floor before my seat. "I want to move, Soph. I don't know how I can be clearer about that."

"Why?"

"Because I want to be with you."

His dark brown eyes bore into mine as he says words I've wanted to hear for so long. But I'm worried it's not enough. He wants to be with me, but I'm *in love* with him. And I'm so tired of always being the one who loves more.

"I want to be with you too." My lip quivers as I fight for control. "So much. But that's the problem. We've been together for four days and I already feel like you could shatter me. And—" I brace myself to put my cards on the table. It's now or never. "—and I love you. Not just as a friend. I love you, all the way. I love you and I'm moving across the country in six months. And what? You're going to come with me? You're going to pack up your whole life here and move just to be with me?"

"Yes," he says simply, frozen in place.

"What if… what if it's not worth it? What if you end up resenting me?" Tears are falling now and I can't stop them.

"I wouldn't resent you." He reaches for my hands but I pull them back. He looks so crestfallen that my heart breaks a bit more.

"Look, Andy, I *want* you to come with me. Of course I do. I want to be completely selfish and take you wherever I go. I just… can't let myself do that to you." My voice breaks. "But I can't give up this dream either."

"I would never ask you to give up your dreams for me," he insists.

"But you want me to ask it of you. You want me to ask you to give up your whole life."

Andy has no response.

"I would hate myself if you changed everything for me and I wasn't worth it."

"You are worth any…" He stumbles again, trying and failing to express his train of thought, and for the first time in our lives I see tears welling in *his* eyes now.

"Okay, Andy, okay." I meet him on the floor, kneeling as I take his face in my hands. Then I kiss him, because I don't know how else to make this better. "I believe you. And I'm so… I don't have the words to express how much it means to me that you would move with me. But I have to make this choice for myself. And if we're together—if it's a choice between doing the program and making you move, or passing on the program and letting you keep your life here—I'm not going to go. It would feel too selfish, no matter what you say, and I wouldn't be able to bring myself to do it. Do you understand?"

He pulls me into a hug, cradling my cheek against his chest where we kneel. "We can't undo it, Soph. Maybe we should have waited another month and started things when everything was more sure, but what's done is done, and I want to be with you. Please, don't end this."

"I'm not ending this," I insist, wetting the cotton of his shirt. "I think I just need a little space to decide what I want to do about grad school, and then when I've decided we can take it from there, okay? I just don't think it's healthy for either of us to make a choice like this under so much pressure. I need time to think about my career path, and you need time to think about all the things you'd be sacrificing if you moved. Okay?"

I feel him take a deep breath, then loosen his hold on me. "And then what?"

"I guess… either we'll decide to be together, or we'll go back to how things were."

"Back to how things were?"

"Yeah, if… if we have to. Whatever we have to do. I don't want this to ruin our friendship."

His hands leave my body, a look of disbelief on his face. "It's already ruined, Sophie. Don't you get that?" His voice rises as emotion gets the better of him. "We can't go back. We can't pretend this never happened and just be friends. It doesn't work like that"

He tries to reach for me again but I flinch away, stung by his words. Andy swipes a hand down his face. "That's not… Soph, that's not what I meant."

I stand and back away from him. "Just stop. Please."

"You have to know what I mean though, Soph," he pleads, following after me. "You're telling me you can really keep living here and pretend we've never dated? Never had sex? You want to be my friend and date other guys and forget about this? That's what you mean when you say you love me?"

With that, time stops. Of all the fights we've ever had, all the petty squabbles and ideological disagreements that have come with almost ten years of friendship, Andy has never hurt me so much as with those last ten words. It's bad enough that I love him more than I should—that I've told him I'm in love with him, multiple times in multiple ways, and he couldn't bring himself to say it back. But for him to throw it in my face, for him to twist my love to win this fight… It's a door closing.

I'm sure my face broadcasts every emotion I'm feeling—hurt, disbelief, then ultimately withdrawal—as I say, "We both need to think about things, okay?"

"Sophie." He tries to touch me again, but I twist away.

"Andy, please stop."

He freezes. I know he knows he messed up, but that's just not enough right now.

"I'm going to stay at Lia's for a while," I say, affectless voice belied by the tears that won't stop falling.

He nods. I grab my purse off the table, collect a few items from my room, and pull on my coat.

And that's all. The door clicks closed and there's nothing but silence.

27

"————— ••• —————"

Andy

I began my morning deep in denial. Coffee. Toast. Brushing my teeth. Staring at the wall.

Despite my best efforts not to think about last night, everything in the apartment reminded me of Sophie. Her sticky notes on the coffee table, her hairbrush in the bathroom, the couch where I held her just yesterday. Ten years of wanting her, all our memories, and I thought for a moment…

But now I'm here.

Robotically, I lace up my running shoes and force my feet to carry me anywhere else—away from the hollow echoes of our brief life together. Yet even outside, Sophie is inescapable.

Ghosts of our past selves stand on every corner. I run past Allston Liquors where I see us as college kids, buying beer where we knew the cashier wouldn't card. I turn onto Comm Ave and see us as adults, moving our friends into new apartments. I see us in the summer, lying in the grass by the reservoir. In the fall, crunching reddened leaves beneath weatherproof boots.

Sophie is so central to my life here that I can't imagine Boston without her. The road arches like the curve of her smile. The Green Line screeches along its track like a shriek of her laugh. I can't even escape her in the sky, as my traitorous mind draws up an image of her in a light blue dress—the one she wore to the Gardner Museum last month.

I know I'm torturing myself, but I stop in my tracks and take out my phone, opening the photos app. My last two pictures are of her. First, her in that blue dress at the museum. It's candid. I don't think I even showed it to her. But she was looking so earnestly at a horrible painting, trying her hardest to find the good in it like she always does, and it was just so *her*. Her body leaning forward, head tilted to one side, open and sincere.

The next picture is worse. The two of us, that night. My eyes are closed, face half-buried in her hair, yet it's so obviously the happiest I've ever been. And Sophie, there in my bed, beaming and bright, the smooth skin of her shoulder, the freckles on her throat, the trust in the way she's leaning against me…

I click off the screen, feeling myself getting lightheaded, chest constricting. I close my eyes and breathe, focusing on the feeling of the ground beneath my feet. I can hear cars driving past and I try to count them. One. Two. Three. Four. I feel the cut of the wind on my face, wishing it would slice me open and let out this heavy grief.

How did I screw things up so badly?

I need help. I know I do. I'm no good at this. But the person who always gives me perspective isn't talking to me, and I definitely can't go to Lia or Nolan. I've been ignoring their texts since last night for a reason. I can't bear their sadness when I'm drowning in my own.

That leaves one option.

Without giving myself time to think, I click on Owen's contact. He picks up after only a few rings.

"Andy? Is everything okay?"

No. "Yeah. Um…what are you doing right now?"

I pinch the bridge of my nose. This is a terrible idea.

"Nothing. I'm working from home but it's a pretty easy day. Do you need something?" Owen is audibly concerned, and of course he is. We don't do this.

Before I can talk myself out of it, I ask, "Could I come over? Now?"

"Of course. Yes. I'll text you my address."

"Thanks." I end the call without a goodbye.

The 45-minute T ride to Owen's apartment could not feel longer. Still trying to think about anything but Sophie, I'm left thinking about Owen. I don't know what compelled me to do this. Maybe some part of my lizard brain still feels like my big brother will look out for me, fix things.

I transfer from the Green Line to the Red Line then walk from South Station. The front desk of Owen's luxury high rise buzzes me in and I take the elevator up, finding his door and knocking twice.

Owen greets me with a simple "Hey, come on in" as I enter his home for the first time since he moved back to Massachusetts.

Owen lives on the 24th floor, with windows directly overlooking the water. It's spacious, if sparsely decorated, with all new appliances. Sparkling hardwood floors, huge kitchen island, flat screen TV the size of my couch. I knew my brother made good money, but this borders on absurdity.

"Nice place," I say, looking anywhere but at Owen.

"Yeah, I got really lucky. There's a balcony too, here check it out."

Owen leads the way through a sliding glass door, and we step out into the late-winter air. The balcony has two patio chairs and a small glass table. I sit in one chair and Owen takes the other.

There's an awkward moment of limbo—neither of us knowing how to talk to each other anymore—before I give up and pick somewhere to start.

"I hooked up with Sophie."

Owen's eyes shoot to me with obvious excitement. It's not like I've ever explicitly told him how I feel about her, but evidently it wasn't hard to figure out. He's been rooting for us—often obnoxiously—since the first time he met Sophie last year. Despite this, something he sees in my body language must tip him off that the story doesn't end well.

"It was bad?" he asks. And I should have known this was pointless.

"Honestly Owen, fuck you." I stand to leave, but he jumps up between me and the balcony door.

"No, Andy, wait." His hands are up in a placating gesture. "I'm not trying to be a dick. Really. I'm just trying to figure out why you're upset. I'm sorry."

I stare him down. It's obvious how hard he's trying to help, he's just shit at it. So, with no other choice, I retake my seat. He does the same.

"Ok then, so it wasn't bad."

"No, it wasn't bad. It was… really good." I can't look at him, so my eyes lock on the place where the sky meets the harbor. "And I think she thought so too. I mean, everything she said made me think she wanted us to really be together."

"What happened?"

I lean forward, resting my elbows on my knees and bowing my head. "She had her PhD interview yesterday and it really freaked her out. She thought it went horribly. So now she's convinced she's not getting into Ashmore and she'll end up with her fallback plan in San Diego."

"And you don't want to do long distance?" Owen guesses.

"No, I want to move with her. I would go anywhere for her. And the thought of her moving away and me staying in Boston is like… for what? My job is remote. There's nothing here for me."

I quickly realize what I just said, and look up at Owen in apology. "I mean, not that—"

He just shakes his head. "I get it."

I exhale. "I tried to tell her how I feel, that I want to go wherever she goes, and she just wouldn't let me. She said she doesn't want me to uproot my life for her, and that she's worried I'll resent her or change my mind. And I couldn't… I couldn't find the words to explain that could never happen. She said we should take some space." My voice tightens and I can't stop it. "Now I'm worried it's over when I just got her." I clench my jaw as hard as I can, but a rogue tear stubbornly streams down my cheek.

We sit in silence for three seconds—three long seconds as my brother figures out what the hell to say to that. Then, to my surprise, he reaches over and places a hand on my shoulder. Without a word, the gesture speaks volumes: he's here, and he knows there's more to it, and he's ready to listen.

"Maybe she's right," I continue, wiping furiously at my eyes. "Maybe it couldn't have worked out. It's not like I've seen a lot of great relationships. Maybe everyone falls out of love eventually. I mean, look at the example we had with mom and dad. They had a great marriage and then he just left. He just changed his mind and left. Maybe that's in my genes. Maybe I'd end up making her miserable."

"Mom and dad never had a great marriage," Owen counters. "You might have been too young to see it but please trust me, it was a good thing dad left." There's a beat where Owen seems to consider saying more, but he changes course. "Besides, you and Sophie are not mom and dad. You would never… you are not dad."

"You don't know that."

"I do know that," Owen pushes, raising his voice. "You might not think I know you anymore, and you're right that I could've been a better brother, but I know who you are at your core and you are not him. You are a good man, and loyal, and you care about everything so much even when you don't let it show. Sophie would be lucky to be with you."

I keep my gaze fixed on the water as I say, quietly, "I don't know what to do."

"You fight for her." When I don't reply, Owen continues. "Andy, I know it's still new but… have you actually told her you're in love with her?"

I huff out an annoyed breath—clearly he's not understanding the point here. "Owen, I promise she knows I love her. We say it all the time. We've said it for years. And it's obvious I'm out of my league here. There's no way she doesn't know."

"Not that you *love* her—your friends throw around 'I love you's like confetti. I mean that you're *in love* with her."

That gives me a moment of pause. But no, yes, of course I have. Because she said she loved me yesterday in the middle of the conversation, and I…

I rub my hands over my eyes, furious and frustrated and edging towards panic again.

"I—I don't know. I feel like I can't keep track of what's staying in my head and what's coming out of my mouth. I have no control around her."

"Did she tell you she loves you since you've been together?"

"Yes."

"And did you say it back?"

I squeeze my eyes shut, trying to catalogue our conversations. She said it twice since we've been together—I remember each time perfectly, along with the feeling of overwhelming certainty that she couldn't possibly love me as much as I love her. In a sprawling, consuming, driving way.

But did I say it back?

I might not have used those exact words, but she knows how I feel. She knows, right? She has to know. I cannot be that much of a fuck up. There's no way.

"I… dammit, I don't know! I don't know if I told her. I should have told her, but maybe I didn't and now it's too late. Fuck." My voice breaks again as I bury my face in my hands.

"You have to tell her now, Andy. All of it, the whole truth. If you don't, you'll regret it for the rest of your life." When I don't reply, Owen continues. "Hey, if you're worried about finding the right words on the spot we can think it through ahead of time. We'll figure it out. I've got nothing but time. But we're not giving up without a fight."

And that 'we' means more than I can say. It's a 'we' I'm so used to hearing only from Sophie, and it's a relief that even without her here I might not be alone.

Maybe it really isn't over yet.

28

Lia's studio apartment is nowhere near big enough for two adult women and one adult bulldog to cohabitate, but desperate times call for desperate measures.

When I arrived on Tuesday night, I framed the request as "crashing for a night or two," when in reality I had no plan whatsoever. At the time, I shared only the bare bones of my situation with Andy: that we're taking some space to think about what we want, and that it's all my idea.

Now it's Wednesday, and Lia's out late at an influencer event. I'm already brushing my teeth and looking through the works in progress along her art table when Lia finally gets home.

The door opens to the merry call of, "Where's my belly boy?"

Archie faithfully trots over, jowls flopping and tail wagging as he greets his mom. Lia crouches down to lavish him with affection. "Were you my bravest boy while I was gone? Did you have an excellent dog evening? *Bravo, mio caro.*" She scratches his butt and he does a little side-to-side dance.

"Huhh Luhh," I say around my toothbrush.

"Hey, Soph. Ugh, I'm exhausted. I either need a drink or to go to bed right now."

I pop back into the small bathroom to spit out my toothpaste before asking, "Did something happen at the event?"

Lia bends down to unzip her knee-high snakeskin boots. "I broke up with Rayna."

"Oh no! I'm sorry. What happened?"

"It's really okay," Lia replies as she tosses her shoes aside, then hangs up her fluffy green coat. "If anything, I'm the bitch here."

I take a seat on Lia's bed and pat the spot next to me. "Tell me what happened."

"This is going to sound terrible," Lia says as she sits, "but Rayna was just too nice for me. Like, I felt like a bad person when I was with her. Sometimes I just want to talk shit and fuck around, and she was not here for it." She flops backwards onto the bed as she says, "I think I have to be with someone who's kind of a dick. Is that bad?"

"Kind of," I laugh. "But at least you know yourself, I guess. You sure you're okay?"

"Yeah, I'm just beat."

"Honestly I'm exhausted too. I'm happy to just call it a night."

For the next few minutes, we bob and weave around each other as we change into pajamas, wash our faces—me in the kitchen, Lia in the bathroom—and let Archie out for one last potty break.

Since Lia's apartment has zero space for a couch, she and I are sharing her double bed for the duration of my stay.

"Hear me out. What if we sleep like Charlie Bucket's grandparents tonight?" I ask. "Like your head at my feet and vice versa. I feel like we might have a little more room that way."

"Whatever you want, babe," Lia says as she joins me on the mattress. "Are your feet smelly?"

"I guess you'll be the judge of that." I stick one out towards her, wiggling my toes in her face. Lia slaps it away and we both laugh, then I grab my pillow and toss it to the foot of the bed. I'm all tucked in by the time Lia turns off the light and crawls in on the opposite side. Archie promptly hops on too, settling directly between our legs and taking up a full third of the available space—which we wouldn't have any other way.

"Hey Soph?" Lia says through the dark.

"Yeah?"

"I have to ask. Are you ready to talk about the Andy thing yet?"

"I don't know how much more there is to say. I just have a really bad feeling about my interview, and I think we need to grapple with the possibility that I don't get into Ashmore."

"Did Andy say anything about what he's thinking?"

I stare straight up at the ceiling as I explain, "He said he would move to San Diego with me."

"Really?" Lia sits upright, faint illumination from the streetlights striping her face through the blinds. "Wait, that's fantastic. What's the problem then?"

"The problem is that's a really big decision," I say, sitting up to mirror her. "And we've been on like two dates. I just worry he just said it because it seemed like what he was supposed to do, but not because it's actually a good idea."

Lia tilts her head, studying my expression in the low light. "What do *you* want? If grad school and moving and all of that weren't a factor and it was just you and Andy, what would you want?"

"Him," I reply without hesitation. "I want him. And I want him to want me."

"Do you doubt that he does?"

Do I?

The answer is more complicated than I can explain in a single murmured secret of a weeknight sleepover.

Do I doubt he wants me? No. He told me he does and his actions suggest the same.

Do I even doubt he loves me? No, it's not that either. But I love him like roots love the earth. I want him to surround me and nourish me and I know that if we're pulled apart I'll be the one to wilt.

"It's not that I doubt him. But it's one thing to want to be with someone—or even to *love* someone—and it's another thing to give up everything else in your life to be with them. I thought I loved Elliot, but he wanted me to give up my education and career for him and it was a complete dealbreaker. I can't turn around and do the same thing to Andy, and ask him to give up his whole life for me on a dime."

"You are doing the same thing to Andy, because you're making the choice for him instead of listening to what he wants."

That statement hits me like a blow. "Lia, that's not—"

"Is there anything he could say that would make you accept he really wants to go with you?"

"Look," I say petulantly, "I just think he jumped to a conclusion without really thinking about it. He would be leaving half of NASA behind. He'd be leaving his mom and his brother. His job is based here. And he loves Boston."

"Andy doesn't care about Boston, Sophie. He barely leaves the house."

I flop back against my pillow with a loud sigh, too drained to keep up the fight.

"Can I be honest?"

"Yes."

I lower my voice to just above a whisper. "I'm scared."

Lia nudges my leg with hers under the covers. "Of what?"

"A lot of things. Of turning into my parents. Of making him move and then watching him realize down the line that I'm not enough. My mom was always miserable on the farm, Lia. She's a city girl who needs constant stimulation. She knew that when she moved there, and so did my dad. She never should've done it. Or she should've changed her mind before it was too late and she was stuck with a baby in a place that made her feel stifled and miserable. And my dad... when she left, he was never the same. I don't want to become my dad. I don't want to make Andy move across the country and watch him end up feeling trapped. I don't want him to resent me. I don't want to keep on loving him so much for the rest of our lives and watch him drift away."

Hearing the catch in my voice, Lia reaches forward and pulls me up to sit. She keeps my hands cradled in hers as she says, "Falling in love is a risk. It always is. But you are not your parents. You're not. Andy is your best friend. Your hot best friend who's crazy about you. If you trust him enough to let him take that risk with you—if you love *yourself* enough to let him—it could end up being the best thing you ever do. And of course there's a chance it won't work out, but there's also a chance it will. And isn't that amazing to think about? There's a chance you're perfect for each other, and you could miss out on all that if you're not brave enough to give it a real shot."

My eyes squeeze shut. "I guess I just want to know that he's thought of everything. All the risks and the commitment. Because I'm so in love with him, Lia, and we just went on our first date last weekend. If he came with me across the country, and then a year from now or ten years from now he realized I was the wrong choice, I think it would kill me."

Lia chews on this for a moment, then says, "I mean, yeah it's kind of fast to decide to move across the country with someone after technically dating them for a week. But you've basically been dating him for eight years." I take a breath to rebut her, but she cuts me off. "I know you've dated other people, and I know you hadn't been physically intimate before now, but think about it. You two have been way closer than 'just friends' for a long time. And plenty of couples wait until marriage to have sex anyway. Sex aside, you're building on a lot of history."

It's *almost* a good point. So close to a good point that I don't know how to respond.

"Do you have a reason to think you won't be compatible? Was… was the sex not good?"

Even in my present mood, that question brings an unbidden smile to my face.

"That!" she yells, pointing at my face. "What is that!"

"Oh my god, Lia, it was unbelievable. I literally didn't let him leave the bed on Sunday."

She cackles. "I want every single detail, but I also don't because it's Andy and that's weird. You know what? I'm just going to pretend you're talking about somebody else. Okay, proceed. Tell me everything."

My face is hot in the darkness, but honestly, I want to talk about it. "He's like, really big. Definitely the biggest I've ever been with."

"How big? Wait, no, nevermind, I don't want to know. Just keep talking."

"And he really talks me through it. He's always telling me how perfect I am and it feels so good and all that. Oh my god, I'm blushing so hard right now." I flop back on the pillow, palms pressed to my cheeks.

"Sophie, you are certifiably insane if you let this man get away."

"I know," I say to the darkness. "I know."

Lia hands me her phone.

"Why are you giving me this?"

"Just read it," Lia says, gesturing at the screen. "I have no idea what compelled him to text this to me, but it seems like something you should see. To be loved is to be known, Soph."

On the screen is a long text from Andy. Our ice skating bet.

> Andy: Hey, I just wanted you to know my top 10 favorite things about Sophie.
>
> 10) She refuses to read nonfiction, but will read the densest, most opaque fiction you could ever imagine.
>
> 9) She has never once made a hot meal for herself, and when other people do it she acts like it's a Herculean feat.
>
> 8) The way she rambles at a million miles an hour when she's excited, or when she's deflecting.
>
> 7) The mischievous half-smirk she does when she's about to outsmart you.
>
> 6) She's gorgeous. I felt like I had to put this in the bottom half in order to remain a feminist but I mean, come on.

She's so beautiful it drives me a little crazy.

5) The stupid bits she always comes up with. I don't think I've ever had a meal with her where the food didn't become a prop in some running gag. We could be staring at a wall watching paint dry and she would still find a way to entertain both of us.

4) She wears all of her emotions on her sleeve. Panic, calm, happiness, sadness. You always know where you stand with her. And seeing her go from panic to calm or sadness to happiness, and knowing you helped make it happen, is the best feeling in the world.

3) The assiduous way she pursues her dreams, even when people who should be her biggest support system try to get in her way. Her determination. Her dedication and drive.

2) Her warmth and optimism. Those sound like two different things, but in Sophie they're one and the same. She finds the best in everything around her.

1) She is the only person in the world who makes me feel like I am okay, and there's nothing wrong with me. She makes me feel loved and appreciated just for being myself, just by being herself. I hope someday I can make her feel that way too.

29

People say March comes in like a lion and out like a lamb, but it never quite feels that way in the Northeast, where March comes in like a dark, roaring blizzard and out like a slushy, unending question mark.

The sun sets a little later, the ice melts a little faster, the B line still experiences 20 minute delays, with shuttles from Sutherland to Boston University East.

I worry about whether I'm making the right choice.

This will be my fourth night at Lia's, and as much as we both love a sleepover, I'm definitely overstaying my welcome. But this time has served its purpose: with each day I've felt more and more sure of what I have to do with Andy. It's just that when I think about actually having the conversation… it's too terrifying. So much history, the tenderest feelings of one of my favorite people in the entire world, all resting on a few minutes of discourse. My head could explode from the thought.

It's snowing pretty hard when I step off the train and start walking towards Lia's building. All-season athletes jog past in bright jackets. A yellowed armchair sits abandoned on the curb, collecting a layer of fine white flakes. The nearby stoplight flashes red as six lanes of cars and two trains honk furiously to claim right of way. An older man in an unzipped coat and a Bruins hat tosses blue salt across the pavement.

Normally I hate all situations that make me cold—snowfall being an obvious one—but this particular, contemplative headspace I'm in makes the storm feel sort of nostalgic.

During my and Lia's sophomore year, there were two days when Ashmore classes were canceled due to record-breaking snowfall and it was an absolute free-for-all. I remember it so well. Andy and Nolan trekked through snowbanks higher than their heads to come over to our dorm room, and we greeted them with boozy hot chocolate and a night's worth of dumb games. Truth or dare, smash or pass, text or shot—the third being our favorite, where you had to either send an embarrassing text or take a shot.

We kept score on a whiteboard with our initials scrawled along the top: N. A. S. A2. I'm pretty sure I squealed out loud when she realized it spelled NASA, and we did bits all night long about being members of an elite scientific community.

It was stupid, but we didn't know it in the drunken haze of a late night with new friends that felt old. And when we re-read the whiteboard in the morning, after falling asleep in various corners of the living room as only college kids can do, it was Nolan who decided the name would stick.

"I love it! N-A-S-A." He pointed to each of us in turn like the meaning wasn't both abundantly clear and recently established. "It was meant to be."

At the time, it really felt like it was.

"Sophie?"

The sound makes me jump, and I'm slammed back to the present.

"Andy, hi! What are you doing here?"

My best friend is standing in front of Lia's door. The snow collected in his dark hair and across his shoulders suggests he's been here a while.

"Is this okay? I wanted to talk, but if you're not—"

"No, yeah, it's okay. It's…" I remind myself to smile. "It's good to see you."

"I did what you asked," he rushes out. "I thought about this decision, and what I really want."

He takes a step towards me, but his posture is as stiff as I've ever seen it. He's nervous, and I am too. God, am I nervous. I wasn't expecting to have this conversation now, didn't have a chance to choose my words, don't know what to say next. So I just ask, "You did?"

"I, um…" He reaches into his pocket and pulls out a piece of paper, folded and crumpled and refolded. "Sorry if this is weird, but I wrote notes." He rubs the back of his neck with a self-deprecating smile. "I didn't want to forget anything, or say things wrong like I usually do."

"Oh, okay."

He unfolds the note, a slight shake to his hands that I pretend not to notice. Then he starts reading.

"I've lived within an hour of Boston my whole life, and I've never liked change. All the big changes in my life have been terrible. My dad left, then Owen left, and I was always worse for it. So I became the kind of person who never changed anything. I had routines and structure and that was comfortable for me. But then you came along."

He looks up at me then, and my heart is a captive animal, beating against the cage of my ribs, restless and feral, even when he breaks our eye contact to look back down at the page.

"When you moved in, it shook up all my routines, and it was the best wakeup call I ever had. Because this past month I realized it's not really change that scares me, it's losing what I love. And that's you, Sophie. I love you. I—"

He meets my eyes again, and whatever he sees there has him stepping closer as he repeats, "I love you. I am in love with you." There's almost a laugh in his voice, like saying the words aloud is a relief. "I am. I'm completely in love with you. I've—"

He suddenly remembers the paper. His eyes dart down, desperate to find his place again, and I think it's the cutest, purest, most lovely thing I've ever seen.

"I have been in love with you for almost a decade," he reads, "and I've spent every day of that time wishing for you. Savoring every moment with you and convincing myself that staying your friend was better than risking it all by telling you the truth. Finding excuses to touch you, and hold you, and speak to you. Brushing your hand and thinking about it for days. Watching other people fall in love with you, and you fall in love with them, and torturing myself knowing I would never be enough."

Tears start to gather in my eyes, thick as clouds.

"Loving you became part of who I am. Loving you made me want to be a better person. Loving you became my deepest, most precious secret, and I'm sorry it took me so long to realize it didn't have to be a secret anymore. I should have told you every day. I should have screamed it from the rooftops and whispered it in your ear and written it in every book I touched. And—"

I take a step closer, something molecular in me pulling towards something molecular in him. The movement catches his eye, and he looks up again. Then, with something between resignation and determination, he shoves the paper into his coat pocket and breaks from the script.

"—and I know I might be too late, or this might be too much. If you don't want me, I get it. But if that's how you feel, I still hope we can stay in each other's lives, because you're the most important person in mine. And if by some miracle you really do want me too, I'd love to go on this adventure with you. I can't imagine my life without you in it. I can't imagine *Boston* without you in it. I barely made it through this week." He laughs again, and I do too, and the sound is honesty and desperation and hope. "And yeah I'd be sad about moving away from Nolan and Lia and my mom, but they'll always be there. And I don't really want to move away right when things are getting better with Owen, but I just love you too much to stay behind." He reaches up to touch me, finally, cupping the sides of my face. "I just love you. There's no future for me here without you. So please, give us a chance. Give me a chance. Please."

I'm left staring in awe at this thoughtful, sweet, brilliant man, standing in the snow loving me so deeply. I've been scared for so long—scared I would never deserve a love like this, that it wasn't in the cards—but here he is, holding out his hand and teaching me how to be braver.

"You love me?" I ask, though it's not really a question.

"I love you," he whispers, still holding my face.

In that moment, I realize there's one thing I want more than anything else in the world. And, for once, I'm not afraid to ask for it. Even though it's crazy. Even though it's asking for too much too soon, I don't care. After years of hesitating and doubting and fighting to make my feelings small enough for other people to handle—I know what I want, and he makes me feel brave enough to go for it.

After so many almosts, maybe we can have one *at last*.

Voice heavy with emotion, I say, "Okay. You can come with me. On one condition."

"You name it. Anything."

I look him straight in the eyes as I say, "Marry me."

A million reactions flicker across his eyes in an instant—disbelief not the least of them. His brow is furrowed and his mouth is laughing as he asks, "What?"

"I'm asking you to marry me, Andy." He goes to respond, but I shove a finger over his lips. "Wait. You had your turn. Let me have mine."

When my finger draws back, he looks like he's wondering whether the words "marry me" have an alternative definition he's never encountered, but I don't give myself time to doubt. I go for it, talking faster than I should to plead my case while I have the chance.

"You're my best friend, and I love everything about you. I love your dry wit, and your unnecessarily fancy vocabulary, and the way you listen so intently. I love your dimples. I love the way you run your fingers through your hair when you're nervous or thinking hard. I love how tidy you are, and how meticulously you follow a recipe. I love the person I am when I'm with you. I can't imagine ever loving anyone else even a fraction as much as I love you. You take care of me, and I feel safe with you. So wherever we are, whether we stay in Boston or move to San Diego or join the first colony on the Moon, I'm asking you to marry me. Please, Andy. Will you marry me?"

I watch his expression melt in real time. And with those final words, Andy is lurching forward, bridging the gap between us and crushing my lips to his. My arms circle his neck as my feet leave the ground. Snowflakes collect on our shoulders as tears streak down our cheeks. All our history collapses into one moment and we're finally here, loving each other so much it hurts, the way we've always loved each other but new and more because it's out loud and forever.

Andy pulls back just long enough to say, "Yes."

30

A loud knock sounds on the apartment door. Andy opens it to find Nolan and Lia standing on the other side, beaming ear-to-ear. They're carrying a giant cake between the two of them with the words *Congratulations I Guess, You Crazy Fucks* written in royal blue across the top. He laughs out loud as he lets them inside.

Of course, we told the remaining members of NASA about our engagement *immediately*, but this is the first time we've all been together to celebrate.

Well, hopefully celebrate. Today is also the day I'm getting my admission (or rejection) call from Ashmore, so I summoned the troops for moral support.

The cake is already helping with my mood. I'm literally wheezing as they set it on the kitchen table and Andy comes up behind me, wrapping his arms around my waist as I catch my breath.

"You guys are going to have to go easy on me," Lia says as she and Nolan take out plates and forks. "I'm not used to seeing you two all lovey-dovey. I'm going through an emotional journey over here."

"Yeah, Lia," Nolan jabs. "Tell us more about how this is all about you."

"I'm serious! You guys are giving the lesbian stereotype a run for its money. Moving in together… what was it? Negative four weeks into your relationship? And getting engaged on day six? Really normal stuff, guys."

Nolan shoulder checks his sister out of the way, then sets the table. Andy just keeps holding me against him, unbothered.

"Also, still no ring?" Lia asks. "I don't even know which one of you I'm supposed to yell at about that, now that we know Sophie is the boss in this relationship."

"She's getting a ring," Andy insists, then turns to me. "You're getting a ring."

"I don't need one. I just need you." I kiss his lips, and see Lia pantomime gagging herself out of the corner of my eye.

"Well too bad. I want the world to know you're mine," he replies, and Lia's pantomime evolves from gagging to hanging. Nolan throws a fork at his sister before cutting four slices of cake.

By the time we've all eaten our fill and put the leftovers in the fridge, I'm ready to explain my game plan. I line my friends up on the couch, marching back and forth in front of them like a drill sergeant.

"I am expecting the call anytime before 7:00. If the phone rings, each of you is *silent*. Not a *peep*. None of you are to look at me while I'm on the phone. You look at your own phones or find a distraction in the room."

This level of militancy probably isn't necessary—I know everyone in this room is as nervous as I am, but they don't interrupt my schtick.

"If it is bad news, I'm just going to say 'Nope', and then we are not talking about it anymore all night. We are going to put on a movie and order junk food and no one is allowed to be sad or even speak to me. If it's good news," I continue, still pacing, "I'm going to say… I don't know, literally anything else. And then we're immediately doing shots and having the best night of our lives. Do you understand? I need verbal confirmation from each person seated in the exit row."

Nolan, Lia, and Andy each comply with an audible "Yes."

With my speech done, I deflate onto the couch, not knowing how else to pass the indefinite anxious minutes until the decision comes in. But Andy knows what I need before my butt even hits the cushion. He tucks me under his arm, then says, "Okay, Nolan. Distract us. What's the craziest thing that happened to you recently?"

Easy prompt. Right away, Nolan launches into a long recounting of how one of his roommates recently almost burned down their apartment making stovetop s'mores, and is just getting to the moral of the story when my phone starts to buzz on the coffee table.

I look around at my friends in horror, then grab the phone. Lia shoots to her feet, dragging Nolan into the kitchen where they can pretend to re-alphabetize the spices or engage in some other inane task. Andy just squeezes my hand and whispers, "I love you."

I answer the call with a shaky, "Hello?"

I stand from the couch as I listen, watching my feet travel back and forth over the rug. Andy takes out his phone too, but I know he's just staring down at a blank screen, trying to hear the other side of my conversation, but all he can hear is:

"This is she."

"Yes, so nice to hear from you again."

"Oh..."

Nolan and Lia lock eyes.

"Thanks for letting me know. When is that?"

"Got it. Thank you so much for the call. I appreciate it."

"You too, bye."

I look first at Lia, then Nolan, then finally Andy, knowing that no matter what, they'll always be in my corner. No time or distance or circumstance can touch what we've made here—me and my favorite people in the world.

And since I love them so much, I decide to put them out of their misery. A smile bursts across my face as I say, "I got in."

Epilogue

Three Months Later

“‘ **T**here’s something very serious we need to talk to you all about,” I say, hands folded demurely at the head of the table like I’m the Godfather. (Though I do think the severity of my tone is belied a bit by my plastic BIRTHDAY QUEEN tiara.)

Of the four people seated with me, only Owen is taking this seriously at all. My fiancé and two best friends just smile indulgently.

“We have started looking at wedding venues for July next year,” I explain, “and we wanted to make sure that timing would work for all of you.”

“Oh my god Sophie, get to the good stuff,” Lia interjects. “Am I going to be your maid of honor, yes or yes?”

“Lia,” Andy scolds, with a look in his eyes that I’ve come to know means *don’t mess with my future wife.*

I love him so much.

"Well actually, speaking of wedding jobs," I say, turning to Lia's right, "Nolan, we were wondering if you would be our officiant."

Nolan takes exactly one second to process my words before jumping up from his seat with a booming "ARE YOU SERIOUS?" He throws his arms in the air triumphantly, attracting the attention of every single other person in the restaurant as he yells, "Yes! Of course!"

"Would you sit down, you lunatic?" Lia hisses with a hard tug on her brother's shirt. He lets himself be pulled back into the chair next to hers, but doesn't let her interruption stop his unprepared speech. "I mean, I get why I'm the natural choice since I'm basically the whole reason you guys got together. Just think, without me supporting you guys in your time of need, would you ever have known true love?"

Andy is getting ready to rescind the offer on our behalf when I cut Nolan off. "Okay, okay, we get it. Now, Lia, to reward you for your patience," I say facetiously, "I was wondering if you would be my maid of honor?"

Lia looks down at her nails as she says, "Mmm, I'll think about it."

I smack her arm, and finally a grin bursts onto her face. "Of course! I would have been furious with you if I wasn't." She stands to squeeze me in a tight hug, and just like that, it's Andy's turn.

He originally begged me to let him do this part over text, explaining that Owen would not care if it was in person and he might say no anyway or not be available or whatever. And—to be clear—I told him he could ask Owen however he wanted to, but *I* was going to ask Lia and Nolan in person, and Andy didn't want his brother to feel like the second string.

They've been talking more often, even hanging out. Things are… good. So now Andy's here, mustering up the courage to push through the next five seconds. He quickly glances over to Owen, then back down at his plate as he says, "And I was wondering if you would be my best man."

To his credit, Owen immediately wraps an arm around his brother's shoulder, clapping him on the chest with the other hand. "That's amazing, man. I'd be honored."

"Great. That's great. Thanks," Andy exhales, and I can tell he's both relieved and excited.

"We have a lot to celebrate," Owen says. "Sophie's birthday, the wedding, your fantastic selection for a wedding party. I'm getting us champagne." He taps Andy on the shoulder again as he stands and heads for the bar.

"I'm getting us champagne," Lia mocks under her breath once he's too far to hear.

"Lia, be nice," I warn. "He's really not so bad, and he's about to be family."

"He was already my family, but that's never stopped you before," Andy mutters.

"I'm sorry, he just rubs me the wrong way. Something about him is just so entitled and dickish and—"

"Has he actually done anything to make you feel that way or are you just a misandrist?" Nolan bravely asks.

"Can't two things be true?"

"I just don't understand what he did to make you feel this strongly," I say. "Like this is not your standard level of misandry."

"Okay, well first he tried to hit on me right in front of my girlfriend the day we met." Lia begins counting on her fingers.

"He didn't know you were together," I rebut.

"Which was heteronormative of him," Lia snaps back. "Then—" second finger "—he kept giving you unsolicited advice about subletting your place with Elliot."

"He's a lawyer and it was actually really helpful."

"Third—" she won't be stopped "—every time we go anywhere with him he's always picking up some random chick. It bugs me!"

"Lia, my love, half the time we go somewhere together *you* end up picking up a random chick."

"Yes, but I do it with respect. There's a difference." Lia sticks her nose in the air, indicating the conversation is over in her mind.

"Okay well, you don't have to like him, but you do have to act civil until the wedding is over. You two are going to spend a lot of time together."

"Alright, I get it, once in a lifetime opportunity to celebrate my best friends falling in love, blah blah blah. I'll handle it."

Lia stubbornly crosses her arms over her chest, but says no more on the matter as Owen approaches the table with a bottle in hand, pouring a glass of champagne for each person. When everyone is served, he takes his seat and raises his glass.

"To my future sister-in-law," he says, smiling in my direction. "Cheers."

"Wait!" Lia interrupts. "I need a picture of our raised glasses. Don't drink yet."

She grabs her phone from where it lays face-down on the table, and catches the tail end of Owen rolling his eyes as she snaps the picture.

"Sorry Owen, did you have something to say?"

"Nope," he says with a saccharine grin. "Can we drink now?"

"Do you have a problem with me taking a picture?" She rests an elbow on the table, leaning in.

"I'm just… surprised," he says in feigned diplomacy.

"Surprised?"

"Amazed, really. That you can't let a moment go by without making things about you."

"Okay!" I interject, because really this is too much. "None of that. My special day, remember?" I glare at each of them in turn, forcing them to pry their death stares off of each other.

"Speaking of your special day," Andy says. "I have a present I wanted to give you."

"Another?"

"Mhm."

Then he reaches into his pocket to pull out a small black box.

Nolan starts smacking his sister's arm, practically choking on excitement. Lia shushes him even though he isn't making any sound. Owen wordlessly takes out his phone and starts filming. And me? I'm tearing up before Andy's knee even hits the floor.

"Sophie," he says, taking my hand in his and speaking only to me, like no one else is here, "I never told you this, but I first realized I was in love with you exactly eight years ago today, on your nineteenth birthday. When we spent the night eating french fries and drinking absinthe and talking about books, and in only a few hours you became my favorite person in the world."

I can only assume that everyone at this table is crying, because I certainly am.

"I realize we're already engaged because you're braver than I am." We all laugh at that. "But I want you to know that if you hadn't proposed when you did, I would have spent every day trying to figure out the soonest possible moment to do it. It's always been you for me, Soph. And selfishly, I want the rest of the world to know you're mine."

He opens the ring box to reveal a shimmering ruby on a gold band—a perfect match to the earrings he gave me so long ago. He asks, "Will you accept this ring, and continue making me ridiculously happy when you marry me?"

I nod enthusiastically. Andy slides the ring onto my finger, and I immediately pull his face into a kiss. Then we're standing and he's lifting me off the ground into his arms. Cheers rise up across the restaurant, and it feels like life can't possibly get better. But I also knew that, somehow, it will. Now that we've finally found each other, with our entire lives ahead of us. And all our memories and chaos and friendship and almosts managed to lead us here—exactly where we're meant to be.